RISE of the SKY PIRATE

The Adventures of Captain Keenan

S.W. Raine

Rise of the Sky Pirate

Published by: S.W. Raine 2022
Cover Design by: Fiona Jayde Media
Editing by: Renee Dugan
Sensitivity Read by: Veronica Vega

ISBN: 978-1-7348795-5-1

For more information visit:
http://swraine.com

To my mum for enduring my books through every step of the process,

and

to Chris for the one sentence that sparked an entire idea.

CHAPTER 1

Benedict Keenan had escaped jail. It wasn't the first time, and he was sure that it wouldn't be the last.

At least his crimes were petty enough to warrant a jail cell as opposed to being taken to prison. He didn't doubt his skills of escaping the latter; he simply didn't wish to test them out.

The moon shone bright and full, but the floating land of Upper London cast most of London Below in shadow. Thankful for such cover, Benedict scaled the buildings with ease, his long legs propelling him from rooftop to rooftop in order to avoid being caught in the streets below, each crumbling slate tile cracking more beneath his feet. The sooner he reached his destination, the better.

The symmetrical rust-colored brick establishment was finally in sight, standing slightly taller than the crumbling stone buildings around it with its familiar pointed arches and steep roof. The tension in his muscles and jaw relaxed as he drew closer to his safe house. Slowing his pace, he carefully calculated his jump onto an extended tree branch nearby and leaped with feline poise, quickly adjusting his footing and balance on the thick limb. Expertly pushing past the split trunk, Benedict stepped onto another sturdy branch before jumping again, calloused hands gripping onto the ledge just beneath the third-story windows.

Progressing to his left, he made his way to a window illuminated by wildly dancing candlelight. The sound of heavy breathing reached his ears as he quietly slid the window open, and Benedict smirked. He'd have to have a talk with Kitch about giving in to her urges while on the job. His toes had hardly touched the floor when Benedict suddenly froze.

This was not Kitch.

His dark eyes quickly scanned the room, finding that he did not recognize the setup or any of the items inside. Had he been gone for so long that he'd forgotten which room was hers? No, that was impossible. He'd only been locked up for a week. Maybe two—he had lost count. Casting a rapid glance over his shoulder to double-check that he indeed had the correct window, he pulled his leg back out as quietly as he could to not alert the worker or her client to his presence and risk being tossed back into the slammer. Shuffling over to the next window, he cautiously peeked inside.

Kitch was not there, either. With a frown playing on his features, Benedict tried a few more windows with no luck. His heart pounded faster. What if something had happened to her? What if she had fallen ill and passed away, or one of her love-struck clients had stabbed her in a jealous rage?

Before he could think up another possible scenario as he reached the next window, a hand snatched his wrist and pulled him inside before he could make a sound.

His mind reeled as he came face-to-face with a pair of glaring blue eyes. "Are you trying to get yourself caught *again*?" she hissed. "The entire world could hear you!"

Though her tongue was quicker than his, Benedict's reflexes were far better honed. As her hand threatened to leave its mark across his cheek, he grabbed her wrist to stop her, glaring in turn. After attempting to yank her arm back without success, the other hand flew up, and Benedict caught her other wrist with just as much ease before shoving her onto the bed and away from him.

Once he knew he was safe from her sudden barrage of violence as she opted for a scowl instead, he took the opportunity to inspect his surroundings. He whistled, impressed. Decorated with rich and regal fabrics of all colors, this cozy room was much bigger than her last. "Who did you—"

"Don't you *dare* finish that sentence," she warned as she got back to her feet, smoothing out her red skirt. "I worked my way up the ladder with honesty, unlike you."

Benedict smirked. "Don't be like that, Kitch."

"I can't keep doing this!" she said, exasperated. "I can't keep being your safe house and covering for you." Stepping over to her vanity table—walnut-colored and bound with brass—she dropped onto the fluffy beige cushion atop the matching bench. Reaching for one of the brass knobs beneath the oval mirror, she pulled open the tiny drawer and grabbed a small round tin that lay nestled in the lush velvet lining. Applying the red salve from the tin onto her lips, she pressed them together before reaching for another drawer, where she pulled out her rouge as she continued to scold him. "The higher I move up the ladder, the more I know and the more I can control, but you are making things entirely too difficult all the time."

Benedict watched her expertly massage the carmine dye into her cheeks. He never understood why she used cosmetics; she was already naturally beautiful and the obvious envy of all women with her perfect porcelain skin. "Are you saying that you're doing this for me?" he asked.

"I'm saying that we've been through a lot, and we deserve better." Kitch put the tins away before reaching for her raven black hair. It was silkier than he remembered it being as a kid. She pinned it up in a fancy chignon and, for a moment, looked so grown-up that it almost hurt Benedict to keep looking at her. "I make enough on my own; I don't know why you keep giving me your wages . . ."

Stepping over to her as she pulled a string of beautiful pearls out of another drawer, he took the ends, his dark eyes on her reflection in the mirror. "Because I want you to have a good life," he replied as he tied the necklace about her neck before delicately placing his calloused hands upon her bare shoulders.

Kitch placed a hand over one of his and continued to look at him in the mirror. "You're straying from your path, Ben."

Benedict didn't want to hear it. Pulling away, he headed for the massive wooden chest against the far wall, where he rummaged through Kitch's various accessories down to the bottom for his spare clothes. He remained quiet as he changed out of the prison linens and into his fancier duds.

Straying from his path? What did she know? He was climbing his own ladder just fine. If she meant the many times that he'd found himself jailed, well, those were learning experiences. One couldn't move forward until all potential obstacles were dealt with. The more he dealt with his own obstacles, the more of a straight shot his final attempt would be.

He finished dressing, adjusting the crisp cuffs of his sleeves as he turned to face Kitch, who now stood before him, her hands locked together in front of herself.

"You look the part, but you don't act it," she commented.

"Are you saying nobles don't get locked up?"

"I'm saying that I can't keep up."

"Looks like you need to hurry and get another promotion," he teased.

"Get out of my room before my next client shows up," she said a smirk on her own painted lips.

Grinning before leaning in, he placed a kiss on her rosy cheek before pulling away, heading to the window to make his exit. He was partially out when he turned back to Kitch. "I saw all the money I've ever given you at the bottom of that chest," he pointed out. "I gave it to you to spend."

"I'm saving it for when I need to bail you out of Coldbath."

"Might want to find a better hiding place."

The last thing he saw of Kitch was a glower before he climbed the rest of the way out of the window and vanished into the night.

CHAPTER 2

Sunlight poured into the room, which only aggravated Benedict's hangover. He groaned as he rolled onto his back, bringing his hands up to massage his temples.

Benedict had made his way right back to the pub for a much-deserved drink after leaving Kitch that night, despite having just been locked up for being drunk and disorderly. He'd kept mostly to himself, hidden in the shadows and surrounded by drunken tomfoolery. As much as he enjoyed his alcohol, he also enjoyed listening in on conversations; the more informed he was, the better he could perform any task and tick another thing blocking his way to the top off his list.

The pull and thud of a door opening and closing caught his attention. Peeking at the intruder with one blurry eye, he recognized Kitch's familiar black hair as she rummaged through the chest against the wall. Shutting his eyes again, he then found himself buried beneath clothes.

"Get up, they're coming to clean my room," she said.

That didn't make his pounding head feel any better. Slowly sitting up with a frown as his clothes tumbled off him, he waited for the hammering against his skull to steady a moment before standing up.

"Quickly," she stressed.

Moving as fast as his sluggish body would allow, he dragged himself through the brothel room window after receiving a testy reminder to stay hydrated. His body protesting, he struggled down the building and shuffled toward the streets of London Below.

The autumn morning was crisp, and the shadow cast by the Upper Lands made the temperature of London Below even more chilly. Shoving his icy fingers into the pockets of his wool frock coat, his aristocratic dress style garnered glances and sidelong looks from the lower working class. Benedict was used to it—ever since the upper class separated worldwide by detaching entire cities from the ground via alchemical infusions, nobles and alchemists were no longer commonly seen wandering among the tech users in the filth and grime of the Lands Below.

Shambling down a cobblestone back alley flanked on both sides with wooden barrels and crates, empty carts, and scattered rubbish, he overheard a child's voice.

"Halt!" it ordered, and Benedict obeyed with a raised brow. "What's the password?"

He didn't know the password; it was one that changed every week, and he had been locked up for a short time. Frozen in place, he swiftly glanced about to locate the source of the voice but saw no one. Tentatively taking a step, the voice chimed in once more.

"What's the password?" it repeated.

"I don't know," he admitted as he flicked his gaze about more urgently for the location of the voice.

"Then you'll have to pay a fine."

"I'm afraid that I don't have the money right now."

"Ben never has money," came a tiny, disappointed voice from another location. Benedict smirked in amusement.

"*Quiet*!" the first voice hissed.

"Put it on my tab," Benedict instructed as he took another step.

A dozen children jumped out from their hiding spots and surrounded him. He grinned. He knew this strategy, as he was the one who'd taught it to them: they'd act all tough and menacing, only to have the smallest one jump on his back to distract while the others used their pick-pocketing skills.

Despite his sluggish hangover, Benedict swiftly turned in time to catch the youngest one, who had jumped from a window.

"Ben!" The small child gleefully beamed and wrapped his tiny arms around the man's neck in a hug.

The younger children followed suit, rushing toward him from all sides, lovingly embracing his legs, almost knocking him over. Trying to keep the remainder of his balance, Benedict laughed as he set the youngest boy down and ruffled a few of the kids' hair. When they had released him and he could stand without teetering too much, Benedict approached the eldest boy, who was leaning against the wall with his arms crossed and a twinkle of amusement in his brown eyes. They clasped forearms in greeting.

"Good to see you, Ben," he said.

"Likewise," Benedict replied. "What's the word at the orphanage?"

The eldest boy stuffed his hands into the pockets of his wool trousers and went through a mental list of happenings from the past few weeks. "Winnie went to live with a real swell family in the Upper Lands. And after all these years, Bates finally got adopted."

"Did he? Good for him," Benedict replied, impressed.

"Bowler got adopted too. Some alchemists chose Briar and Edith to be housekeepers, and Abby is in the kitchens. Close to being Kitch two-point-oh, she is." Benedict smiled fondly at this. "Jax left on his own, Chase is in prison for theft . . . and a few new kids moved in."

Benedict always appreciated the updates. His gaze drifted to the younger children playing in the alley, and it reminded him of his time as one of them. He could practically see himself and Kitch running and jumping around with the lot of them, without a care in the world. They might have been hard times, but things were definitely simpler as a child.

A hiss from the eldest boy broke him from his reverie. "I forgot to tell you . . . Lefty passed."

Benedict's body stiffened. At seventeen, they had urged him to get a job and to find another place to live. As the orphanage phased him out and he was left on his own, he found himself at workhouses—institutions exchanging accommodations for employment—but he had walked away from more jobs than he cared to keep track of, costing him his free lodging each time. Homeless and not wanting all his eggs in one basket, he scattered his items across London Below with keepers. Lefty was one of those keepers, permissively holding onto some of Benedict's items in his small trunk.

"What happened?" he asked.

"He got real ill. Mrs. Aness gave his room to one of the new kids after scrubbing it top to bottom. I tried to salvage the trunk for you, but she had already burned it."

Benedict hissed in turn. Not only did he have some clothes in that trunk, but it also contained the key to his storage box, which held more of his items. Thanking the boy for the intel, he waved goodbye to the children and headed for the orphanage.

Despite being part of the impoverished Lands Below, the structure itself had charm—all things considered—with its decorative iron fence surrounding the property. But to Benedict, the bleak establishment reminded him of the overcrowded rooms, underfunded meals, and punishments such as paddling, caning, and whipping.

Stepping inside, the pressure in his head mounted. He didn't want to have to deal with the owner of the establishment, but he had to.

The lobby looked like a library, its tall wooden shelves filled to the ceiling with thick, dusty tomes of various colors and subjects. Benedict hated those books; they were more often used for paddlings than for education. It was quiet despite the muffled chatter, laughter, screams, and cries of children coming from the back rooms. A bone-thin woman worked at the desk in the front, silver wisps of her tightly pinned blonde hair almost glowing in the sunlight.

"Benedict Keenan," the secretary started in a monotonous tone, never once raising her attention to the man that had just walked in. "Did they let you out, or did you escape?"

"Mrs. Dimper," he greeted with a charming grin, purposely ignoring her question. "How is Mr. Dimper? How are the kids?"

"Mae is expecting again, and Maximus is doing well providing for his family. As a man should," she added.

Benedict's grin faltered, and he frowned. The secretary had never liked him and was exceptionally quick at sending a low jab in his direction as proof. "Now, now, there's no need to be sour . . ."

Mrs. Dimper's blue eyes shot up from her paperwork, and her thin lips practically turned into an invisible line in her discontent. She thankfully did not have time to retort when the back door creaked and swung open. A plump woman strolled into the room on a mission, trailed closely by an unknown toddler.

"Mary, have you seen—" She paused midsentence upon noticing him and veered her conversation with a sigh. "Mr. Keenan, what are you doing here?"

The wee little one, thumb in mouth, fell flat on her rump from colliding with the back of the woman's plump legs. She did not cry, however, and Benedict found that very grown-up of her. His attention moving back to Mrs. Aness, he stood up straight—as she had always instructed him to do in her presence while growing up—despite the fact he had already learned proper noble posture.

"Ma'am, I came to fetch some of my items."

"You have nothing left here, Mr. Keenan," she said coldly as she continued on her mission toward a rolltop desk near the corner bookshelf. Materializing a small iron key from the pocket of her pale brown wool tea gown, she unlocked the desk and opened the roll top, rifling through small drawers and compartments.

"Well, truth be told, I actually had some items left with, er, Lefty. Connor Embers."

"I am well aware of who 'Lefty' is, Mr. Keenan," she replied as she continued her search, "and I'll have you know, as your latest incarceration has obviously kept the world from you, but young Master Embers passed last week."

"I've been told."

Mrs. Aness paused, clearly surprised. Glancing suspiciously over her shoulder, she eyed him for a moment before returning to her search. "Were you also informed that there is nothing remaining of any property that young Master Embers had in his possession?"

"I've also been told," he admitted. The woman's cold shoulder was testing his patience—and hangover—so he jumped straight to the point. "My clothes may be ashes now, ma'am, but I also had a brass key. Did you find one, perchance?"

Mrs. Aness found what she had been looking for: a wooden brush with horsehair bristles, which she used to detangle the knotted mess that was the toddler's black hair. "Can't say that I have," she replied with disinterest.

Benedict inhaled and exhaled deeply, mostly to remain calm, but also to keep his pounding headache from worsening. He knew that chances of the key being separated from his clothes were slim to none. Despite knowing the answer to his next question, he asked, nevertheless. "May I look around the stoves and furnaces?"

Mrs. Aness pulled away from grooming the child. She placed both hands, brush included, on her rotund hips, a grave expression on her face. "No, Mr. Keenan, you may not." She then sighed and relaxed her arms, rolling her eyes back before returning her attention to Benedict. "I have your damned clothes and key in my possession," she finally admitted. "I knew the clothes did not belong to young Master Embers because they were far too big and refined. The key could have been a found trinket, but now I know that it also belongs to you."

The entire experience was making his headache worse. He needed his belongings, and he needed out as soon as possible. "Then I'll take my possessions and be off, if you please."

"And be off you will, Mr. Keenan. This has no longer been your home for eight years. At seventeen, you should have been earning a wage of your own. Today, you should have a home, a wife, and . . ." Mrs. Aness paused, tapping an index finger through the air as she silently counted, ". . . at least three children!"

Benedict laughed dismissively. What was with everyone scolding him with the expectation that he needed to settle down? "Kitch almost said the same thing last night."

"Well, Miss Gladstone is wise, despite her . . . tactless choice of career." Benedict glared at the insult toward Kitch, but as he parted his lips to defend her honor, Mrs. Aness raised a hand to silence him. "I am certain that you are not here to start arguments, Mr. Keenan, so I will fetch your clothes and key."

Stepping away with the toddler in tow, a rather uncomfortable silence hung heavy in the lobby as Mrs. Dimper continued to work without saying a word. With a sigh, he brought his hands up to rub at his temples and ease the pounding in his head. He needed some fresh air.

Mrs. Aness eventually returned, hands full. A crisp white shirt, a golden brocade waistcoat, and a pair of subtle plaid trousers were neatly folded and draped over her arms while she

clutched a pair of shiny, pointed black boots in her right hand. Her left hand appeared empty, but she quickly revealed a rusty old key.

Handing him the items, she then headed for the front door, opening it wide. “Please leave, Mr. Keenan, and do not return.” Benedict blinked in surprise at her boldness. “Please live a wonderful life. Don’t waste it. I have these children handled. I do not need your help.”

Benedict bit his tongue to prevent lashing out. She had no right to forbid him from seeing them. As an orphan himself, he was particularly attached to them. He knew what that kind of life was like, after all. Swallowing his anger, he inhaled and exhaled deeply. There was no point arguing with the woman, especially with his pounding headache. Nodding, he headed out. “Thank you, Mrs. Aness.” Glancing over his shoulder, he called out a little louder, “Thank you, Mrs. Dimper! Give my regards to the family!”

Mrs. Aness swiftly shut the door behind him. With a sigh, he walked away from the orphanage, deciding to return to Kitch—her room had to be clean, by now—to drop off his clothes. He was inconveniently down one location across London Below.

CHAPTER 3

They found themselves in the pub's dark parlor for a pint after lunch. Surrounded by oak wainscoting and a cheerful fire, Benedict updated Kitch on the goings-on at the orphanage, including the regular cold shoulders he received from Mrs. Aness and Mrs. Dimper.

"You wouldn't have had anything to do with that, would you?" he asked as he finished his drink and slammed it down onto the table out of habit. "Awfully suspicious that all three of you are trying to set me straight."

"Heavens, I haven't seen either of them since I left!" she replied, insulted. "You know I hated it there! Besides, I will always get on your case. I will always worry about you and wish for you to just settle down. You know this."

"I know," he said with a sigh.

"You've never been one to settle for what we have in the Lands Below, to settle for what we had growing up. When you made it your goal to join the noble ranks in the Upper Lands, I finally felt a bit of relief. It drives me insane each time that you end up jailed, Ben! I don't know how much more I can handle thinking that your chances of being up there diminish with each trip behind bars!"

"Kitch," Benedict warned. He was both too hung over and too sober for her to continue in the direction that she was going.

"Would it have been different had you married her?"

Benedict's attention wandered off at her words. There was no telling if things would have been different under those circumstances. One thing he was certain about, however, was the return of the pounding in his head.

Kitch leaned closer to him. "What would Lady Catherine think if she were still alive?"

Benedict's attention returned to her, laser-focused, as he hissed his displeasure at the new direction of their conversation. If Mrs. Dimper's blows weren't low enough, Kitch was definitely aiming below the belt by bringing Kate into the discussion. "Kitch," he growled.

"I'm serious, Ben! You think her father hated you then? He would definitely hate you now!"

That was it. Her words made him snap. Knocking his chair over as he jolted up from his seat, he slammed his fist onto the table, spilling some of Kitch's untouched tankard. "I wouldn't be like this if Kate was still alive!" he bellowed.

The entire pub quieted down for a moment, all attention on him as he glared at the prostitute on the other side of the table.

But Kitch did not react. In fact, she looked highly unimpressed. Slowly standing, she straightened the skirt of her wool dress. "Benedict Keenan, I don't know why you self-sabotage like this. I can't keep sticking up for you. I'm risking my career and life each time." Wrapping her woolen fringed shawl about her shoulders, she continued, "I will say this one last time: please take one hard look in a mirror and ask yourself what it is you truly want. Once you figure that out, I want you to act like the Ben that I've always known, and go get it. Reach for the stars as I know only you can. Reach, and don't stray from your path. I know you're destined for greatness. Stop sabotaging what the universe is offering you. Only you stand in your own way."

Kitch walked away, leaving Benedict to sulk over her words.

She was right, as always, and he hated it. Grumbling, he grabbed Kitch's undrunk beer and chugged it down before wiping his foamy mouth with the back of his hand and leaving for the Thames River.

The bright sunlight reflected off the dingy surface of the water, causing what remained of

Benedict's headache to intensify. The putrid stench coming from the Thames—though infinitely better than during the summer months—didn't help, either.

The river was busy, as it had always been when he worked at the piers. Smokestacks atop of paddle steamers of various sizes belched black fumes of fine coal as the ships zigzagged past the queues and tangles of trade ships on either side of the river, transporting business commuters.

Weaving through the whirl and movement of wooden carriages full of subtly fragrant spices, and solid laborers and shady sailors carrying bales, baskets, and sacks of goods, he continued on toward the multiple-story warehouses. His eyes, however, were on the idle sails and rigging of the massive wooden vessels.

Mighty iron steamships were becoming the norm on the seas and in the skies, able to reach their destinations faster, but Benedict preferred the decay-resistant white oak keel and frames to the rusty and corroded metal. Not only was it more visually appealing and reminiscent of the elite and regal Upper Lands, but it didn't conjure up the disgust he had with the industrial abomination that was the Lands Below.

The warehouse was stacked with tons of product in cases and bales, surrounded by various steam lifts with hoists and hydrants, as well as other gear-grinding machinery. The noise did nothing to ease the pounding in his head and instead caused it to intensify.

A man rummaged behind a desk, yelling orders to another. Finally turning around, his eyes widened in surprise before he became serious. “Well, if it isn't Benedict Keenan,” he said, adjusting the firmly woven wool cap that adorned his head.

The man's fashion sense seemed expired by a few years, bringing a smirk of amusement to Benedict's lips. “Mr. Dunesworth,” he greeted with a nod.

“We thought you were dead in a ditch somewhere.” Returning to his search, he continued, “Glad we were wrong.”

“It takes a lot more than that to kill me.”

Finding what he hunted around for, Mr. Dunesworth snatched a satchel of small tools and handed it to a laborer in passing.

Benedict got straight to the point. “If I may, Mr. Dunesworth, I'd like to return to work. You see, I was jailed for a short time—”

“If you don't show up for the job, I give it to someone else, Keenan,” he interrupted as he turned to hand another passing laborer a stack of papers.

Benedict almost spun around to return to the pub and drown his inconveniences away, but he surprised even himself when he parted his lips once more. “What of any other openings? I'm skilled in a variety of different—”

"Might want to try the India docks," Mr. Dunesworth said, cutting him short. When Benedict released a disappointed sigh, he continued, "I'm sorry, Keenan. I really am. But I have a business to run."

"I understand," Benedict replied. "Did you empty my lock box?"

"Not yet, luckily for you. I was waiting to do it this weekend."

"Perfect. I'll empty it and return the key."

"Much appreciated," he replied as he turned to take care of another issue.

The narrow storage compartments were stacked up against the wall in the far back of the building. A thick wooden bench stood nearby, seating two workers in casual conversation while on their break. The younger of the two—a meek boy with shaggy brown hair—produced an audible gasp of surprise upon Benedict's approach.

"Keenan!" he said excitedly as he stood and rushed over to him, clapping him on the back. "We thought you—"

"Dead in a ditch," he quoted with a smirk. "So I've heard."

"Are you coming back to work?"

Benedict cast him a kind smile. He had a soft spot for the klutzy boy—an orphan from the other end of London. "No, I have an offer at the India dock," he lied. "I've simply come to collect my belongings and say my goodbyes."

"Aw, shucks, Keenan, we're gonna miss you!"

"Speak for yourself!" the other laborer jested as he stood up, expertly taking a slow drag from his clay pipe. "Take care, Keenan."

Giving the man's hand a firm yet cordial shake, Benedict then clapped the boy on the back before heading to his locker. Turning the rusty key, he pulled a few crisply folded shirts and trousers from the lockbox, as well as some coins—his pay before going to jail. With a casual wave goodbye, he decided to drop off his items in Kitch's room until he could secure another area. That was two places he had lost. Benedict was running out of keepers.

CHAPTER 4

Kitch was out when Benedict climbed through the window to her room. It was probably best that she was away; he was unsure of what to say after his brief outburst at the pub, and he knew that he would have made things worse had she been home.

Placing his belongings in the large chest up against the wall, he also noticed that the money that was previously hidden was now gone. His heart skipped a beat. Did someone steal it? Did she find a better hiding spot, like he had suggested? Casting a quick glance around the room, he resolved to return later and ask about it.

Heading for the window, he paused at the vanity table when Kitch's words loudly resonated inside his mind: *Take a hard look at yourself in the mirror and decide who you want to be.* Slowly, Benedict turned his attention to the oval mirror and inspected the scraggly, unshaven man with disheveled hair staring back at him through the reflection.

He wanted to be a noble. He had always wanted to for as long as he could remember. The division of the social classes grew by leaps and bounds when the world split into the Upper Lands and the Lands Below. He could still hear Lord Taylor, Catherine's father, scoffing over the "filthy orphan and tech user," notifying him that he would never amount to anything more.

His first step to living the aristocratic life was with proper clothing. It was love at first sight when he laid his eyes on Catherine all those years ago, and he desperately needed to impress her. Stealing shirts and trousers from shops and trading what few possessions he had for a pair of boots, he groomed himself to look like the nobles, to look like an alchemist. Next came training himself on his posture, then adjusting his way of speaking. Soon, he was a whole new man.

He had indeed made a great first impression on Catherine. He could not fool her father, however, who made it known at every occasion that his daughter was too good to be seen around the likes of impostors. And when the world split, Lord Taylor's tongue-lashings were even more savage and heartless.

But that never stopped him. In fact, it motivated him further to sneak onto the Taylors' property and steal a few secret moments with

Catherine as often as he could. He loved her. He wanted to marry her someday and promised her—and himself—that he would follow the aristocratic rules properly to finally be by her side forever. Unfortunately, fate was cruel, and his downward spiral wasn't pretty.

He reached for one of the brass knobs on the vanity, pulling the drawer open and rummaging past Kitch's belongings until he found what he was looking for: his shaving-tackle.

Momentarily pulling his attention away from his reflection, he turned to the nightstand and grabbed the porcelain water pitcher and washbowl. Sitting on the vanity bench, he shaved.

He'd wanted to be a noble. He'd wanted to prove to Lord Taylor that he could join their ranks. Now that Catherine and her father were no longer in the picture, who did he have left to impress? The answer revealed itself the longer he stared at his proper sitting posture and crisp and sophisticated clothing: the rest of the world.

His learned etiquette, his self-discipline, practice, and patience kept him confident and motivated against all the naysayers, all the toxic people who denied, refused, or opposed him, all the skeptics and cynics. He was no longer the same Benedict Keenan from all those years ago; the same orphan who could not—would not—get himself adopted; the same orphan too attached to the other kids in the orphanage—to Kitch—

who constantly got into trouble so that nobody would want him.

A sigh escaped him as he wiped the rest of the soap from his face. Kitch was right: he knew how to reach for the stars and get what he wanted. He'd always known how. He'd been doing it since he was young. The universe was his if he'd only reach for it as he used to. Slowly shaking his head, he chuckled to himself. He was lucky that she stuck out for him for so long. He was indeed making a fool of himself by undoing all his progress.

Shutting his eyes, he rubbed at his temples. This was all annoyingly sobering, and Benedict was going to need a few pints to get him back on track. Opening his eyes, he cleaned up after himself and cast one last glance at the nobleman in the mirror before climbing out the window, headed for the streets of London Below.

CHAPTER 5

Sitting in his habitual corner of the pub, pewter tankard in hand, Benedict nursed his beer after quickly chugging down the first one. The place was busier than it had been around lunch, yet less so than it usually was after working hours and into the evening.

He mentally replayed the events of the day: the orphanage, the docks, and Kitch's words. He was brooding, and he knew it, but he allowed himself a dip into the self-pity of his final downward spiral before taking off like a rocket toward the stars he longed to reach.

His thoughts then shifted to the jobs he could take on to gain enough money to reach the Upper Lands. Unfortunately, every job that he'd ever temporarily worked was never enough. He needed something bigger.

Lifting the tankard to his lips, he drew his attention to two men in a low discussion. Trailing his eyes to the stamped tin plate ceiling, he eavesdropped on the conversation—partially drowned out by the hubbub of the pub—without looking too conspicuous. It was difficult to hear, but he caught a few keywords to string together the gist of the discussion. Casting another quick glance in their direction, he caught a surreptitious exchange of a bulky purse—presumably heavy with coin.

A retrieval mission? Maybe that would work. Rogues were the mercenaries of the world, taking on jobs from whomever had the highest bid. It wasn't exactly honest work, despite the police and military employing them at times, and it definitely wouldn't be simple work. But it was quick money.

Sealing the deal with a handshake, the elder of the two gentlemen stood up, donned his coat and hat, and bid the other farewell before walking away. Following the dark-haired man with his eyes, Benedict downed the rest of his drink before casually walking out of the pub himself. Thanks to his long legs, it didn't take him long to catch up to the rogue.

"Let me join you," Benedict called out.

The man spun around, startled, his downturned eyes wide and his thick, waxed mustache practically bristling. "I beg your pardon?"

"Let me join your mission across the ocean."

"Who the hell are you?" he asked, his surprise quickly turning defensive.

"I am just the person you need," Benedict replied.

"And how do you know what I need?"

"Ships are always in need of skilled sailors. I'm capable of rigging and tarring, and I'm unafraid of heights. I've helped build my fair share of ships, so you can use me for repairs, if necessary. I'm also apt at navigating and an array of other jobs."

Still eyeing him suspiciously, the man was silent for a moment before speaking again. "Your name, sailor?"

"Benedict Keenan, at your service," he replied, extending a hand in greeting.

"Commander Jeremiah Erikson." They shook hands, but the commander still seemed suspicious. "What does a pretty boy like you need this job for?"

Benedict's body stiffened some. So now he was also going to be treated poorly because he played the part of a noble too well? "Why does anybody take on a job such as that?" he countered.

Jeremiah continued to eye him up, then eventually gave a curt nod, satisfied enough. With a sniff, he turned back to leave. "We leave promptly at dawn, with or without you," he called over his shoulder.

"Yes, sir!" Benedict replied with a grin.

Lying on Kitch's bed that evening, he silently stared at the ceiling. He had promptly apologized to her upon his arrival—which she graciously accepted—then followed up by asking her about the money. She confirmed that she had found a new hiding spot, as per his suggestion. When he had asked where, however, she refused to divulge her secret, which made his heart swell with pride.

"A penny for your thoughts," she said as she finished brushing her silky black hair in front of her vanity table.

He wanted to tell her . . . but how would she react? He couldn't figure it out, and that scared him. Did he even know her at all? Why couldn't he come up with a perfect Kitch type of reply? Inhaling deeply, he went for it. It was now or never.

"I took on a rogue mission. I set sail for the colonies at dawn."

He expected her to say nothing, to act like she didn't care. He expected her to scream at him or burst out crying. What he did not expect, however, was the shatter of a perfume bottle dropping to the ground, or the quiver in her voice when she asked, "Why?"

The sudden sound made him blink, startled, and he caught the look of shock on her face as he swiftly turned his attention to her. Getting up, he quickly grabbed one of the silk scarves from the bed and took it to the spilled perfume. He knelt and wiped the floor until he felt a trembling hand touch his cheek. Pausing, he slowly glanced up to see tears threatening to fall from her eyes.

He could tell that she was giving everything that she had to keep herself composed. Kitch parted her lips—perhaps to ask why once more—but only a sharp intake of breath escaped her, like she was bracing against a sob.

"You're the one who said that I needed to rein myself in, that I needed to take a hard look at myself and reach for the stars," he said. "Well, I took a hard look at myself. If anything, it's your fault, because it was in your blasted mirror!" he added with a smirk, pointing to her vanity. This caused her to whimper instead of laugh. With a sigh, Benedict stood up and took her hands, carefully pulling her to her feet. "Kitch. Everything will be all right. I'm overqualified."

He was downplaying the dangers of the mission; there was always the possibility of not making it out alive. But he was confident in his skills and trusted that he'd return to London Below.

Kitch finally shut her eyes, and the welled-up tears fell down her rosy cheeks. While Benedict had expected her to cry, he'd never pictured her fighting it with style and grace; he envisioned the Kitch of the old days, crying like a baby because he had pulled her hair. Ever so gently, he wiped at her tears. She was so strong, but at that moment, she was also so delicate that he might have kissed her then and there in weakness.

"Are you afraid that you can't keep me in check on the other side of the ocean?" he tried. She let out a shaken breath and opened her eyes. More tears flowed down her cheeks, and he wiped them away as well before leaning in and placing a kiss on her cheek. "Everything will be fine," he whispered as he lowered her back onto the bench and returned to the shattered perfume bottle.

Kitch finally spoke when Benedict stood back up to dispose of the mess. "Promise me you'll write every day."

"I promise."

"Promise me you'll stay out of trouble."

"I promise."

"Promise me you'll come back intact."

"I promise," he replied as he turned to her with furrowed brows. What was with all the demands?

"You're such a liar," she said with a tremble in her voice.

"That I am." He grinned.

"Then just promise me you'll come back," she whispered.

Benedict leaned in to be at eye level with her. "Now that is a promise that I intend to keep." When she finally gave a faint nod in acknowledgment, he placed another kiss on her temple.

"Clean yourself up. You don't want your clients or Madam Donnelly to grow suspicious."

And with that—and a tug at his heartstrings when he heard her sobbing once he had climbed out of her window—he left for the rest of his items.

CHAPTER 6

Benedict was at the docks before dawn. His mind hadn't been able to shut off, causing him to toss and turn most of the night. Repeatedly running through his discussion with Kitch about straying from his path, his thoughts eventually shifted to Catherine. He missed her so much that his heart deeply ached. The rogue mission was his chance to get back on track, to show the world—and especially the Upper Lands—what he was made of, and he knew that he'd make Kitch proud . . . if only he could imagine how proud Catherine would be too.

With a small cotton sack of belongings slung over his shoulder, he walked along the Thames in silence, pausing when he approached a galleon. The airship was beautiful, even in the predawn hours. The solid propellers and the mast riggings were exquisite from what he could see, and the wood was expertly well-kept. A peaceful smile found its way to his lips as he envisioned himself captaining such a fine vessel, exploring every corner of the world. He loved the freedom that sailing provided, and it was definitely easier to get to the Upper Lands with an airship than with the elevators that connected every major city in the Upper Lands to their crumbling counterpart in the Lands Below. He'd overheard that the elevators were expensive anyway. Flying was free.

His attention was pulled away from the ship and its dreamy liberties to the low sound of clicks and whooshes that gradually grew louder. Turning away from the galleon, Benedict glanced over to find a figure in a thick black coat unevenly treading along the dock with one tarnished brass peg for a leg. The wool scarf he wore nestled comfortably at his neck, his salt-and-pepper beard appeared to keep his lower jaw warm enough. The man seemed to have tunnel vision; Benedict politely bowed his head in acknowledgment, but the elder man ignored him and continued on.

Benedict followed him with his eyes, watching him board the next airship over. Wrinkling his nose at the unsightly rusty blimp, he froze when a hand suddenly clasped his shoulder. Spinning around to confront the person, his eyes widened in surprise to find the commander with a smug grin.

"Changed your mind, have you?" he asked.

Furrowing his brows, perplexed, Benedict watched as Commander Erikson stepped past him, reminding him they would leave promptly at dawn. His confusion quickly melted away, replaced instead with a heaviness in the pit of his stomach as he watched the commander board the blimp, followed by a few others. Directing his gaze back to the beautiful galleon, Benedict was having second thoughts.

"You have got to be kidding me," he muttered to himself as he turned his attention back to the corroded vessel. He contemplated turning back and finding himself another way to earn money, but the orphan in him—the part of him that was accustomed to filth and broken things—told him to give it a go. Swallowing his pride and dignity, Benedict approached the blimp and made his way up the plank onto the main level of the vessel.

He wasn't sure what smelled worse: the Thames or the bitter oxidation of the metals aboard the ship. Covering his nose until he grew accustomed to it, he tried to stay out of everyone's way as he watched the sailors rushing around.

"Welcome aboard the *Newport Nine*," spoke a familiar voice.

He turned to see Erikson and the peg-legged man from earlier.

"Before you ask, no, you don't want to know what happened to the other eight," said the other in a soft tone, winking. Benedict wasn't sure if he was serious or not.

A forced guffaw escaped the commander. "He jests! Each time we gain a new vessel, we give it a number." Benedict looked back and forth in between both men. Erikson's forced reaction could only mean one thing. "Allow me to introduce you to Captain Abraham Allendale," the commander said. Benedict extended his hand in formal greeting and was met with the captain's firm shake and gentle smile in return. "You are to address the captain as 'Captain,' and myself as 'Commander,' 'Quartermaster,' 'Master,' or 'Sir.' Am I clear?"

"Yes, sir," Benedict replied dryly. Just what exactly was he getting himself into? His eyes drifted to the large rusty turbines near the rear as he changed the subject. "This ship must have been in your possession for a long time, Captain."

"No, we acquired this one about a month ago."

Raising a brow, he inspected the captain's features. There was no wink. There wasn't even exaggerated laughter coming from Erikson. Benedict forced his gut feeling into silence. He was definitely having second thoughts. Parting his lips for some sort of reply, he was grateful when the captain fished out a pocket watch from his thick coat, prompting the commander to end the conversation.

"If you'll excuse us, we must finish our rounds. Head below deck and put your belongings away. While down there, ask for McGee, our gunner. He'll put you to work."

"Yes, sir," he said, and then "Captain," as he turned away, heading for the ladder.

The gun deck was just as busy as the main deck, with sailors buzzing about to prepare for launch. Benedict wandered down the center of the passageway, keeping out of everyone's way as much as possible, his eyes on the dozens of cast-iron cannons. Wondering if they were the least rusty items on the entire ship, he stepped past empty tables and benches stationed neatly in between each one, searching for the gunner.

The clanging of a bell above deck, along with the cheers from the sailors, indicated that the ship had set sail.

"Pardon me, but I'm looking for Gunner McGee," he finally interrupted one of the passing sailors.

"Down in the galley!"

"Much appreciated." Benedict gave a polite bow of his head, despite the sailor already being a few paces ahead.

He easily found the cargo access and climbed down the ladder to the orlop deck. The air was stale, but the strong earthy aroma of freshly brewed coffee was becoming prominent.

Stepping past barrels, crates, and sacks of ingredients, he peeked through a door frame, meeting the steely blue gaze of an old bald man looking up at him.

"Are ye lost, boy?"

"I'm looking for Gunner McGee," Benedict replied.

The old man looked him up and down, eyeing him suspiciously as he scratched at his scraggly gray beard. "Tha'd be me."

"The quartermaster said that you'd put me to work."

McGee continued to scan him a moment before finally nodding. "Set yer belongin's in tha cargo area and help me wi'h breakfast, then."

Doing as instructed with his sack of clothes, Benedict then gathered biscuits from their barrels and pots of marmalade from crates as sailors began making their descent into the galley at the seventh bell.

After breakfast, they gave him the task of securing some barrels near the bilge, which didn't seem like such a bad thing until the barrels started to leak a brown sludgy liquid. Groaning in disgust as the muck easily found its way inside his expensive Turkish shoes and in between his toes, Benedict removed them—mourning the loss of the ruined footwear—opting to continue barefoot instead.

"Tha's why ye get yerself some boots!" snarked McGee. "Tha higher, tha better."

"Duly noted," he muttered as he continued securing the drums amid the sniggering of the other sailors. He ignored their mockery and expertly finished his task. Wiping off his feet with a ragged cloth, he made his way back to the gunner. "What exactly is in those?" he asked.

"Ye don't want ta know," McGee replied.

A sigh of despair escaped him. It was going to be a long few months.

CHAPTER 7

After a few more expertly completed chores, Benedict's slacks and pristine white shirt were filthy with sludge, oil, and grime. They were even torn in a few places. It vexed him when it first occurred, but he continuously reminded himself that he'd endured worse and worn worse growing up. Desperately needing the money to get back on his feet, he swallowed his pride and kept to himself as he moved through each task.

After doing some preventive maintenance to the enormous engine on deck, he spotted McGee topside, deep in discussion with the quartermaster.

"Ah! A man who's not afraid of getting himself dirty!" Erikson exclaimed as Benedict approached. "You should all aspire to be like Pretty Boy over here!"

Clenching his hands into fists, Benedict stopped in his tracks. "The name is Keenan," he called back before he could control himself.

The quartermaster's amusement quickly vanished, and he slowly, menacingly, closed the distance in between them. "Pardon?" he started, bringing an index finger to his earlobe. "What did you say?"

"My name," Benedict clarified. "It's not 'Pretty Boy,' it's Benedict Keenan."

"I didn't catch that."

Was he serious? Benedict stared at the man inquisitively. Was he deaf? Noticing the other sailors gathering around as they sniggered, Benedict realized that this was a power game. Standing tall and straight, he tugged at his filthy shirt to appear more noble and less like the orphan scrub he looked. His dark eyes bore straight through the quartermaster's green ones, and he cleared his throat.

"My name," he said, slowly exaggerating each rhythm in his words while simultaneously allowing his booming voice to carry and bounce off every metal piece so that everyone could hear him, "is Benedict Keenan. And I think the captain needs a different second-in-command if the one he currently has is deaf. It's unsafe for the crew." Erikson glared daggers, but Benedict stood his ground. The sniggering crew immediately ceased, gasping, dumbfounded. As soon as the quartermaster parted his lips to reply, Benedict hit him with the very word the man had been waiting for since the beginning: "Sir." The cherry on the top of the insult. Stepping past Erikson, he headed back down below deck.

He was hard at work scraping the rust off the cannon hooks when McGee came down a short while later.

"Are ye pouting?" the gunner asked after a beat when Benedict did not bother to acknowledge his presence.

"Hardly," he replied as he continued applying a massive amount of elbow grease to his task. "I'm fairly certain I won that battle."

"Heck yeah, ye did!" McGee cried out, causing Benedict to pause and swiftly divert his attention to the man, eyes wide in surprise. "Me an' tha boys have mad respect for ye, Keenan. Mad respect."

Benedict blinked a few times, unsure how to react. Was he supposed to say thank you? He was pretty sure that talking back to a superior was grounds for extra chores until port, where they'd kick him off the ship. It probably even meant that he couldn't get his share of the reward either. "Thanks?" he muttered despite his fluster.

"Ye shoulda seen 'is face!" McGee continued with an amused gleam in his steely eyes. "He went from boilin' over ta shocked. Captain's impressed, which means cranky ol' Jer has no more say." Benedict's heart skipped a beat as the gunner continued. "Ye'll go down in hist'ry as tha man who finally knocked 'im down a peg."

"Wait," he said, trying to gather his thoughts. "The captain knows?"

"Aye. I pleaded yer case. I told 'im yer a hard worker, Keenan. One of tha best volunteers we've seen in a long while. So ye can stay." Benedict exhaled a breath he didn't know he held as McGee handed him a copy of the articles of the ship to sign, as well as a steel nib and a small glass inkwell. "This is only yer firs' day, though, Keenan," McGee warned, his expression more serious. "Don' make me regret it."

"I won't. You have my word. Thank you."

"Now get back ta work." McGee grinned, clapping him hard on the shoulder before walking away.

The rest of the day went by smoothly, and Benedict eventually ended up in the galley, helping with dinner. Joining the rest of the crew for their meal, he sat down to laughter and congratulated applause on giving the quartermaster a taste of his own medicine.

"He's prolly sulkin' in 'is cabin." McGee sniggered as he sat next to Benedict.

"Better him than me," he said with a smirk. "So, what brings you on this journey?"

McGee spooned the steaming meal, shoving it in his mouth as if he had no pain receptors to react to the heat. Swallowing, he then replied,

"Been wit' dis 'ere crew fer a decade now. Not quite a foundin' member if ye will, but one of tha oldest, minus tha captain. I joined fer tha money. I still do it fer tha money."

"A decade's worth of money should see you in a castle, should it not?"

"I give it to tha needy. I've got a few kids. They've 'ad it rough since tha lands split, an' I'm not tha type ta hoard it all ta myself."

"How generous." His brows raised, impressed.

"And you?" McGee asked. "Wha' do ye intend ta do with yer money?"

Smirking, he finally took a spoonful of his food. "First, I'm going to buy new clothes . . ." McGee nearly choked from his chortle before Benedict continued, "then I plan to move to the Upper Lands."

McGee raised a brow and looked him up and down once more, but Benedict offered nothing else. He knew, based on the way the gunner kept eyeing him up, that McGee thought that he already came from the Upper Lands. Parting his lips as if to further inquire, he instead returned to finishing his stew. "Here's ta makin' tha' plan come true."

"Cheers," Benedict said as he took a large swig of his drink.

As Benedict finished his stew, a figure approached, looming. "A word, if you please, Mister Keenan."

Benedict was in no mood for another battle of wits with the quartermaster, but his tongue lashed before he could stop himself. "So, you remember my name."

He didn't see the expression on Erikson's face, but by the looks on the other sailors' faces, it would have been well worth it. The quartermaster cleared his throat. Did Benedict detect a hint of embarrassment? "Captain Allendale wishes to see you."

Benedict didn't outwardly react, though his mind reeled at why the captain would even want to see him. Didn't McGee plead his case? Scooping up his last bite, he stood and finally turned to face the quartermaster, staring him down for a moment, unimpressed. Finally, he spoke. "Lead the way, sir."

Erikson blinked and quickly recomposed, nodding before glancing at the other sailors. "Gentlemen," he acknowledged, then turned on his heels to lead Benedict to the captain.

The interior of the rigid balloon was like night and day compared to the corroded wear and tear of the rest of the airship. His attention stolen by the depiction of well-known cities in the framed paintings adorning the walls, he followed the quartermaster past tables draped in sumptuously luxurious cloth, seemingly set for a lavish ball. Was this what the captain spent his earnings on? Surely, making sure the vessel was in proper working condition was more important than aesthetic frivolities.

"Mister Keenan," Captain Allendale greeted, stepping away from one of the large tilted windows. "You've made quite a series of impressions."

"Such as?" Benedict raised a brow, authentically curious.

"From bold and confident, to classy and charming . . . then I believe I heard the term 'Pretty Boy' being thrown around." Benedict internally groaned. Of course that was one of the impressions. The captain continued, "Followed by conceited and arrogant . . ." Swallowing hard, Benedict spotted out of the corner of his eye a complacent smile on Erikson's lips. "So far, to be concluded with hard-working and dependable. Am I missing anything, Mister Keenan?"

"No, Captain," he replied, his heart pounding.

"Jeremiah here tells me you have quite the impressive list of ship skills. Is this true?"

"It is," he replied, adding "Captain," before he cast a quick glance at the quartermaster. What was he up to?

"Does that include janitorial duties?"

"It can," he replied, raising a brow.

"Then you can start here first thing after breakfast."

Benedict scanned the pristine perimeters, confused, before placing his attention back on the captain. "Forgive me. I'm not sure that I understand . . ."

"You don't understand cleaning?" Erikson smugly asked.

Benedict purposely ignored the quartermaster, his attention still on the captain. "These quarters are spotless, compared to, well . . ."

"Compared to the rest of the ship?" Captain Allendale offered. "Yes. Fools even the best, doesn't it?"

Benedict was definitely misled, but it still made no sense. "It's wonderful knowing that this room will still be pristine when the entire ship corrodes away," he mused.

The captain gave an amused chuckle, which triggered Erikson to follow suit, though boisterously. Benedict didn't understand what was so funny; it was the truth.

"You best get to work on the rest of the ship then, Alchemist," Erikson jested.

Benedict blinked. "What? I'm no alchemist."

The quartermaster's demeanor suddenly changed. His eyes widened in shock before narrowing threateningly. "Come again?"

Benedict watched Erikson for a moment before he turned his attention back to the captain. "I apologize, but I'm no alchemist." Glancing back to the quartermaster, he added, "Did I ever mention that I was?"

Erikson looked back and forth from Benedict to the captain, whose gaze was grave.

"Jeremiah, explain yourself," Captain Allendale said.

Stuttering before he gestured to all of Benedict, he blurted, "But you dress like a noble! Like an alchemy user!"

"Fools even the best, doesn't it?" Benedict countered with a wink before his attention fell back to Captain Allendale. He knew when to retreat, despite his satisfaction of watching the quartermaster squirm. "Thank you for this conversation, Captain. If that is all, I shall return in the morning with cleaning supplies."

"Aye, that is all for now, Mister Keenan. Thank you."

With a nod and one last glimpse at the quartermaster, Benedict walked out of the blimp and down onto the main deck, where the sailors were enjoying the rest of their evening off with alcohol, pipes, and lively chatter. Heading below deck, he glanced about for McGee as he made his way in the galley's direction, where he found the gunner peeling vegetables for the stew the next day.

"Keenan!" McGee shot up from the overturned wooden bucket he sat on. "There ye are. Everythin' all right?"

"Just splendid," he replied. "I am now Captain Allendale's personal janitor, and I'm unsure if that's a promotion or a demotion."

McGee chuckled. "Tha' would make ya 'is favorite, let's keep it at tha'."

Musing on if that comment should have been reassuring or not, he at least comforted himself in knowing that he could possibly overhear some insider information and use it to his advantage.

With a motion of his head, McGee led him to the cleaning supplies he'd need the next morning. As they walked, the gunner alerted him to the strict rules on being caught smoking below deck, as well as the lights-out curfew. McGee then led him to the sleeping quarters, which were nothing but netted slings suspended above the cannons and tables on the gun deck. Benedict had slept in, on, and around a lot worse, so the sight hardly fazed him. In fact, his whole body immediately felt very heavy and sore, reminding him he hadn't slept very well the night before. Suddenly, the hammock seemed like a dream come true.

"Ye joinin' us fer some fresh air?" McGee asked.

"Not tonight," he answered.

Nodding, the gunner began walking away. "Suit yerself, then."

Benedict smirked. Did he detect a bit of disappointment? "Goodnight," he called out after him, receiving nothing but a dismissive wave in return.

Despite quickly falling asleep, it felt like he hadn't slept much at all. Waking before dawn for the morning watch and deck swabbing, the brisk air on the Atlantic Ocean quickly gave him the alertness he needed to get the job done.

After breakfast, Benedict made his way back to the balloon and began setting up to clean. Clean what, he wasn't even sure. There wasn't a speck of dust on anything, let alone dirt or smudges. And so instead of washing everything, Benedict just tidied and set everything up, unwrinkled the cloths, and turned to ask Captain Allendale for more orders when he spotted him approaching.

"Good morning, Mister Keenan. Sleep well?"

"Like a log," he answered.

"I want to apologize for Jeremiah yesterday. He can be a bit . . ."

"Stuffy?" he replied impulsively. "Full of himself? I noticed."

The captain cast him a look of warning. "'Assuming' is the word I was going for." Benedict cleared his throat, embarrassed. It wasn't anywhere near the words he would have used. "So, if you're not an alchemist," Captain Allendale continued, "what's your story?"

"Just a simple man wanting to live the big life and acting as if I've already made it. Nothing more."

The captain watched him carefully, eventually nodding sagely before stepping past him toward the exit. "Carry on then, Mister Keenan."

"Captain," he called out, spinning to catch the man before he left. When Captain Allendale paused and looked over his shoulder, Benedict continued, "What would you have had me do if I were an alchemist?"

"Make the ship better," was the captain's simple reply, with the hint of a smile. Nodding farewell, he headed for the main deck, leaving Benedict to ruminate on his reply.

Pulling himself out of his thoughts, he sighed as he realized he had failed to ask the captain what he needed help with next. Guess it was time to needlessly scrub the immaculate floors.

Benedict was almost done when the captain returned to the balloon. He stopped nearby, inspecting the invisible progress with a content smile.

"Excellent work, Mister Keenan. Finish up, then you're free for the rest of the day."

Benedict blinked as he turned to what he finished of his task. How could the captain even tell what he had cleaned? "If I may ask, Captain," he started, "why am I here?" Captain Allendale raised a brow, and Benedict exhaled deeply. "Cleaning, I mean," he clarified. "The place is already spotless, and I can immediately think of at least a dozen places on the ship that can benefit from an equally good scrubbing, instead."

The captain clasped his hands behind his back, contemplating his answer. "I see potential in you, Keenan," he finally replied. "A widely skilled sailor such as yourself is an asset that any rogue captain would be a fool not to keep close by." It was Benedict's turn to raise a brow, suspicious. The captain hadn't even seen what he was capable of yet. "Also," he started, a mischievous twinkle in his eyes, "it's keeping you out of trouble."

Ah, there it was. "You mean out of the commander's way," he spelled out.

Stepping past Benedict toward his quarters without a reply, Captain Allendale called out over his shoulder, "Enjoy your day off. I don't hand out too many of those."

"Noted. Thank you, Captain," he said, returning to work.

Making his way below deck once he had finished with the floor, he spotted McGee repairing a cannon. The gunner raised a brow as he approached. "Everythin' alrigh'?"

"Seems so. The captain gave me the rest of the day off."

The gunner laughed. "Definitely 'is favorite!"

Benedict smirked at the remark. "Need any help?" he then asked.

"Nah, I'm almost done. Go enjoy yer day off. Tha captain don' grant tha' too often."

"So I hear," Benedict mused out loud as he climbed into his hammock and read from a tattered book he had found for the rest of the day.

CHAPTER 8

They had been at sea for a little over a month, and the days were only getting colder. It had always been damp below deck, but with autumn halfway over, it was more difficult for Benedict—accustomed to less frigid temperatures—to stay warm during breakfast. He huddled into his wool coat as he rubbed at his arms, his attention on the closed gunport he had just peeked through.

He'd noticed the ship slowing for the past few days. Was this a normal occurrence? He couldn't tell; it was slight enough that the other sailors seemed unfazed. He turned his attention to McGee on the other side of the table.

Despite being in the rigid balloon all day long instead of the gun deck, Benedict and McGee had bonded during their time above the ocean. He reveled in the old man's stories of his travels, and the gunner never failed to inquire about his many skill sets aboard a ship. If he could trust anyone's answer, it would be McGee's.

"Why has the ship slowed?" he finally asked.

"Could be we're preppin' fer a storm," the gunner suggested, as he shoveled oats into his mouth.

Benedict frowned. The old gunner was on deck like the rest of them for watch and chores; he witnessed the sunrise and clear skies like the rest of them. "We didn't slow our course until the last storm was right in front of us," he pointed out.

McGee shrugged as he continued with his oats. Surely, his rank aboard the ship would have made him privy to such information? Benedict figured that he'd have to inquire to someone else. Thankfully, he worked right alongside the captain's quarters.

Unfortunately, as the day progressed, his window of opportunity grew smaller and smaller: the captain did not leave the helm or his quarters attached to it, and the quartermaster was with him the entire time. He wanted answers but didn't much care to seek them out around the insufferable quartermaster.

While he was wiping down the already-spotless windows, he finally heard the door open. Turning, he spotted Erikson staring right at him.

"Keenan, report to the infirmary," he ordered.

"Why?" he asked, his question just as defensive as the order was aggressive.

"Just do it!" Erikson hissed.

"Mister Keenan," the captain calmly voiced as he appeared in the doorway, "what Jeremiah is keeping to himself is that Mister Bailey needs help. Since you're so flexible, I thought you the best suited for the task."

Benedict cast a rapid glare in Erikson's direction—who tried really hard to compose himself, as if those were indeed the exact words he had spoken—before nodding. "Yes, Captain."

The quartermaster spun and marched back to the helm without another word. Captain Allendale met Benedict's gaze for a moment before quietly shutting the door between them. Benedict shook his head, the gears within turning. What was going on? Why were the captain and the quartermaster locked in a meeting all day long? Did it have anything to do with the ship slowing down? And while the quartermaster had kept his distance since their battle of wits, why did he seem so tense? Each question prompted more, and he knew he would get nowhere with assumptions, so he headed for the infirmary on the opposite side of the rigid balloon as requested.

Benedict knocked on the hollow steel door, but there was no reply. Banging a little louder, he glanced over his shoulder to Captain Allendale's quarters, secretly hoping that he was scolding Erikson for his attitude. The man had no tact. Bringing his attention back to the unmoving infirmary door, he raised a brow. Didn't Mister Bailey need help? Where was he? Curious, Benedict gripped the handwheel and rotated it to the left. It squeaked loudly, and the door creaked just as noisily as he peeked inside.

The infirmary looked nothing like he'd imagined. Filthy, cramped, and filled to the brim with tools and gadgets, he wondered just how safe the room truly was. Not a single inch of wall could be seen, and he envisioned himself trying to dodge the falling sharp objects during a storm.

"What do you need?" came a voice.

Benedict flinched, startled. So, there *was* somebody inside. His gaze eventually found a scraggly bald man sitting on an upturned bucket, cleaning rust—or was it dried blood? It smelled the same—off tools. "I knocked," Benedict started.

"Nobody knocks in an emergency," the man replied, not once lifting his head. "If you knocked, there was no emergency, therefore I was in no rush to answer."

Was everyone on the damned ship a smartass? "The captain said that you needed help."

"I don't."

Benedict blinked. "Are you sure? The captain said—"

"I don't need help," he repeated flatly.

Still in the doorway, he contemplated just turning around and getting back to work, but he figured that if the captain wanted him to help, then he'd at least offer. "Well, is there anything I can help you with?" he asked. "Perhaps help you disinfect some of those tools?"

Mister Bailey finally looked up, his blue eyes eerily uneven thanks to the multiple looking glasses in front of his face, attached to the contraption atop of his head. Inspecting Benedict from head to toe, he then shook his head and returned to his work.

Throwing his hands up in defeat, Benedict stepped away from the infirmary. Maybe he was mistaken about who it was that needed help? Crossing the balloon back to the captain's quarters, he paused before knocking, frowning as he overheard voices on the other side.

They were speaking about alchemy. Benedict strained to hear, as their voices were very hushed. Retrieving infusions . . . was that what the job was about?

"But it's dangerous!" he heard the quartermaster hiss, clearly displeased.

"All our jobs are. That's why we take them on."

"But Captain, this is just—"

"Listen well, Jeremiah. We are being paid to retrieve this. Nobody knows what it does but those scientists. Not even me."

“All the more reason to turn back now! What kind of mess did we entangle ourselves in?”

“That’s not our concern. Our concern is the retrieval. And if there is even the smallest chance we can catch up—”

“What are you doing?” interrupted a new voice—not coming from inside the captain’s quarters.

Caught off guard, Benedict’s heart skipped a beat. He spun around to find Mister Bailey watching him with a quizzical look—free from the multiple looking glasses—on his features. Benedict parted his lips to speak, but he had nothing. No excuse: he had been caught. Stepping aside, he began walking away. That was it; Mister Bailey would tell the captain that he was snooping, and he’d never hear the end of it from the quartermaster.

He heard the knock, followed by the door opening, as he continued to his job of washing the windows.

“Captain, I am going to need some more acetone and sulfur once we dock.”

“Duly noted, Mister Bailey. Is that everything?”

Benedict glanced over to see the short, scrawny man nod as he headed back to the infirmary without even paying any attention to Benedict. Maybe he didn’t care that Benedict was listening in? Maybe he didn’t know—after all, he didn’t quite seem all there. His attention veered from Mister Bailey to meet the captain's gaze. "He didn't need help," Benedict explained. Captain Allendale mouthed that he knew before quietly shutting the door behind him once again.

Benedict furrowed his brows. So the captain purposely sent him on a wild goose chase? For what reason? Things were growing rapidly concerning, and he didn't like it one bit. Trying to eavesdrop on the conversation from his location by the windows—he even held his breath to see if it would make a difference—he couldn't make anything out. Maybe they were finished talking. Having caught enough to ruminate over, he went back to washing the already-spotless windows.

He barely touched his meal during supper when McGee sat across from him, stew in hand. "Everythin' alrigh', Keenan?"

He had spent the past few hours trying to piece the puzzle together. What kind of alchemical infusion were they talking about? Why did the scientists want the infusion so badly? And the most important question of all: why the secrecy? He faintly nodded in response to the gunner's question before he blurted, "What exactly are we doing here? What are we really getting paid for?"

"It's a retrieval mission, Keenan," McGee sighed as he began eating.

"I overheard some things," he admitted.

McGee's eyes lit up. "Do tell!"

Leaning in, he spoke so low that he had a hard time even hearing himself. "We're retrieving an infusion."

McGee tilted his head expectantly, waiting for more. When nothing came, he inquired. "Is tha' it?" Benedict nodded, to which the gunner pulled away in a huff. "'Ere I though' ye had somethin' good."

Benedict shook his head. As much as he wanted to reveal more, he didn't know how much the gunner was dutifully obliged to reveal to the captain. No, he couldn't say anything more. Judging by McGee's reaction, however, retrieving infusions seemed like a common occurrence and nothing to worry about.

He'd just have to continue to piece the puzzle together himself.

CHAPTER 9

Mister Keenan, I have a job for you."

Stifling a yawn, Benedict set the lantern in the center of the table after dusting the ball shade. The glass glinted in the early morning sunshine, casting caustic reflections throughout the interior of the rigid balloon. Turning to the captain, he awaited his orders.

The captain's attention was on his hands as he picked at his nails. After a beat, he cleared his throat. "The *Nine* has been slowing down."

"I noticed," he replied, eliciting a single impressed nod from the captain, their eyes finally meeting. It had been a few days since overhearing what he had, and each one of those days saw a continued reduction in the airship's speed, as well as decreased altitude, which he had astonishingly overlooked.

"The engine needs repair." This did not surprise Benedict one bit. "I need you to join the team on deck to tend to it."

"Yes, Captain."

He'd just spun around to head to the main deck when the captain continued, "You'll be reporting to Jeremiah." This caused him to pause in his steps with an internal groan. "I trust you to be the better man, Keenan," he added.

The captain trusted *him* to be the better man? That said a lot about Erikson . . . why was he even quartermaster, anyway? Gritting his teeth and soothing the outrage inside of him, he nodded. "Yes, Captain," he said as he walked away.

A beast of a machine, the *Nine*'s cast-iron cylindrical engine took up most of the main deck at its center. Benedict was no mechanic, but he had tinkered with enough things growing up that he could get by.

The team in charge of repairs comprised four other sailors, one having volunteered at port in London, much like Benedict. He was relieved when one of the other team members handed him tools instead of the quartermaster, who stood nearby, observing the happenings on deck. Benedict wasn't sure if he was purposely being ignored or not, but he'd take any opportunity that he could to avoid interacting with the insufferable man.

The air about the engine was hot from the coal-fed fireboxes, as well as from the exhausts and valves. Benedict actually enjoyed sweating versus freezing for a change, though he preferred the heat not be accompanied by singeing his arms and fingers with every turn of his wrench.

"Are you sure this will be enough?" asked the mousey freckled lad from London as he expertly climbed out of a tight space without even burning himself.

"It'll be enough to keep us going," replied the grumpy old man known as Noah, his long gray beard stained with grease.

"'Keeping us going' will not get us to port any faster," the Londoner said. "I don't know about the rest of you lads, but the faster we get to port, the faster we can get off this freezing airship."

"And into the bed of a whore, you mean!" sniggered a hook-nosed man.

Noah joined in on the teasing with a sneer. "Whatever keeps him warm at night!"

The lot of them laughed—even the one being mocked—but the fourth sailor, a normally quiet man in a blue turban named Qasim, eventually spoke up. "We can set it up to go faster, but we'd need infusions."

The laughing trio stopped, suddenly glum.

"But we don't have infusions on board," the Londoner said.

"Of course we do!" the hook-nosed man replied. "What do you think lights our lanterns at night?"

"Are you willing to go the rest of the trip without light then?" Noah grunted. "I'd like to see the gunner catch you with a torch below deck!"

While the trio went on, Benedict pondered the situation. The infusions had to be locked up, and the chances of acquiring permission to use any of them were slim to none. But he suddenly had an idea. Sliding down toward Qasim, he asked, "How much do we need?"

Raising a thick brow, the man made a quick calculation. "A lot."

Benedict pressed his lips tightly together. His idea would no longer work. Glancing about for another plan, his eyes found the horizon. "Can we dilute it?" he asked.

Qasim studied him carefully, suspicious, before his eyes glazed over, deep in thought. His lips moved silently, and eventually he nodded. "I think it can work," he said, his gaze fully returned.

"Perfect." He began climbing down the engine. "I know where we can get some."

Jumping down the rest of the way, he stood up to find himself face-to-face with the quartermaster. His body tensed as Erikson's mouth twisted into a snarl, and he bit his tongue to prevent himself from saying anything that would disappoint McGee or the captain. Thankfully, there was no need for a quick-witted reply, as the quartermaster turned his attention to the rest of the team working on the engine. Breathing easy again, Benedict continued on.

Once inside the rigid balloon, Benedict grabbed the closest lantern atop of the tables. Removing the glass, he picked up the small blue sphere and held it up to the light through the window with his index finger and thumb, watching the infusion swirl inside. He then did the same with the next lantern, and the third and fourth.

"Keenan, what do you think you're doing?"

Casting a quick glare in the quartermaster's direction, he returned to his work. Despite having to report to Erikson for the project, he had been content with their mutual disregard for one another. He did not appreciate the accusatory tone in the quartermaster's voice.

"I asked you a question," Erikson barked.

"I'm doing my job," he snapped in return before he could hold himself back.

"And what job would that be?"

Smoldering in aggravation, he clenched his jaw before replying. "Repairing the engine."

"The engine is on deck, sailor. This looks like theft to me."

Benedict spun around to face the quartermaster, incredulous. So he was being accused of theft too? Biting his tongue hard to prevent himself from lashing out, he turned back to the lanterns. "We are testing a theory that will make the ship faster," he said, using the bottom of his shirt as a net for the spheres, "and we need infusions to do it." It was taking everything he had to remain calm and polite.

"We don't need additional attributes to the engine, Keenan, we just need it to work!"

The quartermaster was maddening. Clearly, his hatred was clouding his judgment; who wouldn't want to get to land quicker with the onset of winter? And the faster he could get away from Erikson, the better. "I'm—"

"Put the orbs down," he harshly interrupted, "or I'll—"

"What's going on here?" The captain cut in from the doorway, his eyes shifting back and forth from both men before settling on his second-in-command.

The quartermaster cleared his throat. "That's what I was investigating, Captain." Benedict rolled his eyes as he waited for the lie. "I followed him after he left his team to find him stealing orbs."

"With all due respect, sir!" The rage in Benedict's voice echoed through the rigid balloon, the venom with which he spoke the quartermaster's title dripping with animosity. Though he was addressing Erikson, he honestly didn't care enough to turn around to face him. "How you have your fingers stuck in your ears and still manage to point accusingly baffles me! If you could get off your high horse long enough to listen to someone other than yourself, you'd realize you're not the only one trying to get us out of our current predicament."

"We don't need improvements!" the quartermaster hissed.

"I'm sure the captain would like to reach land sooner rather than later."

Erikson took a breath to retort, but Captain Allendale, his ever-composed attention on Benedict, raised a hand to stop the quartermaster. "Your argument, Mister Keenan?"

He waited for the quartermaster to squeeze something in, but surprisingly, no words came. He almost wanted to turn back to the man just to see his expression. With a nod to the captain, he went on. "We're testing a theory that will make the ship faster. We need infusions, and I figured the infused orbs in here were our best bet to test it out. I apologize for not asking permission first, Captain."

"They have satisfactorily repaired the engine, Captain. I have a list of other tasks that need—"

"I think that's a grand idea," the captain said, causing Erikson to pause.

"But Captain . . ."

"Any opportunity to make up for lost time is always welcome in my books," said Captain Allendale. Benedict held back a victorious grin and regretted not being able to see the expression on the quartermaster's face. "Carry on, Mister Keenan. May your theory prove true. A word, if you will, Jeremiah?"

"Thank you, Captain." Benedict continued collecting the infused orbs, ignoring the feeling of Erikson's eyes burning holes right through him as the quartermaster made his way to the captain's quarters, shutting the door behind him.

Benedict inhaled and exhaled deeply. Oh, how that man made his blood boil. Quickly gathering the remaining orbs, he made his way back to the main deck and to Qasim.

CHAPTER 10

The blanket of fog was particularly dense before dawn, casting an eerie and filthy obscurity around the lanterns on deck. Benedict hated it.

It had been a few days since repairing the engine. Qasim—who, Benedict found out, had learned a thing or two about alchemy from a distant cousin during religious gatherings—had been correct in his calculations; diluting the infusions gave the ship an added oomph to her journey, even if a tiny one.

The airship's brass bell chimed loudly as a warning to any potential vessel in the distance, but it also caused an annoying reverberation through the steel ladder he stood on for his watch halfway up the rigid balloon.

The tension aboard the *Nine* was just as thick as the fog. The moist air, with its briny tang—and previously so bitterly cold—clung to

Benedict's hair, beard, and clothing, weighing him down. Keeping a sharp eye out for shapes along the horizon was a difficult task through the mist, forcing him to squint. The air about him suddenly turned stale, and he frowned at the stench of burnt wood and tar. What was on fire?

"Debris, sir!" a sailor on deck called out to the quartermaster.

Benedict's eyes left the horizon for the surface of the ocean below as Erikson rushed to alert the captain. What happened? His attention was on the floating fragments, barely visible through the hazy whiteness, when he spotted something else. He focused his gaze, and his muscles became rigid. Was that . . .? "Man overboard!" he cried.

The constant cautious chimes of the bell became more urgent, alerting all aboard of the emergency. There, collapsed upon a plank, was a body.

The airship slowed to a halt and descended, hovering just out of reach of the water. Benedict rushed down the ladder and made his way to the edge of the ship, his attention never once leaving the body at sea.

"It's our target ship!" bellowed the quartermaster in irritation. "Bring him in!" he ordered as he rushed back to the captain.

A few sailors rushed to lower a yawl for rescue, and the ship's keel slowly dipped into the

Atlantic. Benedict's eyes widened as the act caused large ripples in the water, teetering the body aboard the plank, causing it to partially slip into the frigid ocean. If the crew failed, he was out of his share of the bounty. But there might just be a chance . . .

Time was running out, however; if the man was still alive, he wouldn't be for much longer.

Swiftly removing his wool coat, he uncoiled the nearest roll of tightly woven ropes, tying one end to the metal cleat and the other end about his waist. He hopped onto the gunwale before anyone finally noticed.

"Keenan!" the sailor lowering the yawl bellowed. "Get down, you'll be—"

"He won't make it!" Benedict shouted back before diving off the edge of the ship after a quick calculation of his descent.

He cried out in shock below the surface as the ice-cold water surrounded his entire body. Skin tingling and mind blank as his body protested in response, he quickly forced himself to get his bearings now that there was less air in his lungs. Trying to determine up from down, he followed the rope around his waist and eventually broke the surface with a loud gasp and cry.

Instantly regretting his actions, his entire body shivered uncontrollably as he tried to focus. He dove into the ocean for a reason and desperately needed to rein his mind back to the task at hand. Glancing through the fog for the man on the broken plank, he caught sight of the white shirt just as it slipped below the harsh ripples.

Benedict dove under, clumsily kicking his feet as hard as he could despite the numbness setting in. Urgently swimming after the body, he tightly clenched his jaw to fight the desperate need to extinguish the sensation of a growing fire in his lungs. He didn't even want to imagine the drowning man's own water-filled lungs. Reaching out, he barely gripped the body's shirt with his numb fingers before changing direction for some much-needed air. Benedict had a split-second moment of panic. He didn't know if he'd make it.

His body gave in, and he took a breath. Thankfully, he'd broken the surface, and the gulp he took was air instead of water. Gritting his chattering teeth as his entire body protested, he held the man up to his body as tightly as he could with one arm and haphazardly pulled himself along the rope with his other hand until the yawl reached him.

Two sailors pulled the drowned man into the boat first, then Benedict, who collapsed as he gasped for air. His entire body violently trembled from the shock of the frigid water, and he felt the darkness creep in, but he knew that he only had a few seconds left before the man was lost forever.

The sailors' voices were muffled, as if he was underwater once more. They tried pulling him away from the body, but he clumsily fended them off, his limbs feeling excessively heavy as he did so. Why were they pulling him away? He needed to help! Benedict began applying pressure with both hands when the body convulsed and the man coughed up a gallon of water, choking and gasping for breath. Benedict fell back as one sailor shoved him out of the way. Taking much-needed breaths himself, the darkness quickly closed in. Everything became indistinct before he passed out.

The nauseating scent of blood surrounded him as he came to, and an intense tingling sensation buzzed throughout his entire body. Gritting his teeth to counter the discomfort, he slowly opened his eyes, instantly wishing that he hadn't, as a blur of rusty tools and gadgets hanging from the ceiling of the infirmary greeted him. A groan escaped him as he shut his eyes once more.

"Glad you've returned to us, Mister Keenan," spoke a familiar voice. Benedict's eyes shot open before he blinked away the blurriness, revealing the form of the captain holding up a small trinket attached to a chain, inspecting it from all angles. "It seems they attacked our target ship in the middle of the night," he added. "And though purposely diving into the Atlantic in the winter was a careless move, it just might have secured us our bounty."

"'Might'?" Benedict croaked, followed by a coughing fit that resulted in hisses and groans as his muscles tensed and screamed in protest. His thoughts reeled as his actions replayed in his mind.

"He's breathing," the captain replied. "And we have you to thank for that."

Benedict turned his attention to the next bed. Wincing at the effort as he lifted himself up to rest on his elbows, his eyes fell on the man with the mop of black hair. "Who is he?"

Deep in thought, the captain set the trinket down onto the table as his attention traveled to the form hidden beneath heavy wool blankets. After a beat, he finally replied, "I don't know. We'll find out soon enough." Turning back to Benedict, he added, "Get some rest. I expect you back on your shift tomorrow."

"Yes, Captain." Hissing through clenched teeth to keep from crying out, he adjusted himself to lie back down. Shutting his eyes as Captain Allendale left the infirmary, Benedict inhaled and exhaled deeply, ready for more rest, when someone whispered.

"Thank you."

Benedict questioned whether he had really heard anything at all. Perhaps he caught a voice from outside the infirmary?

"Thank you," the voice repeated, and Benedict darted his full attention to the man on the next bed over. "For rescuing me," he continued.

There was no movement from the man. His eyes stayed closed, and his body remained unmoving beneath the heavy covers, with no signs of panic or distress. If Benedict hadn't distinctly seen the man's lips move, he could have easily convinced himself that the man was still in a coma and that he was hearing things. Parting his lips to reply, Mister Bailey interrupted him upon entering the room.

"Captain says you're awake."

Continuing to watch the unknown man for a moment, he finally replied, "I am."

"Good. How do you feel?" he asked, reaching beneath Benedict's own covers for his wrist, verifying his pulse.

"Like I've been run over by a horse and carriage."

"Perfect," came Mister Bailey's reply, causing Benedict to raise a brow. "It means that you're alive."

"Good to know," Benedict said with a wince.

The doctor made sure that Benedict was kept warm before moving to the rescued man. Checking his vitals, he eventually nodded to himself, satisfied, and turned to his makeshift seat, where he fiddled with an inkwell and fountain pen.

Benedict's attention darted back to the stranger, who still expertly did not move. Was he still awake and listening in? Had he fallen asleep or back into a coma? Benedict didn't know, but one thing was for certain: the captain was going to want answers, and he wanted to be there for it all.

CHAPTER 11

It was the voices that woke him up.

"Where are they?" It sounded like the quartermaster.

"I don't know what you're talking about," came an unfamiliar mutter.

"You know very well what I'm talking about!" Erikson hissed. "Where are the infusions?"

"Like I said, I don't know what you're talking about."

"You best search that brain of yours, or—"

"Hey!" Benedict interrupted, slightly louder than he had expected, causing him to cough. "The man says he doesn't know what you're talking about. Leave him be," he croaked.

Startled, Erikson spun around with wide eyes to face Benedict's glare. The rescued man took the opportunity to snatch something from the quartermaster's hands. After briefly turning his attention to the survivor, Erikson quickly returned his gaze to Benedict. "You best mind your business, Keenan."

"My sleep was my business," he countered, "and you woke me up. I'd like to get back to that sleep, if you don't mind."

When Mister Bailey stepped into the cramped room, the quartermaster hissed, discontent, before stomping out.

"What just happened?" Bailey blinked in confusion.

"I pissed him off," Benedict casually replied with a yawn. "As usual."

"You certainly seem to have a knack for it," the doctor muttered offhandedly.

"Why did you tell him I was awake?" the stranger asked with a frown.

"Simply following orders," Bailey replied.

"Whose orders?" Benedict asked. With his question ignored, he had a feeling that it wasn't Captain Allendale who had instructed the doctor to alert them when the stranger awoke.

"How do you feel?" Bailey asked the unknown man.

"Completely dehydrated," he replied.

"I shall get you a drink then," Bailey said, stepping back out of the infirmary.

Benedict watched the stranger sitting on the bed fiddle with the trinket he had snatched from the quartermaster. "How did he know you were awake?" Benedict asked.

The man's attention shifted from the object in his hand to Benedict, and it took him a moment to reply. "My respiratory rate and heart rate," he said. "They are extremely regular when comatose and quite variable when awake."

Benedict blinked blankly and slowly sat up, hissing from his sore muscles as he did so. "Those are some pretty big words you're using," he pointed out. "Where did you learn them?"

"I'm a surgeon," the man replied. Benedict's brows raised, impressed. He was certain the man could dance circles around Bailey. "Doctor Mathias Darley," he introduced.

"Benedict Keenan," he said in turn.

Mathias's brown eyes traveled about the infirmary, and he scrunched his nose in disgust. Good; Benedict wasn't the only one who thought that the room they were in was unsafe. "Where am I?" he asked.

"You're aboard the *Newport Nine*," came Bailey's reply as he returned with two steaming mugs of liquid, handing Mathias one first, then Benedict.

"What happened?" Benedict asked before taking a sip of his broth. It warmed his insides, and he was happy to let it do so. "Why did we find a surgeon floating among debris in the middle of the Atlantic?"

Mathias shut his eyes after a few sips. If the broth's warmth felt wonderful to Benedict, he could only imagine how the surgeon felt. Eventually, a sigh escaped him. "I was aboard the *Sweepstake*."

The *Sweepstake* was a galleon in service to the Queen. "You're a royal?" Benedict asked.

Shaking his head, Mathias corrected the thought. "I am a surgeon for the Royal Medical Services stationed in Elgin." Bailey, who had been scribbling down some notes, glanced up from his work, surprise etched in his features.

Benedict remembered the captain mentioning that their target ship had been attacked. Was it because of the infusions on board? But all airships had infusions, so what made the *Sweepstake* a target?

Shaking his head and muttering medical jargon, Mister Bailey left the infirmary once more. Benedict needed to hasten and take advantage of being alone with the man. Hopefully, the surgeon wouldn't be reserved with his answers toward the man who rescued him. "Why was an airship full of medical practitioners attacked?" Benedict asked.

Mathias frowned again. "I . . ." he started, but never finished the sentence. What was he hiding?

"Does it have anything to do with the infusions the quartermaster was going on about?" Mathias said nothing, and Benedict figured the silence meant that he knew something, after all.

"What's with the piece of jewelry?" he then asked.

Mathias swiftly pulled the trinket beneath the covers and out of view, more than likely shoving it into his pocket. "It's nothing. Why are you asking so many questions?"

"Just trying to figure out if you're friend or foe," Benedict lied before sipping more of his broth.

Captain Allendale entered the infirmary while Bailey stood in the doorway. The captain's blue eyes set on Benedict first. "Is he well enough to be dismissed, Mister Bailey?"

"Aye, Captain," the doctor answered.

"I am going to need some privacy, Mister Keenan," he said. "Mister Bailey will help you to your hammock."

Benedict watched the captain for a moment. He wanted to be present and overhear what Mathias had to say, but he knew Captain Allendale wouldn't make an exception just for him. Finally, he nodded. "Yes, Captain."

Bailey aided Benedict to his feet. His muscles screamed in protest, and he clenched his teeth with the effort. Casting a last glance at Mathias, whose attention was on the liquid in his mug, he limped out of the infirmary. The door shut behind him, and that was that. He'd never know what was being said.

Below deck, Benedict limped toward his hammock as McGee rushed toward him. "Yer alive!"

He chuckled with a wince. "Yes, that's the general consensus."

"Wha' about tha man ya saved?"

"Alive and well, from what I can tell," he replied.

"Mister Keenan needs his rest, please," Bailey cut in. McGee nodded and returned to work.

The climb into his hammock was ridiculously difficult, and relief washed over his screaming muscles once they finally settled. He truly hoped that they'd quiet themselves by morning if the captain demanded that he return to work. Bailey made sure that he was kept warm before taking his leave, and hundreds of possible conversations between the captain and surgeon played out in his mind before he fell into a dreamless sleep.

CHAPTER 12

A shout startled him awake. Benedict's eyes blew wide, searching for the source. He saw nothing but darkness before a loud explosion rocked his surroundings. Where was he? What was going on?

Sailors leaped from their hammocks and rushed to put out the flames as best they could via the portholes as McGee made his way to the gun deck, roaring orders. It took Benedict a moment to regain clarity amid the chaos: it was nighttime, he was aboard the *Nine*, and they were under attack.

Gritting his teeth against the lingering soreness of his muscles, Benedict flipped out of his hammock and dashed for the stairs. Had the ones responsible for destroying the *Sweepstake* returned? If his suspicions were correct, then the assailants were after his reward: the surgeon.

The main deck was a mess of scattered debris and burning fires amid sword clashes and gunshots. Swiftly glancing about to assess the situation, he spotted three small floating wooden brigantines tethered to the *Nine* and hissed his displeasure: the telltale sign of sky pirates. Ducking and shielding himself from flying wreckage as an enormous explosion boomed overhead, Benedict watched as a body hit the deck, impaled by a thick fragment of rusty steel. The ship would not last much longer.

Snatching the gun that slid near his bare feet, he shot to disarm but did not quite hit as many pirates as he would have liked. Guns were definitely not his specialty. Growling in annoyance, his attention darted to the stairs to the balloon above, where the quartermaster fended off the enemy. Rushing toward them all, Benedict fired, hitting one pirate in the shoulder and another in the back while Erikson slashed out at a third attacker with his sword and kicked them into a fourth.

"Where's the surgeon?" he demanded as he approached the quartermaster.

Erikson nodded his head in the direction of the captain's quarters. "With the captain."

Benedict heard the approaching shout at the same time as he saw Erikson's gaze shift and harden. Spinning around, he pulled the trigger, resulting in a point-blank shot into the oncoming pirate's chest.

Dread washed over him as the body hit the deck, unmoving. Suddenly envisioning himself imprisoned in Coldbath Fields Prison, his thoughts traveled to poor Kitch and the disappointment upon her features during each of her visits. Another explosion nearby broke him from his shock. He didn't have time to think about that; he had to protect his reward. Turning back to the quartermaster, his eyes fell on the stairs as he spoke. "Let me up."

For once, Erikson did not argue and stepped aside. Rushing up and into the balloon, Benedict skidded to a halt, his eyes widening as he came face-to-face with a sharp and rusty blade.

Still tightly gripping his gun, his hands flew innocently to the sides of his head as he tried to convince Bailey that he was not the enemy. "It's me, it's me!" he said, taking a step back. The doctor glared, looking so much fiercer without his multi-lensed goggles upon his head. Pushing the blade away from his face, Benedict rushed past the doctor to the captain's closed door, pounding loudly. "Captain, it's Ben!"

Within seconds, Captain Allendale opened the door and looked at Benedict before casting a quick glance over in Bailey's direction. He nervously scratched his scalp, motioning for Benedict to enter with a cock of his head before slamming the door shut behind him once he was fully inside. "Report?" he asked, passing his sleeping quarters and heading straight for the helm.

Benedict followed until they stopped inside the cramped cabin room. Levers vibrated from the balloon's acoustics, and buttons blinked the problems on deck, emphasized by the steaming pressure gauges revealing trembling dial needles beyond their danger zones. "Three ships are tethered, and Commander Erikson is fending them off at the bottom," he said. "They seem to be pirates."

"You would be correct." The captain glanced over his shoulder at the surgeon.

"Are they here for you?" Benedict asked Mathias, who watched them both from the captain's cushioned chair.

An explosion shattered the windows in the cabin just as Mathias parted his lips to answer. Ducking and shielding their heads from the glass, Captain Allendale growled as he stood back up. "Stay here and keep an eye on him, Mister Keenan," he ordered, pulling his gun from his holster. "I need to protect my ship."

Benedict nodded as the captain left, then turned his attention back to Mathias, who nervously fidgeted with the item in his pocket while staring toward the door.

He hoped the captain could turn the tide of the fight, because he wasn't sure how much more the *Nine* could handle before crumbling beneath their feet. And when he heard Bailey's battle cry and the sound of steel against steel, his stomach dropped; their chance of escape was getting slimmer by the second. Remaining in the captain's cabin was a death sentence, and he'd be damned if he'd break his promise to Kitch.

Glancing about for something—anything—his attention paused at the windows. Holstering the gun, he reached for the surgeon's arm and pulled him out of the chair. "I know the captain said to stay here, but . . ." Jumping atop the console, he climbed out the window and grabbed the rope above his head that fed through multiple retainer rings along the outside of the rigid balloon. "Hope you're okay with heights," he added, holding out his free hand for Mathias to take.

Despite the chaos on deck beneath him, he heard the hollow thuds against the door separating the attackers from the captain's cabin. It wouldn't be long before the door burst open and pirates flooded in. He had to reach the ladder. If he could climb to the top of the rigid balloon, he'd have some semblance of an advantage. Or so he hoped.

"Come on!" he urged. Mathias jumped, startled, tearing his attention away from the oncoming calamity to scramble up the console toward the window. Benedict grasped his hand just as the door blew off its hinges. "Grab the rope and walk along the rim. Hurry! Follow me."

Eyes on the ladder, he shuffled uncomfortably along the lip that was so narrow he could barely rest on the balls of his bare feet. Knuckles white from his death grip on the rope, he clenched his jaw shut so tightly that it hurt. Carefully, he made his way along the edge of the balloon, glad that his muscles had stopped screaming now that adrenaline had kicked in.

A gasp escaped the surgeon, and Benedict turned his head to see the man's fearful gaze upon the battle on deck. "Don't look down," he snapped, and Mathias was quick to clamp his eyes shut. "Quickly! This way!"

The steel rungs within reach, Benedict grabbed hold and pulled himself onto the safety rail. Upon turning to Mathias, a feeling of dread washed over him as his attention focused past the surgeon. He even let a very unnoble curse slide past his clenched teeth.

"What's wrong?" Mathias asked, eyes wide in fear.

The pirates were following them, climbing along the rim toward the ladder. Time was of the essence. Brows furrowed in determination, Benedict began climbing. He just had to reach the top. "Come on!" he called out after Mathias. "Follow me!"

Their attackers rapidly catching up, Benedict urged Mathias to move a little faster. Once at the top of the balloon, he dropped to his knees and reached down for the surgeon, grabbing him by the wrists and hauling him to the top. Removing the gun from the holster on his belt, he pulled the trigger and shot at the first pirate, who fell from a blow to the shoulder, knocking some others down along with him.

Jumping to his feet, he rushed to the next closest safety rail of the six, only to find the enemy climbing that one as well. A dash to the next ladder revealed they were surrounded.

"Ben . . ." There was a concerned quiver in the surgeon's voice.

Benedict spun around, his eyes hard on the approaching pirates that had finally reached the top, brandishing their weapons menacingly. Great. There was no time to form a plan—not that there was much to plan for while being surrounded at the very top of a doomed airship. Gritting his teeth as the enemy advanced, he took aim and lunged forward as Mathias dropped to his knees in the middle of the balloon, covering his head with his arms. Benedict fired three times before one bullet finally hit, collapsing a heavier-set balding man. Ducking down next to Mathias, he swiped the dropped sword and struck his arm forward defensively, stabbing a freckled marauder right through the stomach.

He knew that each body slain was earning him a longer sentence in Coldbath, whether it was out of self-defense or not. He couldn't dwell too long on imagining Kitch's reaction, however; he needed to stay alive.

Jumping to his feet, he kicked the impaled body off his new weapon before turning around and clashing with a brawny man that had approached from behind. At this rate, they were as good as dead. He couldn't fend them all off on his own.

"Here!" he said, handing the gun to Mathias after slicing a gash along the pirate's midsection. "Use this!"

Somehow, Mathias's horrified eyes widened even further. "I've never used a gun before!"

"It's simple," he said, swiftly pulling the gun back away from the surgeon to fire point-blank into a wide-shouldered man's chest. "Just point and shoot!" he added, shoving the gun in the surgeon's arms.

"Because that has *clearly* always worked so well for you," Mathias pointed out, fumbling with the weapon.

"Minor detail!" he hissed, exasperated, using both hands to block a powerful blade swing. The clang from the force at which the blades hit rang in his ears, and he felt the reverberating buzz all the way to his shoulders.

Kicking the kneecap of a lanky assailant, he bounded over the collapsed man, leaping forward and slashing out at another before he heard Mathias cry out. Spinning around, he found the surgeon continuing to fumble with the gun as he scampered away from a pirate. With a growl and renewed panic, Benedict lunged toward the man to save the surgeon.

The downward stab of the pirate's blade narrowly missed Mathias's leg, pinning his wool trousers to the rigid balloon before the marauder's body collapsed atop of the sword, crimson liquid seeping from the wound Benedict slashed in his throat. How many more were there? Where did they keep coming from?

He needed out—preferably with Mathias alive—but the surgeon was completely useless at fending off the attackers, and though Benedict had thinned the herd ever so slightly, the odds of success were not in his favor alone. Spotting an opening away from the crowd, he hooked his arm around the crook of the surgeon's elbow and forcefully dragged him away, shoving his shoulder and elbow into a nearby body, causing the recipient of the blow to topple over.

A loud gasp escaped Mathias as his pinned pocket tore from the movement. "The infusion!"

Benedict's attention fell to the trinket as the surgeon tried to reach for it. Unfortunately, Mathias had drawn the sky pirates' attention to it as well, and they began barreling toward the item. There was no way he'd be able to reach it in time and fend off the attackers. Yanking Mathias a little harder, he continued to drag him to the edge of the balloon, sword extended defensively, wishing for a distraction.

Another explosion rocked the *Nine*, causing many to fall to their knees. Benedict stayed upright; he'd managed much worse while drunk.

The cannonball wasn't the interference he had in mind, but he'd take any opportunity that he could. Pulling Mathias to his feet, he quickly swiped the gun from his grip, holding him captive against himself with the blade of the sword to his throat and the barrel of the gun at his temple, resulting in a yelp from the surgeon. "One move, and I'll kill him," he lied as the group slowed to a stop and one marauder picked up the trinket, much to the surgeon's dismay. "Then you'll never know how to activate it."

Looking particularly proud of himself, the pirate grinned a nasty smile, complete with random missing teeth. "We'll take our chances," he said with an amused snicker as he shoved the item into his own pocket.

Benedict internally growled at his failed idea. There were two more things his mind had come up with on the fly, and he really hoped that he didn't need to resort to the last one. "Guess I'll just keep him as my captive," he said nonchalantly, as he moved the gun away from Mathias and fired at the pirates.

He missed the first shot—what else was new—before a series of clicks alerted him to his weapon being empty. Perfect; now he had no choice but to execute the last idea. With a grumble as the wave of pirates bull-rushed them, there was no time to mentally prepare for the next move. Dropping the gun, he wrapped his arms around Mathias and lunged backward, off the airship, without warning.

Mathias tensed up in panic from the fall, but Benedict didn't let go. As random as it seemed, his jump was expertly calculated. The landing, however, was what truly concerned him, as it was bound to be a little rough for the both of them. "Grab on to my waist!" he ordered, and the surgeon latched on so tightly that Benedict thought he'd be crushed. Allowing his back to fall into one of the sails of the tethered brigantine below them, it temporarily slowed their fall long enough for him to grab at the rigging and effectively cut it with one slash of his sword. "Tuck and roll when I tell you to!" he instructed, before being met with Mathias's terrified gaze.

"Are you out of your mind?!" Mathias snapped.

As they swung down toward the middle of the ship, Benedict cast a split-second assessment of the situation. There were two bodies aboard that he could immediately see. Tossing his sword like a throwing ax at one of those figures, the blade effectively sliced through flesh, embedding into the shoulder.

"*Now*!" he bellowed to Mathias, whose eyes were so dilated in terror that Benedict could no longer see the color of the irises through the light of the fires aboard the *Nine*.

Mathias released his death grip and dropped only a few feet onto the deck of the ship. Counting down his aim, Benedict released the rope, landing on the other pirate he could see from above, successfully crushing him beneath his weight from speed and momentum. Tumbling from the inertia, he jumped back to his feet once he came to a full stop, his vision spinning. Attempting to quickly blink it away, he glanced about, despite the dizziness to locate the surgeon, finding him flat on his back, rubbing his head. Good, he was still alive.

Benedict swiftly made his way over, but not before first raising his fists and getting in a few punches on his oncoming angry victim, blade still embedded in his shoulder. Once Benedict knocked him down, he grabbed the hilt and pulled the bloody blade free.

A roar from behind caused him to spin around and slash out at a third man's face, causing the aggressor to crumple with a cry of pain before Benedict stabbed the blade through him. How many bodies did that make now? He'd lost count and preferred to keep it that way, for poor Kitch's sake.

Finally reaching Mathias, he extended his hand to help the surgeon to his feet. "We need to secure the ship," he started, but noticed the surgeon's gaze was on something else. Turning his attention to the *Nine*, he watched as the enemy clambered down the balloon on their way to the brigantine.

Another explosion occurred aboard the rusty airship, and both men shielded themselves from some of the flying debris. Mathias cried out as the airship jerked violently, knocking him to his knees. Benedict's attention returned to the *Nine* as it dropped toward the ocean . . . taking the tethered brigantines with it.

Benedict rushed for the tethers, cutting the ropes and grappling hooks, releasing them from the doom of the *Nine*. He figured that the other ships might do the same and would eventually come for them. They needed to get the hell out of range.

"The infusion!" Mathias was still on his knees, his voice soft, almost fragile in his despair. "They have the infusion . . ."

Benedict knew what he had done. Even if—through what he had overheard—their mission had been to retrieve the infusions, handing over the only survivor could still potentially earn him the reward.

Maybe.

Hopefully.

The most important reason behind his decision to jump, however, was to make good on his promise to Kitch. He knew the risk. "Come on," he urged, trying to get the surgeon out of his daze. “We need to secure the ship, and we need to get out of here.”

“Where will we go?” Mathias shook his head, still in a state of hopelessness. “They have the infusion! This could spell disaster—”

“Don’t be so dramatic,” he interrupted. He didn’t have time for this. Marching to the helm, he sincerely hoped that if there were any pirates still on board, they weren’t secretly planning a coup down below deck.

Gripping one of the mahogany handles, he felt the grooves at the tip, which meant that the rudder was dead straight to the hull. Perfect, right where he wanted it. Using the brigantine’s effortless maneuverability to his advantage, he gave the wheel a hard turn to the right, and the airship followed swiftly and smoothly, all sails but the one he had cut the rigging to billowing in response. Pushing a lever forward on the console nearby, the mechanics of the infused engine roared to life and thrust the brigantine forward at full speed.

“They’re following,” Mathias warned as Benedict straightened the wheel.

“Damn,” he muttered under his breath.

“What’s your plan?”

Plan? All his plans from the night thus far were only a bunch of crazy ideas that were either successful or weren’t in keeping them alive. “To lose them.”

“Obviously. How do we do that?”

"I haven't thought that far ahead yet," he replied.

"Are you just making this all up as you go?" Mathias asked, incredulous.

"Would you shut up and let me think if I said yes?" Benedict hissed through gritted teeth.

He felt Mathias's tight-lipped glare before the surgeon turned and headed below deck. Irritation melting in the silence, Benedict could finally concentrate.

His gaze traveled up to the masts and sails in the darkness—to what little he could see of the system of ropes, cables, and chains—then followed the shrouds down to the main deck before him. Perhaps his "great" last-resort idea wasn't that great after all. Sure, the initial point was to get away from the pirates, but what he didn't consider was that he was on a ship that required a minimum of thirty people to properly sail, and that he was, unfortunately, only one person.

Mathias reemerged and made his way to the bodies on deck, checking for a pulse before dragging and shoving the corpses overboard. Benedict could do nothing but watch the surgeon between dancing shadows cast from the lanterns. The adrenaline must have been wearing off because he was starting to feel the sting of each cut received in battle, the stiffness of his protesting muscles, and the sharp stab and viscous sensation of something on the soles of his feet. He remembered inconveniently being barefoot when the windows in the captain's cabin shattered during the attack. The pain was really getting to him now.

Dropping his attention to his feet, he realized the wet and sticky consistency was a small puddle of blood. Following the trail of crimson footprints with his eyes until they disappeared in the darkness, he noticed them also scattered along the deck and wondered who the blood really belonged to. He'd have to check out the damage come morning.

Taking a step back, he almost cried out in agony when his leg gave out, dropping him down to one knee. His entire body refused to cooperate as he tried to get back up, the shooting pain making him nauseous. Gulping for air, his head suddenly started spinning.

"The ship is secured—" he heard Mathias say before gasping.

Benedict fell forward, losing all control of his body. It refused to listen. He felt himself collapse into Mathias before he lost consciousness.

CHAPTER 13

Somebody was talking. What happened? Where was he? Whose voice was it? Benedict's body throbbed, stung, and ached a million times worse than any hangover he'd ever had, but he willed it to silence itself and forced himself to breathe slowly to quell his racing heart and not give away the fact that he was awake. After all, if Mathias could do it, he figured he should be able to as well.

"I'm staying with him." It sounded like Mathias, and the tone in his voice was not pleased.

"You have no say in this," another voice spoke.

"He's my prisoner. I am claiming my reward, and am not letting him out of my sight," Mathias informed.

Who was he talking about? What prisoner? Had there been a pirate below deck with a price on their head? Benedict continued to listen in, curious.

"Who is he?" the other voice asked after a long pause.

"His name is Benedict Keenan," Mathias said. Benedict's blood ran cold at the mention of his name. He didn't understand; why was there a reward on his head? Had they placed a bounty on him when he escaped jail? "Don't tell me you don't recognize the infamous sky pirate?"

His body lightly twitched, and his heart galloped so loudly he thought they could hear it. Pirate? He was no pirate. What on earth was Mathias talking about?

"Never heard of him," the voice replied. "I'll alert the captain to the situation. In the meantime, you are not to venture outside of this room."

"I won't," Mathias replied. Was that a bit of animosity he detected in the surgeon's voice? Footsteps grew fainter, and a door opened and closed somewhere. Was it safe? Was he alone with Mathias? "I know you're awake," the surgeon said quietly. Well, that answered that.

Benedict's eyes shot open, revealing the steel beams of the room's overhead compartment. He was no longer aboard the seized brigantine. "What happened?" he asked, trying to sit up, only to hiss from the pain as his body refused to cooperate. Mathias was instantly by his side.

"You suffered a syncopal episode—" he started, but Benedict cut him short.

"In *English*!" He didn't have the mental clarity or the patience to deal with the surgeon's big words.

"You passed out, I patched you up," came his simple reply.

Benedict's gaze swept over the sterile room lined with steel cabinets and shelves that were filled with boxes upon boxes of medical supplies. The bed he lay on sat in the middle of the room, while another bed rested against the far wall. "Where are we? How did we get here?"

"We're aboard a military airship called the *Amaroq*. I signaled for help, and they were nearby."

"Luckily for us," he scolded. "The pirates we were trying to outrun could have intercepted that signal!" Honestly, Mathias might have meant well, but he clearly had put no thought into it.

"Don't worry, I used the Royal Guard's channel."

A brow raised as he eyed the surgeon suspiciously. "Where did you get that information? Do they teach you that in med school?"

"The lieutenant you overheard me speaking with is my brother."

A sigh escaped him as his eyes fluttered shut. "Wonderful." If there was a price on his head for escaping jail, the military wouldn't be involved.

The surgeon's fabricated lie about him being a pirate, however . . . that was definitely their jurisdiction.

"I had no choice. There was no way to properly sail that ship on our own," Mathias pointed out. He was right. If the pirates hadn't caught up and finished them off, a storm could have easily spelled the end instead.

"What's your plan?"

"We're headed back to Elgin. Captain Fitzgerald is arranging for the Newfoundland colony to form a barricade at the gulf. Hopefully, I can get the infusion back . . ."

Was he still going on about that damned infusion? That was the furthest thing on Benedict's mind. What he really wanted to know was what the surgeon's plans were for him. Parting his lips to speak, the door interrupted him. His gaze moved to the three figures that stepped inside, making the room much more cramped.

"Good, you're awake," one of them said as he approached Benedict, checking his pulse.

The medical officer was speaking to him, asking questions, but Benedict's attention was on the tall man with dark hair. The man was unmistakably related to Mathias—sharp jawlines and deep-set tapered eyes—though far more serious in expression.

"Lieutenant Darley says that this is your prisoner?" the third man asked, his piercing green eyes on Mathias.

"Yes, Captain," Mathias replied. "The infamous sky pirate Benedict Keenan. Of the Doom Crusaders."

Where did the surgeon come up with this stuff? As the medical officer continued to fuss over him, Benedict's attention shifted to Mathias. If he was so freely able to lie to the military, what else had he lied about?

"Can't say I've heard of him," the captain mused, his gaze momentarily falling to Benedict. "A word, if you will, Doctor Darley?" He gestured with his head for the surgeon to follow him out of the infirmary, but Mathias stood his ground.

"I've already stated that I'm not leaving my reward, Captain."

"Matt . . ." his brother started.

"I am serious, Lieutenant," Mathias countered, not once dropping the formalities.

"Doctor Darley," the captain cut in, "you have my word that we will not take the reward from you. It will only take a few minutes. I need to ask a few urgent questions—"

"With all due respect, Captain, you can ask it here, or not at all."

Captain Fitzgerald blinked, surprised. "I would prefer this criminal not use this information against us."

Benedict bit his tongue; they had only jailed him for being disorderly while drunk. Hardly worth the title of criminal. But he said nothing, continuing to watch how this played out.

"You can't change my mind." Mathias didn't bite.

"Lieutenant Darley can keep watch," Captain Fitzgerald offered. "If you're so convinced that something will happen to your reward, who better to trust than your own brother?"

The lieutenant, as serious as ever and already standing tall, straightened even more with pride. Mathias's eyes flashed with anger—something Benedict had not seen before—and his hands turned to fists at his sides. His gaze fell to Benedict, and their eyes met briefly as the surgeon contemplated the offer before he turned his attention back to the captain.

"Very well," he said in a resentful tone.

Benedict's brows rose in surprise. It seemed that despite the strange tension between the two, Mathias still trusted his brother more than anyone else.

The captain exited the room, followed by Mathias. Neither brother looked at one another. When the door shut, Benedict turned his attention to the lieutenant, who whispered something to the medical officer. Scribbling down his medical notes, the man nodded and quietly left the room, leaving him alone with the lieutenant.

"Who are you, really?" he asked, his voice low, not to be overheard. "Why is the doctor covering for you?"

Benedict frowned. "Excuse me?"

"I've looked up this so-called 'infamous' Benedict Keenan and have only found multiple records of drunken disorderly behavior and an escape warrant."

He couldn't fault the lieutenant for being thorough, but Mathias had never shared his reasoning behind the lie before they were interrupted. "I don't know why he's covering for me." He shrugged.

Lieutenant Darley watched Benedict in silence, his expression stone as usual. "You're lying."

"Am I?" he challenged, his eyes narrowing. Sure, he lied from time to time—and was damned good at it—but he had nothing to work with, and he sure didn't want to ruin whatever Mathias had up his sleeve.

"Why should I trust you?"

"Why don't you ask your brother, since he so easily lied to your face? You said it yourself; I'm no pirate, I'm a disorderly drunk."

"How do I know your name is actually Benedict Keenan?"

An irritated frown finally made its way to his face. Benedict parted his lips to speak when the door opened, and Mathias walked back inside, alone.

"Thank you, Lieutenant. I'll handle it from here," he said, renewed calm in his voice.

Lieutenant Darley, however, didn't budge. "Why did you lie to me?"

Mathias didn't take his brother's bait. "I assure you I don't know what you're talking about," he replied, stepping past the both of them toward the counter, where he picked up a slew of fresh bandages and began prepping them.

The lieutenant followed and leaned in threateningly close to the surgeon, finally breaking his stone-like posture. "There is no 'notorious' sky pirate or Doom Crusaders. Why are you lying? Why didn't you return aboard the *Tombola* like you were supposed to? What—"

Slamming the bandages back onto the counter, Mathias glared, but did not meet his brother's gaze. "Drop it, Frank!"

Benedict blinked his surprise away. It was the first time he had heard Mathias drop formalities when addressing his brother. The lieutenant, however, didn't skip a beat. "I'll ask one more time: why did you lie to me? You know it's a federal offense to lie to—"

"Only if I'm withholding information, which I'm not," Mathias cut in. The surgeon was, in fact, lying, but Benedict did not want to be the one to get in between these brothers. "I'm aware of the rules just as much as you are, don't act high and mighty. He is my prisoner, I will claim my reward, and that is all you need to know."

The lieutenant stood straight once more, but just when Benedict thought the man was done, he spoke again. "Christ, Matt, did you get kicked out of med school?"

Mathias shot his brother such a deathly glare that Benedict wondered how the man was still standing. With a harrumph, the lieutenant spun on his heels, exiting the room without another word or glance. Mathias sighed and shut his eyes. He looked exhausted.

The newly instilled silence would have been deafening if it wasn't for the jumble of questions floating around his mind. He needed clarification on a lot of things, but was slightly reluctant, what with having witnessed the brotherly display. His need to know outweighed the hesitancy, however, and after licking his dry lips, he tried. "What did the captain want?"

Having returned to prepping bandages, Mathias's reply was calm. "He wanted to know what happened."

"Did you tell him about the infusion?"

"Yes."

"Did you tell him the truth about me?"

Mathias only shook his head.

So the surgeon alerted Captain Fitzgerald to the infusions. The same infusions that were, supposedly, the entire reason Benedict was at sea. But why was Mathias still calling him a pirate? Was that what he truly believed? "What's your goal?" he asked.

"My plan is to—" Mathias started, but Benedict cut him off.

"That's not what I asked," he said. Mathias shot his head up, his attention fully on him. "I asked you what your goal was. You've lied to the military, I'm pretty sure that you've lied to me . . . What is your end goal?"

"My end goal, Mister Keenan, is to prevent the sky pirates from using the infusions on the world. My plan, if you'll hear me out," he added sharply, "is to have the Royal Guard take it from them in the gulf."

"And where do I fit in all of this?"

Mathias's expression softened. "You saved my life. I'm trying to keep you with me so they don't throw you in jail—or worse—once we reach Elgin. Knowing my brother, he would have done his research, regardless. Seeing as they can override me at any time, you would have gone straight to the constable. However, jurisdiction over pirates or not, they have no say until I have claimed the reward."

Benedict raised his brows, impressed. That was quite the clever and thorough scheme he had thought out. And so, this meant that if he ever got forcibly separated from the surgeon, that was the ruse he'd stick to. "Benedict Keenan, infamous sky pirate of the Doom Crusaders. Where did you even come up with that stuff?"

Mathias actually chuckled as he shook his head. The sound of his soft laughter warmed Benedict's heart. "If it wasn't for constantly trying to please my parents, I may have actually become an author."

He'd gotten to see many sides of the surgeon in the short time since plunging into the frigid ocean to rescue him, and this side—the amusement, as faint as it was—made him seem all the more human. He hated to have to ruin it, but he needed the rest of his questions answered. "Are you going to tell me who you really are?" he tried. The soft smile on Mathias's painted lips instantly vanished. "Why were you on a different ship? Why was a ship full of medical practitioners attacked? All airships have infusions, so what's so special about these?"

The surgeon's gaze slowly fell to the bandages as the corners of his mouth drew downward. "I'm just someone who was in the wrong place at the wrong time." After a pause, Mathias brought his attention back to Benedict. It was unfocused at first, as if he was lost in thought. "I am truly a surgeon," he added.

Benedict nodded. "I gathered that much when the captain called you doctor."

"And I truly attended a medical conference in Upper London, but I did not return with the rest of my colleagues," Mathias admitted. "The following week was the science conference. Doctor Garfield Marsden was the lead research scientist on a breakthrough revelation . . . and a dear friend. I stayed in London and boarded to return home with him and his colleagues when we were attacked at sea. It was a bloody massacre."

Mathias shut his eyes, no doubt reliving the events. Benedict could only imagine the pure slaughter based on how completely terrified and useless Mathias had been while fending off pirates aboard the *Nine*. Easy pickings. "I'm sorry," was all he managed to mutter.

"Doctor Marsden gave me the original recipe and told me to protect it with my life as he hid me under sacks in the laundry room below deck. There was an explosion. I tried to fend off hypothermia, tried to stay alive while floating alone at sea . . ." Mathias finally opened his eyes, his gaze finding Benedict once more. "Next thing I know, I'm in a room that reeks of rust and disease with you, only to immediately relive my pirate experience—though it ended differently, thanks to you—but . . . at the cost of failing my friend, and possibly the world."

He didn't know what else to say; Mathias had gone through more than he'd thought. Additional questions swirled in his mind. This wasn't the first time the surgeon mentioned the fate of the world regarding the infusions, so just what was in them? He figured that he'd wait to ask; if the surgeon was anything like him, he needed time to process. "You didn't fail," he gently pointed out. "I forced you to leave it. It's entirely my fault."

Mathias didn't confirm, nor deny. His eyes fell back to the bandages in his silence for a moment before he spoke again. "What about you, Mister Keenan?" he asked. "Who are you, really?"

After everything that was said, a playful smirk found its way to Benedict's lips. "Do you mean to say that you don't believe I'm a notorious sky pirate?"

"Hardly," Mathias quipped back, a twinkle of mischief in his eyes. "Where did you learn to shoot?"

Ouch. So he wasn't a sharpshooter. Last he knew, he didn't need to be a proficient marksman to do tasks around the docks. "At least I didn't fumble with the gun," he teased. "But if you truly must know, I am but a simple disorderly drunk."

Mathias watched him for a moment, his eyes slightly narrowed as if weighing the answer against whatever image he had in his mind. Benedict wasn't lying . . . nor was he telling the full truth. He wasn't yet fully convinced he could trust Mathias, and he was sure the same thoughts were going through the surgeon's mind as well. Finally, either satisfied with the answer or not willing to delve deeper into the conversation, Mathias changed the subject.

"Get some rest," he instructed before returning to work on prepping the bandages.

Benedict watched him in silence. Despite being physically exhausted, his mind spun dizzily over the remaining questions from their conversation, as well as running over the events since rescuing Mathias. He didn't think his mind would ever quiet down, but eventually, he succumbed to slumber.

CHAPTER 14

True criminal life was nothing like Benedict imagined it to be: instead of sitting in a strict, dingy prison cell, he spent his days lounging on a luxurious leather chesterfield sofa with his feet up.

Mathias remained with him at all times, just as he'd originally played it out, impressively sticking to his script. After a few days, they moved to the briefing room—more for Mathias's comfort than his own.

Lieutenant Darley stopped by multiple times a day, claiming to be "checking up" on his brother. Benedict often wondered if there was an underlying motivation to his actions, such as waiting for the surgeon to cave and reveal he'd been lying the whole time. The tension between the brothers didn't get any better as the days went on, but it never got any worse, either.

"What's his story?" he asked after one of the lieutenant's visits.

Mathias, who had been silently reading in one of the matching chesterfield chairs, slowly closed his book and set it on the polished round walnut table before meeting Benedict's gaze. "Lieutenant Darley is an ambitious man. With big dreams."

"How big?"

Mathias's eyes fell distractedly back to his book. "Big enough to get into the Royal Guard with ease."

"Why do you keep calling him Lieutenant?"

Mathias raised a brow, his attention back on Benedict. "Because that is his title."

"But you're his brother. Shouldn't you be calling him by his name?" Mathias's eyes narrowed, but Benedict continued before he could say a word. "Why are you always so formal? Loosen up a bit!"

"Mister Keenan, I believe that it's none of your—"

"Ben."

Mathias blinked in confusion. "I'm sorry?"

"Call me Ben."

"R—right. Ben."

"Is there any alcohol on this ship?" Benedict suddenly asked. How long had it been since he last drank himself into a stupor? After everything that had happened, after everything that he had been through and witnessed, he was long overdue. So much so that he was starting to feel agitated and irritable, and that was very unlike him.

"I seriously doubt so," Mathias said, returning to his book.

"Actually, there is," came a voice. Benedict and Mathias turned their attention to Captain Fitzgerald as he entered, a thick stack of papers under one arm. "But none of it is for you," he countered to Benedict.

"It's not for me," Benedict half lied, "it's for him. He needs to loosen up." Mathias narrowed his eyes slightly, but Benedict could tell that the man was clearly in denial.

"I was doing my rounds and came to make sure that everything was orderly in here."

"Everything is well, thank you, Captain," said Mathias.

"Are you sure you wouldn't like a change of scenery, Doctor?"

"I am certain."

With a single nod, the captain turned to walk out. "Don't hesitate to ask if there's anything you need," he said over his shoulder.

"Thank you." Mathias glanced down to his book but did not open it. His lips thinned and his fingers drummed the cover before he quickly added "Captain!" to the man, who turned around, his attention on the surgeon. "Could I have some of that alcohol, please?"

Benedict couldn't hold back a smirk, which swiftly progressed into a grin. So the surgeon wanted to loosen up, after all. Captain Fitzgerald raised a brow at the request before his gaze shifted to Benedict. He wasn't even going to pretend like he didn't enjoy his power of persuasion over the surgeon's decision. He was damned proud of it! The captain finally nodded to Mathias and continued on down the hall to fetch the surgeon a drink.

And it didn't take long for Mathias to get tipsy.

For Benedict, half of a bottle of gin was nothing compared to what he normally drank, but two drinks definitely stripped away the surgeon's formalities and gave him loose lips. The truth was ripe for the picking.

"Frank was always an overachiever," Mathias admitted. "Mum and Dad's favorite child. The do-gooder, the—" He paused as he clumsily spilled some of his drink onto the leather cushion, appearing deeply remorseful as he attempted to wipe it off with the palm of his hand. Whether that guilt was for the loss of alcohol or associated with his story, Benedict couldn't figure it out. "I tried, but I could never be as good as him. So, I enrolled in medical school to prove to them I was just as good."

"Are you sure you did it just to prove it to your parents?" Benedict asked. From what he knew of the surgeon so far, Mathias seemed like the type who wanted to prove it to himself, as well.

Mathias didn't answer, stuck in his mind. "Frank got into the Royal Guard, and I . . . I couldn't keep up. I couldn't hop across that divide he had created. So, I settled. I settled with the fact that Frank was leagues away and was going to keep going. I settled on simply being the best surgeon that I could be. Settled on earning my fortune that way, and I eventually found myself liking it."

"What's Upper Elgin like?"

"Oh, Ben, it's breathtaking," he replied, closing his eyes. Benedict wondered what kind of drunken vision the surgeon was seeing in his mind's eye. "The best parts of Elgin are the waterfalls. There are scientists in the United States who are on the brink of a breakthrough discovery called hydroelectricity. Imagine harnessing the force of water in motion to power entire cities! It'll be bigger than alchemy and technology together!"

"That sounds completely ridiculous," he scoffed, but what did he know? Alcohol ran through his veins, not science.

"And you?" Mathias asked, changing the subject. "What high society did you fall from?"

Benedict's amusement faded. He definitely wasn't drunk enough to answer this, and much too sober to be thinking about it. Did Mathias really believe that he was from the Upper Lands?

Eyes falling to his bare, freshly bandaged feet, they trailed up his torn trousers and stopped at his bloodstained shirt. He was far from upper class. He was just as he had always remembered himself: an orphan of London Below through and through. Despite that, he and Mathias weren't too different; while Mathias tried to impress his parents, Benedict spent his time trying to impress Catherine—then her father once he had succeeded with her.

He was determined to live in the Upper Lands. For years, he'd convinced himself that he was made for the bigger and better, that he could join the ranks of the rich and noble, and played the part fairly well. However, it wasn't good enough, no matter how hard he tried . . . or was it? Mathias believed him to be a member of the Upper Lands. Hell, even Captain Allendale, Commander Erikson, and Gunner McGee believed it. How many others had he fooled without realizing?

He liked this surgeon. With every word Mathias spoke, Benedict grew fonder of him. It was such a strange connection, it almost reminded him of . . .

His thoughts traveled back to Kitch. She had tried to keep him afloat after losing Catherine, tried to keep him from spiraling out of control. Maybe she knew he had already "made it," and maybe she was trying to tell him that everybody could see it but him. Kitch couldn't be fooled.

"What are you thinking of?"

The voice pulled him from his thoughts, and his gaze found the surgeon once more. "Hmm? Oh . . ." He took another swig of gin. "I was thinking of a friend back home."

"A woman friend?" Mathias asked, a ditzy smile creeping to his drunken lips.

"It's not like that," he admitted, allowing the heat of the alcohol to wash over him. Shutting his eyes, he imagined Kitch at her vanity table, applying her makeup as she did every night.

"Sure," Mathias teased.

Peeking through one eye with a smirk, he then opened his other eye. "We grew up together. She's tough as nails, that Kitch. We called her Kitch because she helped in the kitchen. She could bake the world's best bread. You've never tasted bread until you've had some of Kitch's fresh loaves. And her other meals were just as delightful. When Kitch was in the kitchen, never was there even a scrap left for the dogs. Never."

Mathias smiled. "She sounds like quite a woman. Where is she now?"

He envisioned her getting up from her vanity table and walking toward him, hands on her curvy hips, as if ready to scold him. How he missed her so. He remembered how she made him promise all these things that he would never agree to. Thinking back on it now, after having a brush with death, the urge to write her a letter as soon as he disembarked in Elgin was strong. A sigh escaped him before he brought the bottle back to his lips, taking a large gulp of gin. "She's still in London," he replied. "She didn't want me to leave." His heart still ached at the memory of her sobbing as he left.

"Are you certain there aren't feelings involved?" Mathias playfully asked.

"It's not like with Kate—" Benedict froze upon realizing that not only had he given away too much, but that it was some very personal information. Mathias looked at him expectantly, but Lieutenant Darley walked in, and Benedict couldn't be happier about the interruption. He couldn't bear going down that memory again. And it was well worth it, as the lieutenant, normally so stoic and stone-faced, actually twitched.

"What is going on here?" he demanded.

Mathias, still very tipsy, snorted a laugh toward his brother. "Frank, you should see your face."

Benedict smirked at the surgeon's comment, and the lieutenant immediately shot a nasty glare in his direction, as if all of this was his fault. Of course, it kind of was. Shrugging, he brought the gin to his lips but paused, then offered the bottle to the lieutenant instead. "You could loosen up some, as well."

Lieutenant Darley marched over to his brother and snatched the gin away before recomposing himself as best he could. Mathias appeared offended at first, knitting his brows together in a frown, but then snorted again in amusement. "It's true," he said.

Benedict could tell the man was fuming on the inside: he was having a hard time keeping his serious, stony features together as every single emotion flashed through his eyes. Benedict had to admit a certain sadistic delight at watching this—it was so much better than the knife-cutting tension in between the two. With a huff, Lieutenant Darley spun around and stormed out of the room. Seemingly unaffected by his brother's sudden departure, Mathias stood up and staggered toward Benedict, reaching for the bottle of gin. Amused, Benedict held it away at an arm's length.

"Give it here, Ben!" Mathias said with a hiccup.

"I think you've had enough."

"Nonsense. I can still formulate formulas . . ." he started, then paused. "Sentences," he corrected with a shake of his head.

"My point exactly," Benedict said with a chuckle. "Sit down before you hurt yourself."

"Bah." Mathias sat—more like dropped—on the ground next to the sofa. With a chuckle, Benedict ruffled the surgeon's hair after handing him the gin. Mathias took a long swig. "I'm still cross with you," he said matter-of-factly.

He hadn't even known that Mathias was angry with him to begin with. What ever could he be irritated about? "How so?" he asked, a brow raised in curiosity.

"You kidnapped me."

Genuinely amused laughter sounded through the briefing room. He supposed this was true. "What, would you rather I'd let them kill you?"

"I would have rather you not put a loaded gun to my temple and threaten my life," he mumbled before suddenly slouching over, quiet.

Benedict sat up straight, his heart skipping a beat, brain fuzzy from the alcohol. What had just happened? Reaching out for the surgeon, he sighed in relief when he heard the obnoxious snore coming from the man. Chuckling to himself, he settled back down. It looked like he was right: Mathias had imbibed more than enough alcohol. He felt a slight pang of pity—the surgeon was going to have a killer hangover later—but he would not let the surgeon live that moment down. He'd hold it over his head for as long as he could.

CHAPTER 15

Whatever paltry image Benedict had envisioned of the falls was nothing compared to what he was currently staring at.

After spending a few more days over the Atlantic, they had finally arrived in British North America. Mathias was kind enough to give him a brief history lesson, but he had paid little attention, instead opting to look out the windows. Everything was just so white in the Lands Below, painted with splotches of green. Nothing like the dump that was the junk and rust and dirt from back home. But what did he expect from such a large British territory still being colonized?

The *Amaroq* had docked in Upper Elgin. Donning a heavy coat, he then slipped his healed feet into a pair of wool-covered leather boots.

Attached to the narrow-toed section of the footwear, flat soles slapped the steel floor as he followed Mathias. Not only was it a fashionable extension, but Benedict had been told that the slap sole increased surface contact, preventing the shoe from sinking into the snow and mud. He thought it was purely ingenious.

As they made their way through the ship, the rumble of thunder in the distance since their arrival grew louder, until it turned into a prodigious roar as they disembarked. Where was that noise coming from? Pulling away from Mathias, he followed the sound until he spotted the culprit.

An ever-so-slight gasp escaped him, his eyes glued to the three majestic falls from the Lands Below. Literally breathtaking. Strolling along the dock until he reached the edge, he found himself unable to turn away from the grandeur. The mist danced high, reaching for the Upper Lands as the water tumbled over the edges and onto the rocks at the bottom. How could something so stunning belong to the tech users?

Mathias stopped next to Benedict with a soft smile painted on his lips as his attention fondly followed to the gorgeous waterfalls. "Told you they were beautiful," he said.

Benedict was speechless. Not only was the view something out of a fairy tale, but the air was clean. Crisp. And cold. An involuntary shiver passed through him, and he quickly forced down the uncomfortable memories of having jumped into the ocean. He shuddered an exhale, the vapor from his breath imitating the mist from the falls. Mathias turned to him.

"The temperature here is quite drastic from that of London. It took me a few years to adjust, and I admit it still catches me off guard."

"How cold does it get?" Benedict asked.

Mathias's attention shifted back to the falls. "Cold enough that I've seen people walk across the solid surface of the falls."

His eyes finally tore away from the falls to Mathias, incredulous, before he frowned. "That is a lie," he stated. Why was Mathias making up stories again?

"It's true," came a voice from behind: Captain Fitzgerald. Benedict glanced over his shoulder as the captain approached, his eyes on the view before them. "An ice bridge forms from the mist. People walk across from time to time." Benedict couldn't imagine such a thing; temperatures so cold that raging waters freeze? The captain returned to reality, clearing his throat. "Are you certain you don't want us to take him into custody for you, Doctor?" he asked.

Forever keeping up with his ruse, Mathias shook his head. "No, I can handle it. He won't go anywhere or do anything." He finally turned to Captain Fitzgerald. "Leverage," he added. "But I appreciate your offer, Captain. Thank you." The captain nodded, shook the surgeon's hand, and walked away, but not before narrowing his eyes in silent warning to Benedict. "Come," Mathias said, stepping away from the edge of the docks.

It was the first time Benedict had gotten to see the exterior of the military airship since he had awoken inside of it. The official navy-and-white emblem flags from Queen Victoria's Royal Guard rippled around the sleek metallic body of the zeppelin, which reflected the sunlight like the sparkling snow around them. It wasn't as large as some he'd seen, but it was extremely well-kept; definitely a sight to behold compared to the hunk of junk that was the *Nine*.

A part of him regretted deserting the rogue airship. As much as he and Commander Erikson didn't get along, he had enough respect for Captain Allendale and Gunner McGee to feel a twinge of guilt mixed in with grief over their loss. But he just couldn't let his bounty go down with the *Nine*. Earning that payment was a little more difficult now that he was in British North America; he couldn't just force Mathias with him back to London. Maybe he'd ask for payment, instead? The man was a surgeon from the Upper Lands. He had to have the money.

Making their way into the village, the combination of ice and mud along the path sloshed with each step. Spotting a carriage approaching, Mathias rushed forward before setting into a slight jog. The vehicle stopped, and he exchanged a few words with the driver before turning to Benedict with a smirk and a motion of his head to get inside.

Amused and suspicious all at once, he approached the gold-and-black painted carriage, careful to watch his step and maintain his balance with the ice. Mathias gave the driver, bundled up at the back of the vehicle in between two stacks of belching steam, an address as he stepped into the pristine interior of plush velvet and dark stained wood. Benedict climbed in after him—he almost felt bad, what with how filthy he was—and the vehicle moved, hidden gears grinding from the effort.

"How did you do it?" he asked.

Mathias raised a brow. "Do what?"

"How did you get the carriage without paying?"

The smirk that had played on Mathias's lips returned, though it appeared like he was trying his best not to let it show by firmly pressing his lips together. He looked out the window for a second before fully embracing his amusement, allowing a smug grin to form. "I told him that Frank would pay for it."

Benedict blinked in surprise before chuckling. He was amazed by the man's cleverness but was more so relieved that he had actually referred to his brother as Frank. Was he finally trusting Benedict enough to get comfortable around him?

The six red carriage wheels struggled in the slush despite their leisurely pace, making the trip particularly bumpy, albeit peaceful. Mathias seemed lost in thought, eyes glazed over as he silently gazed out the window. Benedict, on the other hand, was awestruck. Even with the mud along the path, everything was so clean, so pure. The village buildings were less rustic than those back home, and the mansions were far apart from one another, giving everyone the privacy they knew they deserved.

A part of Benedict wished that he would have come here sooner. Kitch had always wanted him to settle down and start a family. Here—in British North America, in Elgin—he could envision it perfectly. He made the next mansion they passed along on their trip his in his mind's eye and imagined Catherine and himself sitting by the fireplace, so in love, so alone and free to do whatever their wildest dreams desired.

The stretches of forest between each home were magnificent, especially with the evergreens adding drama to the landscape—a beautiful backdrop amid the blanket of shimmering snow. A wedding in the woods would have gone against everything Catherine's father stood for, and that thought alone gave Benedict immense satisfaction. Catherine, with wildflowers weaved through her beautiful blonde curls . . .

"Where are you taking me?" he suddenly asked after a large bump caused the carriage to rock violently. How long had they been traveling? Mathias had said that he'd get jailed—or worse—if he didn't follow, so where exactly were they going?

Mathias's attention never left the scenery. "The infusion sample I had is traceable. With Garfield gone, there is only one scientist left that I fully trust. We're going to see if he is home."

This, again? Now Benedict definitely wanted to know about the infusions, and he would not allow Mathias to divert the conversation any longer. He deserved to know but was interrupted as the carriage slowed to a stop. Body suddenly tense, his heart skipped a beat. Mathias seemed just as confused and concerned as he peeked out the window, which only slightly comforted Benedict.

"It looks like there's been an accident," he said before opening the door and rushing out. What kind of accident could occur this far out into the wilderness? Benedict followed. Fires crackled high and hot, and Benedict's eyes went wide as Mathias skidded to a halt with a gasp.

From the looks of the burning remains scattered about, it seemed to have once been a rogue airship. The sound of cannons thundered from above, and Benedict glanced up just in time to see falling debris. Yanking Mathias by the arm, they jumped out of the way as a large sheet of steel impaled the ground at their feet mercilessly, slicing through the earth as if it were nothing.

"Go!" he urged, shoving Mathias back into the carriage before climbing into the seat next to the driver, pushing him to the side and grabbing the steering wheel. They needed to get out of there. The steam belched stronger as the vehicle lurched forward, heading straight for the burning airship.

"Ben!" Mathias warned as he opened the window and peeked his head through.

"I've got it handled!" he shouted back, veering the vehicle to the left, gritting his teeth as he almost lost control when one of the back wheels hit up against a large rock.

"Ben," Mathias called out again. "Up above!"

He glanced up as another sheet of steel came tumbling down faster than he could react. The metal sheet narrowly missed the vehicle, but a rod, originally hidden from view due to the larger piece of debris, sliced through the carriage like a hot knife through butter. Benedict's stomach dropped.

"Matt!" he cried out in a panic, desperately hoping it didn't touch the surgeon.

"I'm all right," Mathias called back.

Relief flooded through him at the sound of Mathias's voice. "Be my eyes in the sky!" he said, keeping his focus ahead to safety.

He tried to maneuver through the snow around the rocks and debris, but the carriage zigzagged out of control. Every hit on the wheels made him wonder how much longer they were going to last.

"Ben! The ship!"

Benedict glanced up to see an airship hurtling for the ground. What exactly was going on up in the skies? Back in England, the airships sailed evenly alongside the Upper Lands, as if on a sea of clouds and air. A battle above the Upper Lands was unheard of. Coming from the Lands Below, the tech users were used to falling debris. Were the colonial Upper Landers prepared for this? Did they know how to handle tumbling scrap and crashing airships?

The flaming airship, like a meteor, crashed into a mansion and continued on, eventually coming to a stop as the surrounding wreckage settled from the impact. The fire continued to dance with the downed ship, spreading into the trees. Screeching the vehicle to a stop, Benedict then saw Mathias rush out of the carriage. He jumped down and ran after him.

"Matt, stop!"

"I have to see if there are any survivors!"

Benedict snatched him by the wrist—almost missing entirely—and Mathias practically lost his footing from the snap back. "There are no survivors."

"You don't know that!" Mathias countered, jerking his arm back and breaking free. He started running again.

As a last resource, Benedict tackled him to the ground. Mathias tried fending him off, but Benedict was solid despite his lithe form. Hopelessly angry, Mathias tried to punch him in the face, but he easily grabbed the surgeon's fist.

"Get off of me!"

"No!" Benedict growled. "You can't go there, Mathias! There is nobody left to save!"

"You don't know that!"

"Yes, I do." That was a lie. There very well could have been survivors, but he couldn't afford to let the surgeon verify. Mathias tried for a punch with his other fist, but he caught it as well. "Stop fighting me!" Benedict snapped in irritation.

"Ben, you don't—" Mathias cried out in pain from their struggle. "You don't understand! I made a vow to save lives! I can't stop until I know for certain—"

"If you go, you'll wind up dead, and I'll never get my payment." He felt Mathias's body go rigid beneath him as the surgeon's eyes went wide in realization. "Everything I endured these past few weeks would have been for naught."

Mathias cast him a deadly glare. "Don't you *dare* make this about yourself!"

"I can and I will! Now stop fighting; we need to get out of here. Who knows what else could fall from the sky!"

Getting to his feet and wiping at the snow on his clothes, he rushed back to the carriage, leaving Mathias on the ground. Acknowledging the driver, who'd moved back behind the wheel, he spun around to make sure Mathias hadn't run off despite everything. Fear etched across Mathias's features as his attention fixed on something in the sky. Benedict's eyes followed to see an airship gently hovering, lowering itself over the battlefield.

Sky pirates.

CHAPTER 16

"Matt!" Benedict warned, rushing over to him.

He had no weapons. He wouldn't be able to fend off sky pirates if he didn't have any weapons. Their chance of survival was slimming. Skidding to a halt next to Mathias, he grabbed him by the arm and pulled him away, only to trip over a hidden rock beneath the blanket of snow. A thick tangle of netting fell atop of them as they tumbled, causing them both to hit the ground in surprise. He hissed his discontent: he had nothing, not even a dagger hidden in his boot to help him out.

He could hear the ruckus aboard the carrack as the crew prepared to anchor. Pirates swung down ropes and climbed down ladders, fanning out, possibly checking for other survivors.

A figure approached steadily on impossibly long legs, stopping before the trapped pair.

Benedict trailed his gaze up the bundled body to find a gorgeous face staring down at him: deep brown irises set in bright white eyes, high cheekbones beneath smooth umber skin with jewel undertones, downward-turned sable-colored lips. He cast her a charming smile, which quickly vanished once the pointed tip of a blade aimed at his throat. Mathias garbled a cry and shrunk back behind Benedict.

Something else approached—a hulking sort of monstrosity. What was it?

"What do you say about letting us go?" he asked. He could probably charm his way out of the situation, right? "We can talk this over—"

"Don't trust that one, Ajani," came a voice from behind her.

The hulking creature continued to approach until Benedict could see that it was no creature at all, but a mangled man with machinery for arms and hands. Benedict wrinkled his nose in disgust. Who would do such a thing to their body? But once his attention rose to the face—with its pink scar running from forehead to chin, right across a red cybernetic eye—his eyes widened in madness.

"Thomas Davies!"

In an instant, every buried emotion—the rage, the grief, and everything in between—resurfaced, abruptly overflowing. He scrambled to get to his feet despite the netting, livid, so blind in his craze for revenge that he didn't even feel the warning gash to his cheek from the woman and her blade. Benedict then found himself tackled to the ground—not by any sky pirate, but by a tangled surgeon frantically yelling his name.

"Let me at him!" Benedict bellowed, seething. "Let me—"

Grief temporarily washed over him, competing for the position of top emotion against the raw anger. Preventing his heart from completely shattering a second time was all Benedict could do as the torrent of memories of Catherine in his arms nearly drowned him. He heard Mathias speaking to him, but he couldn't distinguish what was being said. The fury returned. He had placed full blame and responsibility of that whole night on Davies: every panicked scream, every crackle from the roaring fire, and losing the only person who ever truly mattered. All because the ruffian was bored.

"Benedict Keenan," the cyborg cackled. "Fancy meeting you here!"

"Unfortunately," Benedict growled, still held back by Mathias.

"Oh, come now, don't be like that! How long has it been? Ten years?"

"Try three," he spat.

"Such a shame you're actually keeping track," Davies tsked.

"Wha' we waan' do wid dem?" asked Ajani with a Caribbean accent.

"We'll take them with us," instructed the cyborg, as he turned to leave.

"You're not doing anything with us or taking us anywhere," Benedict said defiantly. "We were simply passing through. We have nothing you want."

A faint chuckle rang with amusement as Thomas swiveled back around. "Still as uncooperative as ever, eh, Keenan? So, what have you been up to? Looks like you've been in a rough patch by the look of your clothes." He pointed to the tears in Benedict's trousers. "Did we start a fire without your permission again?"

Gritting his teeth, Benedict went to lunge, but Mathias held him back. All he could do was glare. He wanted Davies dead. There had to be a way out of the net . . .

An explosion from the recently crashed airship caught everyone's attention, save for Benedict. Fueled by revenge, he took the distraction as an opportunity to follow the netting with his eyes, finding his escape route while Thomas, irritation on his features, gestured with his head for Ajani to investigate.

He was almost out. He hurried while keeping his focus on his exit until something else caught his attention: a nice, sharp piece of steel lying flat in the snow. His eyes on the new prize, he could almost taste the sweet victory.

"Not so fast," Davies said, catching him red-handed.

Benedict didn't give him much time to react as he grabbed the shard and stabbed it right into Thomas's leg, who bellowed out in pain.

"Ben!" Mathias cried out, desperate.

"Stay there!" he warned the surgeon before quickly ducking, narrowly avoiding a blow from one of the thick cybernetic arms.

"Whatcha fighting me for?" Thomas taunted as he swung an arm out again. "Got something to hide?"

"Hardly!" he hissed through his teeth as he continued to dodge. He didn't enjoy being on the defensive, especially not in the snow, while wearing a thick wool coat that made his labored movements feel sluggish. "You were the one who had *me* trapped, remember? I was the innocent bystander!"

"Innocent? That's very unlikely."

Benedict couldn't keep dodging the pirate. He needed the upper hand. He just had to win this. For Mathias, who helplessly watched, still tangled. For Kitch back in London, anxiously awaiting his return.

And for Catherine.

With a burst of adrenaline, he launched himself at Thomas, but the pirate was built like a brick house—and felt solid like one too. Benedict bounced off and hit the snowy ground hard, the wind knocked right out of him. He could've sworn that he saw stars.

Thomas cuffed him by the collar with his sharp metal digits. The clunky articulations in the cybernetic arm flexed, revealing thick wires and tubes as he lifted him up with ease, gearing his other cybernetic monstrosity of an arm to punch Benedict's head clean off. But before he could, a bent pipe clumsily flew out at Davies, clanking against his shoulder. The pirate paused and turned his attention to Mathias—still entangled in the ropes and looking very guilty and frightened by what he had just done.

Benedict did not waste any time. With both feet, he kicked off hard against Thomas's chest, pushing the pirate back as his wool collar tore from the robotic grip, landing Benedict back onto the ground. Before he could react, he found himself pinned by a boot to the chest from a familiar long leg.

"Let him go," Davies ordered, wincing as he rubbed at his bleeding leg while his crew scrambled back onto the airship.

"Captain?" Confusion was apparent in Ajani's voice.

"Let him go, darlin', let him go. The Royal Guard are on their way," he added, pointing out in the distance before looking down at Benedict. "You've got some gusto, Keenan," he chuckled. "Wouldn't want to join my crew again, would you?"

Getting back to his feet, Benedict glared as he internally seethed. Join Davies's crew? He wanted nothing more than to chop him up into tiny pieces for what he and his crew had done.

"We're all set, Captain!" called out a pirate from the ship, but Thomas's attention never left Benedict.

"It's a shame," he said, from the lack of a reply. "You were good, Keenan. I could make you great."

"I don't call that 'great,'" Benedict said, pointing to the man's cybernetic eye and arms.

Thomas thoughtfully inspected his one thick cylindrical arm, then the second, more mechanical one. "These are just a prototype," he said offhandedly, bringing his clawed fingers to his red eye. "They're much better than my regular body parts. Stronger, deadlier, more focused . . . I can do so much more than you could even imagine." He looked at Ajani, who offered him a dangling rope ladder. "Let's go." He climbed a few steps before he called out, "The offer still stands, Keenan!"

Benedict's hands clenched into fists as he watched the sky pirates escape. He wanted to murder Davies, and he was more than glad to risk finding himself in Coldbath just for that. But he had nothing to work with, which only added fuel to his internal fire.

The airship took off, and Benedict finally turned to Mathias, helping him out of the netting.

"Who was that?" Mathias asked.

"It doesn't matter," Benedict growled under his breath, then stomped off toward the steam carriage where the driver cowered inside. He was angry—not just with Thomas, but with himself too. He'd thought that burying his grief would help him get over Catherine, but it had only festered, transformed while lying dormant, waiting for the right conditions to turn Benedict into a beast hell-bent on revenge.

The sound of an approaching motor pulled him from his thoughts. Spinning around to figure out where Mathias was, he saw a lone dirigible gliding low to the ground toward them. His body grew tense with concern.

"It's Frank," Mathias said with a sigh of relief.

The lieutenant slowed the small military dirigible and gave Benedict an untrusting once-over before coming to a stop in front of both men. "Get in," he ordered, and Mathias climbed inside. Still stone-faced, Lieutenant Darley added, "You too," to Benedict, annoyance in his voice.

Benedict would have rather not; all he wanted to do was kill Thomas Davies. He was no longer interested in playing Mathias's little act, supposedly being blackmailed to not leave his side in order to claim his reward. But he knew better. He was in a foreign colony with foreign laws—and temperatures so cold, people could walk along an ice bridge atop the grandiose falls.

Shivering at the thought, he climbed inside and sat in the chair next to Mathias. The heat radiating from the steam-powered motor instantly began defrosting his frozen extremities, the tingle uncomfortable.

"What the hell happened back there?" Darley asked as he set sail, his dark eyes fixing on them through the vibrating mirror to his left.

"We don't know," Mathias admitted.

"Why were you both conveniently around airship wreckage?"

Mathias blinked, and Benedict could see the surgeon's shock at being accused in his face. "You can't possibly believe that we had something to do with it!?"

"I don't know what to believe anymore, since you've been lying to me from the start."

"How do you expect the two of us to take down two airships?" Mathias asked, defensively.

"I don't know. Why don't we ask your sky pirate friend? The Royal Guard are on that ship's trail as we speak—or did you think I hadn't noticed the carrack?"

Benedict glared. He hated the tension between both men, but he didn't like to be brought into other people's business. As Mathias and his brother bickered, Benedict piped up. "I'm no pirate, and you know it."

"Ben!" Mathias hissed in warning as his eyes narrowed, akin to one whose secret cover was just foiled.

"It's all right," he said to Mathias, holding his hand up to stop him. "He did his research. He knows who I am. Might as well also tell him I saved your life, and that's why you won't allow them to take me to jail."

Mathias's eyes went wide before he frowned, deeply offended. While Benedict hadn't revealed everything to the lieutenant during those few moments in the infirmary together, he currently needed everyone to be on the same page before things got wildly out of hand—like they were starting to. And so, he revealed enough to remove the target from his back. Mathias sighed and shut his eyes, his silence confirmation enough.

"So now that that's out of the way," he said, chipping away at the awkwardness as frigid as the temperature outside, "you know we had zero involvement in taking down those airships."

"I trust you about as far as I can throw you," the lieutenant said. "And right now, I don't trust the doctor much either, since he continuously lied to me." Mathias, his eyes still closed, hung his head in shame.

The rest of the trip was in thick, uncomfortable silence. Mathias wouldn't even look at him, which stung slightly, but Benedict had said what he needed to; not only to prevent further complications with the lieutenant, but especially to avoid any association with the monster Thomas Davies.

Buildings started becoming more frequent in the scenery as they approached a village. Benedict still did not know where he was; there was no familiarity at all for him to latch on to. His attention landed on the small two-story brick building before them as the dirigible slowed to a stop. Lips pressed tight, Mathias's eyes fell in disappointment as he stood up and got out alongside Lieutenant Darley. Giving the brothers some space, Benedict watched them walk toward the entrance before stopping, conversing in hushed tones. Casually, he left the warmth of the dirigible for the crisp air, where a familiar thunderous roar sounded in the distance. Good, they were back in or around Elgin—he couldn't remember hearing the falls after Thomas's escape.

Two men in dark uniforms came out of the building and approached the brothers. Benedict's body tensed as he carefully watched them speak with Mathias. They were constables. His heart raced. Were they coming for him? After a few minutes, Mathias stepped away from the group and approached the dirigible.

"What's the plan?" Benedict asked hesitantly, pushing off against the spot where he had been leaning. The worry he felt grew stronger as the surgeon continued to avoid eye contact with him. "Matt?" he asked, concerned, but Mathias stepped past him silently.

"Mathias!" his brother called out.

"Go ahead!" he called back over his shoulder. "Take him into custody."

Benedict's heart skipped a beat in his confusion. Who was getting taken into custody? As Mathias got back into the dirigible, the constables approached, and Benedict immediately understood that the one the surgeon spoke about was himself.

Since the military took care of pirates, the fact that he found himself at the constabulary only meant one thing: he was getting turned in for his warrant. He cast a quick, panicked glance in Mathias's direction as he raised his hands defensively. He attempted to take a step back but found himself trapped against the vehicle. Wasn't the ruse meant to *not* get him arrested? Why was this happening?

"Gentlemen," he tried. "I'm innocent . . ."

"Escaped convict is hardly innocent," Lieutenant Darley said behind them.

A constable grabbed his wrists while the other fastened on adjustable wrist bars, his thick black mustache wiggling from whatever he was saying. Benedict wasn't listening. His mind swirled in his confusion. Escaped convict? He wasn't a convict; he was simply a drunkard who became disorderly and placed into "time outs" to think about his actions.

He really wanted to resist and protest, but he couldn't; he was on foreign land with a whole different set of rules than those he was used to in London.

"Matt," he cried out, trying not to resist too hard. He wanted to hear the surgeon's reasoning. "Speak to me!" Mathias said nothing as the constables led Benedict away. "I saved your life!" he bellowed. "At least tell me why. You owe me that much!"

Mathias finally looked at him for the first time in a long time, regret and shame pouring over his features.

"How much was the reward for?" asked a voice.

Benedict spun his attention back to the lieutenant, frowning. "Excuse me?"

"The whole reason you kept Mathias alive," he clarified. "How much was the reward?"

His head was swimming. He was drowning, trying to make sense of everything as the constables continued to pull him away. He didn't know how much the bounty reward was for; all he knew was that rogues got paid excessively well. But none of that explained why Mathias had changed his mind.

"*Mathias*!" he roared.

"Mister Keenan," Mathias started—there he went with the formalities again—his composure regained, ever looking the part of the Upper Lander he was, "while I thank you for saving my life . . . your services are no longer required."

"Services? What services? *Matt*!" he bellowed as the lieutenant, having climbed back into the dirigible, began sailing away.

CHAPTER 17

Deportation is such a hassle."

Benedict sat on the cold pine planks of the wooden floor in the cell, pulled from his thoughts when Officer Tass sighed in frustration behind his desk with a stack of paperwork. He watched the constable for a moment before returning to his thoughts.

He just didn't understand. How could Mathias turn him in like that? Was it because the surgeon felt betrayed that he had exposed the ruse to the lieutenant? Was he still angry at Benedict for keeping him alive solely for a bounty reward?

Despite all the confusion, Benedict was remorseful. Deep down, he was fond of the surgeon enough to have him questioning his own loyalties and morals. But if Mathias was finished with him and his services—whatever that meant—then there was still one thing he needed to do before being deported on the next ship back to London: kill Thomas Davies.

"Cloke just came back from out of town," said a constable as he walked in, a gust of frigid air momentarily dropping the temperature in the room and scattering some papers on the desks nearby. "Said an airship crashed, right here in the Upper Lands!"

Officer Tass briefly lifted his gaze. "How is that even possible?"

"They were flying overhead," Benedict replied offhandedly.

Both men looked at him before the other constable, Officer Kelsey, said, "Airships don't fly over the Upper Lands. And how would you know anyway?"

"Just because they *don't*, doesn't mean that they *can't*," he drawled. "And I would know because I was there right before being turned in." When both men raised their brows in surprise, Benedict felt the need to clarify. "No, I wasn't the cause of it. A man named Thomas Davies was."

The constables looked at each other, then back to Benedict, suspicious. "Thomas Davies, as in the sky pirate?" Kelsey asked.

"What of him?" Tass followed up.

"He was there. Saw him with my own eyes, as did Mat—Doctor Darley," he said, quickly correcting himself.

"How do you know Davies?" Officer Kelsey asked, while Tass quickly reached for a paper and fountain pen to write the information.

Thomas had been a bully. He and his gang of ruffians preyed upon people who ventured down the wrong streets in London. Having disowned his parents—or so he claimed—he began intermingling with the orphans. And when Benedict had been kicked out of the orphanage, Thomas and his goons had taken him in. It was like being granted access into the coveted cool kids club, where lying, cheating, smoking, drinking, and stealing were the ultimate activities of living the life of freedom without responsibilities—as long as you didn't get caught. Each time Benedict lost his job, he found himself right back in with the crowd.

"Because he's originally from London, like me," he replied. Tass and Kelsey mumbled to each other while a brilliant idea struck Benedict. What if he bargained his way out? After all, he had the perfect leverage. The quicker he could get out of the small building—and even smaller cell—the better. "Gentlemen, I will give you all the information that I know about the man, in exchange for my freedom." When they didn't bite, he added, "It'll save you the hassle of filling out the paperwork."

That instantly won Tass over. "Kelsey," he started, desperate, "I'm going to the chief."

Officer Kelsey and Benedict followed Officer Tass with their gaze. Once the door shut behind him, Benedict closed his eyes. If the chief agreed to his bargain, then he wouldn't be a wanted man, and he could get away with showing his face around Elgin without being hunted down like in London. He liked that idea; nobody would question his motives while he searched for Davies.

The door creaked after a few minutes, and Benedict opened his eyes to see Officer Tass with the constable chief in tow. Getting to his feet, he approached the wrought iron bars separating them, wrapping his hands around the rugged surface.

"What do you know?" asked the chief, his blue eyes looking up at the man on the other side.

"Ah, first I need to know if we have a deal."

"I'm sorry, Mister Keenan, but I cannot clear your warrant in London from all the way here in Elgin."

He cast a quick glance at Tass. How did he get that out of the offer? Lightly chuckling, he shook his head. "I never asked for my record to be cleared." The chief, Tennett according to his badge, turned his attention to Officer Tass, who cleared his throat, uncomfortable, and shifted his posture.

"I—" he started, but Benedict saved him further embarrassment.

"In fact, I do not wish to return to London," he lied. "I simply said that I would tell you everything I know about Thomas Davies in exchange for my freedom . . . here. In Elgin." Chief Tennett watched him carefully, probably weighing his words and the pros and cons to the deal. It effortlessly won Officer Tass over with the promise of forbearing the deportation paperwork, but could the chief be as easily swayed? "I'm only a habitual drunkard with an escape warrant in London. I have committed no other crimes than that. You can ask Lieutenant Darley and Captain Fitzgerald. They've looked me up."

Benedict could practically see the wheels turn as the chief continued to think about it. Tennett then turned to the other constable—the more trustworthy of the two officers—and tilted his head in the door's direction. "Go look it up," he said.

"Yes, sir," Kelsey replied.

Tennett's attention shifted back to Benedict. "I'm not sure I have any interest in a disorderly drunk rampaging about Upper Elgin."

A charming grin made its way to Benedict's lips. "I'm a changed man," he tried.

The intermission before Kelsey's return was both the longest wait he had ever had, and the shortest. He wanted to vocalize both moments of "Finally!" and "Already?" when Officer Kelsey returned, handing the report to his superior.

Chief Tennett flipped through it agonizingly slowly.

Benedict wasn't too concerned with what Tennett would find; he had nothing to hide. He had admitted that he was a disorderly drunk, and that was the truth. The fact he had been jailed over two dozen times was irrelevant.

"I agree to your terms, Mister Keenan," Chief Tennett eventually said as he handed Kelsey back the stack of papers. "In exchange for information on Thomas Davies, we will release you. However, I must inform you that in order to remain in Elgin, or anywhere else in the province for that matter, you must follow our laws. One wrong move, drunken or not, and you're on the first ship back to London."

Benedict bit his tongue. He had no interest in being legally tied down. Killing Davies was not just a step over that line, but an entire leap. But he needed this over with. With each second wasted, the distance between him and the sky pirate was growing. "I accept," he said begrudgingly.

He spilled everything: from Thomas's last known occupation in London to the name of his gang. He was going to make the sky pirate's life a living hell before killing him. Kelsey scribbled down the information for the chief, who had Tass get the keys to unlock the cell.

"Is that everything?" Chief Tennett asked. Benedict nodded. "All right. You're a free man,

Mister Keenan. Thank you for your cooperation."

Officer Tass inserted the large iron key into the keyhole and unlocked the door, which groaned as it swung open. Heart racing in anticipation of catching back up with Thomas, he could practically taste his victory over the pirate. Slowly and carefully, as if expecting that this was all some big backfiring con, Benedict lifted one foot and set it down past the cell's threshold and into the rest of the drafty room.

He then fully stepped out, a free man.

Well . . . freer than he would have been back in London, at least. But he had to admit, it was still a pretty satisfying sensation.

Bundled back up and followed closely by Tennett, Benedict found himself outside again, where he took a deep inhale of the freezing, clean air as the sound of the falls rumbled in the distance. Now all he needed to do was hijack himself an airship and find out what was above Elgin. Benedict took only a few steps before turning back around with a burning question on his lips.

"Chief!" he called out, and the man paused just outside the constabulary, turning to face him. "What's in the sky above Elgin?" Benedict asked.

Chief Tennett raised a brow and shook his head. "Nothing," he said.

Somehow Benedict doubted that, but he would not say anything more. If something really was above Upper Elgin, he didn't need the constables or the military messing up his plan.

CHAPTER 18

Hands in the pockets of his wool coat and bearded chin nestled warmly against his chest, Benedict made his way down the streets of Elgin, his boots crunching in the snow and ice. As cold as it was, the temperature dropped as the sun set, causing the man to speed up his pace.

Elgin was a quaint little village growing in size, based on the proximity of the buildings to one another compared to the outskirts. Most shops were closed for the evening, leaving only the pubs and taverns open for business.

His stomach growled distractingly loudly; he hadn't eaten since disembarking the *Amaroq* that afternoon. He needed to thaw out his frozen extremities, he needed information, he needed food, and most importantly, he needed money.

His gaze fell on a small gathering outside the pub, the patrons deep in discussion about the crashed airships from earlier. Monitoring them as he approached, his gaze occasionally drifted around in search of potential distractions: fights, displays, scholars, protestors. He had learned fairly quickly as a little scamp of an orphan that the human being could only focus on one thing at a time, which made them prime victims for losing their coin purses. Alas, distractions were pretty scarce in the evening, so Benedict had to rely on another tactic.

Slowing to a stop in the middle of the gathering, he patted his waist before raising his voice. "Someone stole my money!"

Out of the corner of his eye, he watched the group automatically reach for their own coin purses to make sure they were still present.

Perfect.

Rushing off with a huff, he brushed by one of the taller men before purposely knocking into his portly victim with his shoulder. Spinning around and apologizing, he made sure the man's brown eyes locked on his own by placing a hand on his arm while the other pulled at the drawstring with ease before slipping the small purse into his pocket and walking away.

Slipping down an alley, he checked the acquired purse. There were only a few coins, which were enough to get him fed, but not enough for an inn for the night. It was getting too late to try again—he'd have to spend the night in a church, instead. Emerging from the passageway, he continued on.

He then found himself at the closest tavern—a dainty little joint, which didn't surprise him, what with being in the Upper Lands. Unlike his dig back in London, there really wasn't much for shadowy, out-of-the-way spots. Everything was well illuminated with candles in glistening hanging chandeliers and ambient lanterns infused with alchemy on each table.

The hot stew did wonders not only to his body but to his mind as well. It had been a dreary last few weeks, and though he had been well taken care of on a military ship with three meals a day, it just wasn't the same.

Unfortunately, the drinkery he ate in wasn't nearly as busy as the pub, making for a horrible spot for people-watching and listening in. He'd have to apply a different tactic: one he actually enjoyed using.

When the pretty barmaid returned to his table to refill his ale, he put on the charm.

"Thanks, love," he said in his best exaggerated accent. "Much obliged."

The corners of her defined lips tugged into a smile, and he could see the rosiness in her cheeks as she raised her hand and tucked a loose strand of blonde hair behind her ear before fussing with the messy bun at the back. "You don't sound like you're from around here," she said.

"London, actually," he confirmed.

"Gosh!" she gushed. "I've always wanted to visit! My parents came here when they were little and haven't returned. Will you be staying long?"

"I haven't decided yet, but the scenery is gorgeous. Especially the falls!"

"Oh, those? Yeah, they're beautiful and all, but . . ." she started, taking up a seat next to him at his table, the multiple layers of her skirts swishing from the movement. "I'd love to hear more about London!"

This was not going as planned. She focused on him instead of on herself and the answers to his questions. She was probably expecting him to describe London from the Upper Lands rather than from the Lands Below. Of course, he could easily describe it, as he had been there more times than he could count, and especially more times than Catherine's father, Lord Taylor, cared to know about. But he wouldn't entertain the maiden here. He needed her back on track, and fast.

He cast her a charming smile. "What's your name?" he asked, changing the subject.

"Elizabeth Price," she replied with a faint blush.

"What a beautiful name," he said, watching her rosy cheeks turn even redder. "Tell me, Miss Price, what else is there to see and do around Elgin?"

"Oh, um, well . . . there are plenty of shops, there's Prospect House, and there's Goat Island on the American side . . . I guess it depends on what you're looking for."

Benedict feigned pondering for a moment, all part of his act. "What about tours? Is there a way to get a view of the village from above?"

"From above?" She raised a brow in confusion before giggling, covering her face with both of her hands as an accidental snort sounded, which Benedict had to admit was quite cute. "Heavens, no! We *are* from above! Why would we—what exactly do they do over there in London?"

Well, he'd tried. What had been going on with Thomas Davies and the destroyed airships? He knew he didn't imagine running from the falling debris and dodging the cyborg's attacks. Unfortunately, Miss Price was far too naive or far too smart. He couldn't quite tell which. But for her to not grow too suspicious, were she of the latter sort, he gave her a soft smile and quickly recovered. "No. No, you're right, we don't do that in London. But how else is one supposed to enjoy the beauty of Elgin? How else is one supposed to be convinced that perhaps they should make the colonies their new home?"

Elizabeth watched him with her big blue eyes, her cheeks hot from blushing. "Gosh, you just make everything sound amazing," she said dreamily. "If you do find such a place for tours, promise you'll invite me? I'd love to witness the beauty with you."

His charming smile turned into a grin. "Of course," he lied. "I'd very much enjoy your company, Miss Price."

A patron interrupted, requesting a refill. She flushed, embarrassed, and stood back up apologetically. "I'm sorry, I must get back to work."

"The name is Ben Keenan, by the way," he added. She blinked in surprise. "You gave me your name, but I never gave you mine."

She smiled. "It's nice to meet you, Mister Keenan," she said, giving him a slight curtsy before casting a rapid glance in the patron's direction. "Do you have plans?" she asked, her voice hushed. "Will you be here a while?"

"Is that a request?" he asked. If he could get more out of her, he'd play along for as long as needed.

Giggling, she nodded. "If you don't mind. Of course, if you have other things to do . . ."

"I have no plans, Miss Price," he acknowledged. "I will stay if it pleases you."

"Oh, it very much pleases me," she gushed, flushing before glancing back over her shoulder to the displeased patron watching her. She curtsied again before spinning around to return to work.

Benedict turned his attention to the thirsty man. "Apologies," he called out. "I kept her from her duties. You see, I'm new here—"

"Yeah, yeah," the man dismissed, and that was that.

Returning to his ale, Benedict downed about half of it before setting the mug back down. He mentally readied a bunch of questions for his next round with Elizabeth, mostly including ones about the sky pirates Thomas Davies and Ajani. Deep in thought on ways to slyly incorporate his questions to make it seem like natural curiosity, a name he recognized pulled him back into the present moment: Doctor Darley.

Watching two tenants of a nearby table out of the corner of his eye to not seem suspicious, he strained to listen in on their hushed conversation.

The older of the two shushed the other and cast furtive glances about to be sure that nobody had overheard.

"But I saw him with my own eyes!" the younger said. "He's back at the hospital!"

"The boss is definitely going to want to hear about this," the older man mused. "Guess we'll have to pay dear Doctor Darley a visit."

Both men snickered into their drinks—as if that wasn't suspicious at all—and Benedict's heartbeat started racing. Why were they speaking about Mathias like that? What did they want with him? He'd figured that, after having him taken into custody, the surgeon wanted nothing more to do with him. However, he felt a certain sense of obligation to warn him.

Finishing the rest of his ale in a few swift gulps, he casually stood and approached Elizabeth in the room's corner by the bar counter, who smiled warmly at him before it faltered.

"Are you leaving?" she asked.

Benedict gently took one of her hands in his and brought her knuckles to his lips, causing her cheeks to flush once again. "Miss Price," he started, "I am terribly sorry. Something came up and I must go, but I need your help."

"Of course," she replied.

"I need to see a surgeon," he started, and Elizabeth's eyes grew wide. Stepping closer to her, shielding her from view from the two men, he quickly added, "I don't want to draw attention to myself, love, so please, let's keep this in between us, hmm?"

Elizabeth nodded, concern etched on her beautiful features as she looked up at him. "Are you all right?" she asked. "What's wrong?"

"It's complicated," he said. "But I really need your help in telling me where the nearest hospital is."

"Do you need me to hail you a carriage?" she asked.

"Focus, Miss Price," he urged, seeing the panic making its way in her gaze.

"Um . . . it's to the east of here, on the other side of town, past the medical school."

Perfect. He could stop at the school first, just in case. "Thank you," he whispered with a wink. "You might just have saved a life."

He turned around and casually walked out of the building, careful to avoid catching the eyes of the two men discussing the surgeon. He needed to find Mathias before they did, and now, he had a pretty good idea where to start.

CHAPTER 19

He was a man on a mission.

Hands shoved into his wool coat, Benedict hustled down the icy street, the mud and slush frozen over since the sun disappeared beyond the horizon. What was he even looking for? He had no idea if the hospitals and schools in Elgin looked like the ones back in London. Benedict had to find the surgeon, though, and somehow get there first. He couldn't just stand back and do nothing; he had risked his own life saving Mathias in the Atlantic Ocean, after all.

An airship sailed on above, and Benedict squinted to make out its allegiance, but couldn't see it in the night's darkness. Did it belong to the two men in the tavern? His stomach dropped, and his gaze fell to the street. Time was running out.

Speeding up his pace, he saw a steam carriage ahead and suddenly got a brilliant idea.

Dashing for it, he skidded to a halt before the vehicle, arms outstretched to hail the driver, whose eyes widened in surprise and fear.

"Help!" he cried out urgently. The driver applied the brakes, and the vehicle skidded to a stop. Benedict grabbed hold of the sidebar, leaping into the seat next to him, and shoved the stolen coin purse and whatever money remained into the driver's hands as compensation for the trouble. "I need a surgeon! Please!" he insisted, his voice trembling in a fake panic.

Stuttering and nodding, the carriage operator released the brakes, and the vehicle lurched forward, steam hissing from the stacks on both sides of the back bench due to the sudden increase in power and speed.

Clenching his jaw, Benedict focused on the road ahead. There was a sensation in the pit of his stomach—a deep ache lodged in his chest—telling him that the ship flying overhead in the Upper Lands was none other than Thomas Davies. It had to be, if it was such a rare occurrence. And if that was the case, then Benedict desperately needed to get to Mathias first. Who better to take a foreigner where he needed to go than a local? He trusted the driver knew where he was going.

He sincerely *hoped* that the driver knew where he was going.

"What's going on?" the carriage operator asked, fear as clear as day in his dark eyes.

"Just drive!" Benedict urged through his teeth. "Hurry!"

Shifting the gears as far as they would go, the stacks belched high and hot as the carriage reached its speed limit. It didn't take them long to find an anchored airship in front of a large brick building. That had to be it.

"There," Benedict said, pointing to the wooden sloop—known to be a sky pirate vessel.

The driver started to protest, but Benedict jumped off before the carriage even slowed. Tumbling, he expertly rolled on the ground until he could jump back to his feet in one swift motion—something he'd had lots of practice doing when escaping Lord Taylor's security guards each time they caught him with Catherine.

Darting for the building, silhouettes of people came into play, and he was quick to not only recognize Mathias standing with his hands by his head but also the familiar long legs of Ajani, who pointed her sword at the surgeon's throat. Benedict clenched his jaw, his brows furrowed, and willed himself to run like the wind. He needed to save Mathias.

His footsteps were heavy—it was no surprise that Ajani spun around and slashed out at him, having heard him coming a mile away thanks to the crunching of the ice beneath his feet. Barely dodging the blade, Benedict ducked down into a knee slide and grabbed the pistol from her belt before aiming it at her.

She slashed the blade downward as Benedict pulled the trigger, but the gun did not fire. Instead, it went flying from his hand from the hit, and he soon found himself staring once more at the tip of her blade.

Catching his breath, palms out in front of himself to get her to pause, his eyes never left Ajani's brown ones, even when he spoke to the surgeon. "This is where you flee, Mathias!" he hissed.

It took Mathias a second, but he spun around and darted back inside the building. Ajani turned to stop him, and Benedict spotted the perfect opportunity to take her down. Weaving past the sharp blade tip, he lunged out at her, knocking her to the ground. She cried out in both surprise and pain as her dropped blade skidded to a halt just out of reach. She struggled, but Benedict kept her pinned down.

"Get offa me!" she growled in her thick accent as she continued to free herself.

His eyes widened, and a cry escaped him as a flash of white-hot pain exploded throughout his body, especially in his thigh, where a dagger Ajani had pulled from her belt lay deeply embedded halfway up the shiny blade.

Hissing in agony, he tried silencing the pain receptors—tried silencing the blood rushing in his ears. He couldn't afford to give the stinging and throbbing the time of day. He couldn't let it stop him.

Ajani attempted to knock him off her while he was distracted, but he didn't budge. Eyes growing dark—he didn't have time for this fight, he just had to take her down and get to Mathias—he grabbed the embedded dagger by the hilt and pulled it from his leg, slamming it right into her shoulder blade in return. Her shriek echoed through the night as he leaped off her and scrambled to her sword, swinging it with all his might as he spun around after grabbing it, missing the woman as she dodged.

She was just as adamant as he was as she tried kicking the blade out of his hand—if not more so. Ajani was far more impressively agile, barely allowing him time to pull away. He couldn't even get to his feet before she attacked again.

As she kicked out at his face, Benedict gritted his teeth and jumped back just in time as a hidden mechanical blade in the tip of her boot extended and brushed his cheek. He was certain that the sharpness of the blade effortlessly cut some hairs from his sea beard. He desperately needed a shave, but this method was not what he'd had in mind.

Another kick with the damned hidden blade cost him the sword due to a cut running the length of his thumb. But he didn't have time to lament; there, by his knees, was her gun. Swiping it, he aimed and pulled the trigger.

Still nothing.

"Why won't this thing *fire*!?" he cried out in exasperation, as Ajani went to strike once more but tumbled forward, falling to her knees.

Benedict blinked in surprise—the carriage driver, in an attempt to help, stood behind her with a metal sidebar in hand that he had broken off the carriage. Unfortunately, he hadn't hit her hard enough. Bringing a hand to her head, Ajani spun around, shock on her features before instantly turning into a glare. The driver took a step back upon realizing his mistake, but it was too late. A gasp escaped him as Ajani picked up her sword and stabbed it right through him.

She was distracted, and he had the upper hand once more. And as much as he wanted to end the fight then and there, he had to find Mathias. Bolting for the building as fast as his limping form could, he then heard the unmistakable accent in an angry cry.

"Fyah di cannon!"

Cannon? As in singular? Glancing over his shoulder with a raised brow, he slowed his pace to a stop and turned to see large brass gears and a wide barrel rise from the airship. A white light shone down the barrel's bore, gearing up for an alchemy-infused attack. Stricken with panic, he rushed to the building, nearly pulling the door off the hinges, and thankfully spotted a terrified Mathias to the left, by the window.

"Get down!"

Diving for Mathias, he toppled him to the ground, knocking the wind out of the poor surgeon. Jaw clenched as he braced for impact, he crawled over Mathias just as the explosion occurred, shielding him with his body as debris covered them both. He winced at the weight that had fallen on top of him.

"Are you all right?" he asked Mathias, who swiftly nodded in response. "Come on!" he instructed, struggling to unbury himself.

He could hear panicked cries coming from elsewhere in the building. Poking his head up, he saw the cannon gearing up for a second hit through the destroyed front wall. Hissing his displeasure, he placed his hands on Mathias's shoulders and shoved him back down as the cannon fired once again. More debris fell, and Benedict could feel the foundation trembling, ready to crumble and collapse.

Lifting himself from the debris, he clasped Mathias by the wrist, pulling him to his feet. Benedict's whole body hurt, but they needed to get out of dodge, and fast. Mathias turned to head deeper into the establishment, but Benedict's grip yanked the surgeon back. He would have none of it.

"But the injured—!" Mathias protested.

"*I'm* injured!" he hissed, trying to ignore the throbbing, stinging pain of his stab wound and cut. Rushing as fast as he could, despite his limp, he pulled the surgeon after him.

He was thankful that Ajani hadn't fired a third time. Was she out of infusions? Was she setting a trap? He didn't like her lack of action one bit, and the longer nothing happened, the more his stomach churned with anxiety. Noticing more airships surrounding them, an unnoble-like cuss played on his lips before he realized, by their sleek paneled designs, that it wasn't more sky pirates, but the military that had come to the rescue. Relief washed over him instead. That meant Ajani would be busy—and indeed, she was. This didn't fully ease the sensation in the pit of his stomach, however: with Ajani here, Benedict was certain that Davies wasn't too far away. And he didn't want to have to answer to the military and lose his only lead . . . so, what if he took the ship instead?

Benedict began leading Mathias in that direction. Unlike the hijacked brigantine, a sloop could handle a tiny crew sailing it—even just one person. With his expertise, he could get it up and running in the blink of an eye. Then he could take it somewhere quiet, where he could demand Mathias answer his questions.

Mathias gasped and tugged his arm, trying to get free. Turning to see what had caught the surgeon's attention, Benedict's heart sank as the man called for his brother. "Frank!"

Mathias tried running, but Benedict wouldn't let him. He *couldn't* let him. His grip still tightly around the surgeon's wrist, he scooped up the discarded gun nearby and aimed it right at Mathias's head, who came to a rather sudden stop.

"Get on the ship," Benedict ordered, finally releasing the man's wrist. Mathias didn't move, stunned by Benedict's actions. "Get on the ship, Mathias!" he yelled.

"You wouldn't shoot me," Mathias said, furrowing his brows.

"Do you want to test that theory?" Benedict said with a glare. Mathias didn't need to know that the weapon didn't work; he'd use that leverage with all his might. "*Get on the ship*," he repeated, every word emphasized. But still Mathias didn't move.

Irritated by the lack of compliance, he aimed at the ground in between the surgeon's feet and fired a warning shot. The weapon, despite failing twice before, finally succeeded—the projectile landing inches away from Mathias's right foot. Biting down his shock, he was glad he'd tested his shot elsewhere. Immediately aiming it back at Mathias's head, he cocked it once more, and Mathias, eyes wide, finally obeyed.

Mathias climbed aboard, and Benedict followed close behind. "Secure the ship," he ordered, and Mathias cast him a glower before obediently heading below deck. Limping to the side of the sloop, Benedict weighed anchor before heading for the wheel to set sail.

Unfortunately, the military began following. That was the last thing Benedict wanted and needed. He easily maneuvered the ship, racing toward the falls.

Mathias resurfaced from below and found his way to Benedict's side, confusion etched in his features. "Ben, stop!" he started. "The military—"

"I refuse to get caught again," Benedict said, speeding up. But instead of going where he could see, Benedict halted the sloop rather suddenly in the mist and clouds, cutting the engine, floating in the cloud coverage.

Nothing could be heard but the thunderous roar of the falls. Visibility was poor, and the mist was slowly soaking through his wool coat, causing him to shiver. Or maybe the trembling was because of the pain now that his adrenaline was wearing off. He couldn't tell. All he could do was silently hope very hard that the clouds were thick enough that the ship wasn't poking out from the top or the bottom.

Without warning, his injured leg gave out, but he caught himself on the wheel to keep himself standing. His stab wound was getting particularly painful.

He heard Mathias rummaging about but paid little attention to exactly what the surgeon was doing. It wasn't like he could go anywhere; they were miles in the sky. So, when a hand clamped down on his leg, Benedict jumped, startled.

"What are you doing?" he hissed down to the kneeling surgeon.

"Treating your injuries."

Benedict parted his lips to protest but clamped them shut at what he thought was the sound of an airship motor. He couldn't tell because of the falls, so he remained perfectly still and quiet, even holding his breath—as if that would help any. He couldn't see anything through the haze, and that both relieved him and worried him. Once he had convinced himself that they were safe, Benedict let out the breath that he was holding, and Mathias returned to inspecting the leg wound.

"It's pretty deep," he said, tearing strips from some linen he'd found below deck. "I'm going to need you to sit down."

"No," Benedict said, which brought Mathias's eyes up to him. "You and I have some discussing to do."

"You can still talk while sitting down," Mathias pointed out, growing cold again. "Besides, there's nothing to discuss."

"Oh, I think there is," Benedict said. "I'd love to know what was going through your mind when you turned me in, but that can wait, because what I'm *really* interested in knowing is why the pirates were still after you despite having your infusion." Mathias said nothing, and so

Benedict continued, "They mentioned you by name."

Grabbing a bottle of some unidentified liquid, Mathias silently poured some onto the strip before applying it to the stab wound. Benedict wobbled some and winced again as the pain shot through him. Alcohol. It was definitely some kind of alcohol. "You need to sit down, Ben," Mathias said.

With an ever-so-faint nod, he settled down on to the deck. Raising his leg to be above his heart, Mathias tore open the cut in the trousers to get to the wound.

"I don't know why they're after me," Mathias quietly admitted as he patched up the wound. "And I turned you in because . . . because I was angry with you."

Benedict could feel the surgeon's eyes on him, but he didn't meet them. He knew he had been in the wrong. He knew all he had been focusing on was the money. How could he not? Not only had his ticket to living the good life in the Upper Lands vanished with a sinking ship, but that same ship could no longer take him back to Kitch. Even so, using Mathias that way was wrong. He'd have been angry too, were it the other way around.

"I don't know how much cloud coverage we have left," he said, changing the subject.

"Nor do I."

"We need a place to lie low, Matt," he added. "And I don't want it to be where the military has the upper hand."

"I know where we could go," Mathias mused as he finished wrapping up Benedict's leg. "There. It's far from perfect, but it'll do for now." Benedict tried to get up, but Mathias stopped him with a gentle shove back in place. "What do you think you're doing?" he asked with a frown.

"I was going to take the helm."

"No, you need to rest, so I'll do it."

He smirked. "Whatever you say, Captain."

"Oh, no," Mathias said as he stood up. "You're the pirate, not me."

"Pirate?" Benedict snorted. "How so?"

"Pretty sure I'm your hostage aboard this stolen ship, so . . ."

Benedict could only chuckle.

CHAPTER 20

Mathias had carefully navigated the sloop away from the falls. They hadn't been followed, which meant that the military had thankfully lost them in the clouds. The skies were dark, but Mathias did not show the faintest sign that he was lost. And this made Benedict slightly nervous.

"Where are you taking me?" he eventually asked.

"Somewhere safe where I can take a better look at your leg," Mathias replied, his attention focused ahead.

"We can't go to the hospital," Benedict pointed out. "They'll be searching for you."

"That's not where we're going."

"Don't take me back to jail," Benedict groaned.

"We're not going there either."

Benedict raised a brow. Just where *were* they going then? Was Mathias turning him in to higher authorities? The Royal Guard? Did he have a rogue-ish bounty on his head?

Mathias continued to sail, and Benedict remained silent and shivering with his injured leg propped up. It hurt too much to do anything but sit there with his thoughts as company. Was the surgeon still angry with him? After all, Benedict had never apologized.

His thoughts veered some, and he suddenly wondered where Mathias had learned to navigate airships. He had impressively sailed them some before hailing the Royal Guard after their escape from the *Nine*, and he was doing splendidly at this very moment as well. Did surgeons even have time for sailing lessons?

The sloop descended until it eventually came to a stop. Mathias stepped away from the helm and dropped anchor, lowering the gangway before returning to Benedict with an extended hand.

"I cast anchor a mile out from the village to not draw suspicion. I hope you're up for the hike."

Benedict didn't have a choice. He was completely at the surgeon's mercy, and far too sober for his liking. Grabbing Mathias's hand, he winced as he pulled him to his feet.

The walk was the longest thirty-five minutes of Benedict's life. Even with leaning on Mathias for support as he limped, he quickly grew winded from the effort. By the time Mathias pointed out the porch lantern of their destination, a sheen of sweat coated Benedict's brow.

Trying to focus on the lantern ahead, his eyes couldn't help but fall to the debris littering the cobblestone streets and the mountains of junky springs and cogs and rusty scraps of metal scattered about, illuminated only by the flickering glow of poorly infused streetlamps. If he didn't know any better, Benedict would have thought himself back home in London.

"Where are we?" he asked.

"In Thorold, just outside of Elgin Below."

"Lower Elgin?" He blinked, shocked. "What does a man like you know of the Lands Below?"

"The same thing that a man like you knows of the Upper Lands." Sharp witted, Mathias didn't skip a beat. A smirk of amusement crept to Benedict's lips and, secretly, his heart swelled with pride.

Upon arrival, Mathias helped him up the cement steps of the crumbling and decaying house, rapping against the wooden plank that substituted as a door. The place was in shambles, and Benedict could only wonder what they were doing here. A struggling voice on the other side interrupted his thoughts.

"I'm coming, I'm coming," the voice grumbled, as what sounded like the rattle of chains slithered across the back of the plank. The door opened to reveal a short, skinny man adorned in various mechanical devices all around his arms and head. The irked expression on his face instantly changed to confusion, then shock. "Doctor Darley, what a . . . what a surprise!"

"I am terribly sorry for the late-night intrusion, Mister Dirk, but it's kind of an emergency . . . could we please use your lab?"

The man blinked, his brown eyes jumping back and forth between Mathias and Benedict. "Yes, of course!" he said, stepping aside. His eyes fell to Benedict's leg as he limped inside, and the man frowned. "Ella! Fetch a bowl of hot water and a cloth!" Benedict felt the surgeon's shoulders stiffen.

"Yes, Father!" came a voice from the back room.

"Right this way," Mister Dirk said—more to Benedict than to Mathias—as he led them to the back, down the cramped hall decorated with hundreds of sculptures and assemblages made from junk scraps and random items. The cellar waited at the end of the hall, its staircase so narrow that it forced Benedict to release Mathias and lean against the wall for support, trying his best not to cry out in pain. Benedict thought he was going to pass out by the time he reached the bottom. His leg was both numb and painful, his thumb, much the same.

The lab was beyond the cellar and vastly different from the exterior and what little he had seen of the interior of the house. Benedict limped past nameless gizmos and gadgets hanging from the ceiling, large magnifying glasses, and needles as thick as his fingers and as long as his arms. Tech, as well as numerous vials of liquids, solids, and colorful gases, littered the tables and desks. There was barely an inch of flat surface that was empty.

Mister Dirk pulled out a chair from beneath a table for Benedict to sit on, and Mathias reached for a kit beneath another as if he had done so a hundred times before. As soon as he sat, a light that almost imitated the sun in intensity blinded Benedict. Squinting and raising a hand to shield his vision from the glowing magnifying device overhead, he found Mathias's familiar silhouette standing before him.

"What the hell is this?" he asked.

"It's alchemy," Mathias casually said as he rummaged through the kit.

"And technology," Mister Dirk followed.

"Together?" Benedict asked, incredulous.

"Not necessarily," Mister Dirk replied. "While fusing both technology and alchemy together is impossible, accentuating technology is doable . . . to a certain extent."

"It seems brighter and more stable," Mathias pointed out, as if this was not his first time seeing the device.

"I've been working on it," the man confirmed. To Benedict, he added, "Let's get your coat and shirt dry, shall we?"

Benedict removed the articles of clothing and handed them to Mr. Dirk. He thought he'd be freezing, but the heat emanating from the magnified light above kept him nice and toasty.

Draping the coat and shirt over his arm, Mister Dirk looked at Mathias. "Need anything else?"

"Alcohol," Benedict tried. "I'm far too sober for all of this."

Mathias chuckled as he pulled what he needed from the kit, while Mister Dirk gave a knowing smile. "If he gets too out of hand, Mathias, there's some ale and such in the other room."

"I'll take some of that 'and such,'" Benedict piped in.

"I think I have what I need, Mister Dirk. I thank you, and I apologize again. There is one other matter—"

Just then, a girl came down with a steaming bowl of water in her hands and a few cloths draped over her arm. Kneeling next to Benedict, she placed the bowl on the floor between his feet before soaking a square of fabric. She was a pretty thing, maybe fifteen or sixteen years old, looking at Mathias expectantly with her large blue eyes as he kneeled beside her, silent. Mathias only nodded in thanks as he grabbed and wrung out the cloth, cleaning the wound.

"Thank you," Benedict said, feeling obligated to, since Mathias didn't.

"Is that a stab wound?" she asked, mostly to Mathias than anyone else. "It's pretty deep," she added, coyly playing with a strand of her long blonde hair.

Mathias didn't acknowledge her, which caused Benedict to frown. He'd seen Mathias cleverly keep to himself. He'd seen him irate with his brother—and frankly, he couldn't blame him. Hell, he'd even seen him scared out of his wits while escaping pirates. So, watching him downright ignore someone was definitely new.

"Come, Ella," Mister Dirk said, extending the arm containing Benedict's draped-over clothes. "These need to be set out to dry."

Her gaze dropped to the ground, saddened, before she eventually got to her feet. "Yes, Father," she said before heading toward the man, taking the damp clothes, and disappearing up the stairs.

Mister Dirk went to move, but Mathias's voice stopped him. "The sample was taken." Placing the bloodied cloth in the bowl, Mathias turned away from Benedict, his eyes on those of his host. "Sky pirates took the sample," he specified, and Mister Dirk stared back at his guest, his lips thin and his expression unreadable.

"I'll track it," he eventually said, nodding slowly. Benedict could tell that the metaphorical gears in his head were turning. Eventually, he headed up the stairs, leaving Benedict alone with the surgeon.

"What was that about?" Benedict asked as Mathias expertly threaded a needle.

"What was what?" Mathias said with disinterest, focusing on his work.

"The infusion. The exchange in between the both of you," he added, gesturing back and forth with his index finger.

"Doctor Marsden made the sample trackable for exactly this reason."

There he was, being formal again. Benedict furrowed his brows. He was going to get his answers tonight, one way or another. "Why are they after you?"

"Because I had a sample of the infusions," Mathias said as if it were the most obvious thing in the world, though a frown had made its way to his face.

"They didn't know you on the *Nine*, so try again." Benedict said, calling him out.

"Has it ever occurred to you that maybe they did?"

"You're going to need to convince me. Go on, I believe I have all night."

Mathias finally looked up at Benedict for a moment, slight irritation in his expression. Inhaling and exhaling deeply, his eyes fell back to the wound. "I told you earlier that Doctor Marsden was my friend—brace yourself, this won't feel good," he added, sticking the needle through the skin. Benedict bit down on his fist to stifle a cry of pain. "Our friendship was no secret to anyone in or around Elgin, in the Upper Lands or the Lands Below."

"He must have been pretty popular," Benedict said, wincing with each stitch after having pulled his fist from his mouth.

"He was the lead scientist and was on the brink of the most important discovery yet: an infusion that can control the mind and, in turn, reveal one's deepest, darkest thoughts. A sort of truth serum, if you will."

Finally. Trying to get him to open up about this infusion had been like pulling teeth—which was more difficult than he wanted to admit, what with not being an actual surgeon, unlike Mathias. He whistled, impressed, before it turned into a hiss of pain as Mathias poked through another spot. "That definitely earns popularity points."

"He did so many interviews for various newspapers, he studied under famous doctors, alchemists, and scientists—including Mister Dirk, among various others."

Their host was famous? That made little sense. "But Mister Dirk is from the Lands Below," he mused, trying to connect the dots.

"How perceptive of you," Mathias countered, reaching for a blade as he finished sewing the wound shut.

Benedict forced himself to ignore the smart remark, despite really wanting to throw in a snide comment of his own. He couldn't afford to lose what he had going on with the surgeon; he couldn't afford Mathias putting his walls back up. "What's his story?"

"Sometimes fame and fortune don't bode well for some people," Mathias replied before getting to his feet and reaching out for Benedict's thumb wound.

He wasn't sure exactly what that meant, and he wasn't sure he wanted to ask. Given the state of the exterior of the house, he guessed some things were better left unsaid. So, he stayed quiet, ruminating over everything Mathias had revealed as the surgeon worked to clean the sliced skin. It was all starting to add up—until the point where Mathias had turned him in.

"You mentioned no longer needing my services," he started.

"I was going to have you help me get the infusion back. You seemed pretty good at holding your own in fights. However, when I learned of your true motives—that I was nothing but a bounty to you—"

So that *was* the reason the surgeon was angry. Rightfully so—Benedict still hadn't apologized. Why hadn't he apologized? Upon careful consideration, he didn't need to: he had kept Mathias alive for his reward, sure, but the surgeon, just as exploitative, had been using him too. If anything, it was Benedict who should be mad.

No. No, he couldn't be angry with Mathias. "Why are you helping me?" he eventually said, irritation clear in his voice. Mathias was ridiculously nice, and *that* part just didn't make sense after everything he had put him through.

"Because it's my duty to help the injured."

"But I held you hostage."

"Twice," Mathias agreed.

Benedict smirked. "Yet you still helped."

Mathias met Benedict's gaze. "Why is it so hard for you to understand that my only goal in life is to help people?"

It was Benedict's turn to not answer.

CHAPTER 21

"Why did you come back for me?"

Benedict's wounds had been properly cleaned, stitched, and bandaged, and the two had remained in silence—Benedict, slouching in the chair, forgoing all proper noble posture, and Mathias, leaning against one of the many tables piled high with gadgets—for what seemed like forever before Mathias finally spoke. Eyes trailing from the tear in his trousers up to the surgeon, he watched him.

Why *had* he gone back for Mathias? The man had left him high and dry at the constabulary, on his way to be deported—though, granted, Benedict had a hunch that the lieutenant had a little sway in that decision. Benedict had decided then and there that he didn't care, that he'd be okay if he never saw the surgeon again. So why did he go back?

Well, for one, Benedict wasn't heartless. Though it might have seemed that way after repressing all his emotions after losing Catherine, he still wasn't cruel. No, Kitch would have put him in his place long ago were that the case.

"Why did you come back for me?" Mathias repeated. "After everything that I did . . ."

Was Mathias being remorseful about his actions? The surgeon had nothing to apologize for. But the longer his eyes stayed focused on Mathias, the more his reason was becoming clearer.

His heart began to race, to ache. He knew someone who was just like him.

"Because you remind me of someone."

"Kitch?" Mathias asked, raising a brow.

"No. You remind me of . . ." Catherine. Mathias reminded him of Catherine.

Shutting his eyes, he inhaled deeply, and when he exhaled, it came out as a shudder. He missed her so much, always had. But he had repressed those feelings—locked them up, threw away the key, and buried them deep enough that they would never hurt him again—until one single look at Thomas Davies had caused a flood of emotions. Everything resurfaced instantly.

Kitch mentioned her by name every great now and again, mostly as a figurative slap in the face to get him back on track after he strayed. Other than being irritated, he had never had such intense fury over her loss . . . until now.

Benedict opened his eyes. Even just thinking about speaking her name to Mathias had his heart in a vise. He breathed in and out, desperately wishing for some liquid courage to help him deal—to help him forget. Or, at least until morning, when he'd curse himself over his splitting headache.

"Kate cared deeply about everyone and everything," he finally said, his voice slightly wobbly with her name, but it straightened out quickly afterward. "From the smallest creature, to the elderly, and everything and everyone in between."

Mathias was quiet for a moment. Was he silently judging him? "She sounds like quite a woman," he eventually said, his voice soft and kind—just like Catherine. "Who was she?"

"The daughter of a nobleman," he explained. "I saw her one day, and she was just . . . gorgeous. She took my breath away."

Benedict envisioned her in his mind's eye so perfectly it hurt: her long ringlet curls that glistened in the sunlight like spun gold, silky soft lips that melted his heart with each smile, blue eyes that glittered like sapphires whenever she was happy or amused. He could even hear her laughter like the tinkle of bells on the wind.

"I had to talk to her. I had to make her notice me. But how could I? I was nothing but a dirty tech user of an orphan. And believe me, even with new clothes and learned etiquette, her father never let me forget it."

Mathias, arms crossed over his chest, shook his head slightly as he listened intently. Benedict's thoughts shifted to Catherine's father, Lord Taylor. He was a hard man to please, wanting nothing but the best for his daughters—nothing but the best for himself. He hated Benedict with a passion, and Benedict was pretty sure it was because he didn't come with a dowry were they to wed.

"After a few tries, I managed to get her attention," he continued. "But I could only steal glances here and there, some words, never more than a few seconds at a time because her father was always hovering, practically stifling her."

Lord Taylor's hovering never stopped him, however. If anything, it made Benedict more determined, more eager to see just how far he could go and how long it would take before Lord Taylor found out.

"When the lands separated, I knew I had to do something. I couldn't let it tear me any further from Kate. So, I worked as a sailor and learned the ins and outs of airships, as well as earning an income to get me closer to living among the nobles. Unfortunately, her father still hated me and constantly chased me away from his property, so Kate and I had to be sneaky about it." Lord Taylor's security had yet to actually physically catch him, and if Benedict was proud of nothing else in his life, that fact would be enough.

An amused smirk found its way to Mathias's lips, and he pushed off the table, walking into the next room, disappearing. Benedict sighed. The memories were painful. How he missed her touch, how he missed her lips . . .

Mathias returned with a bottle of alcohol in each hand. He handed Benedict the gin, keeping the whiskey for himself. With a lopsided grin, he watched the surgeon return to his spot up against the table.

"I know I'm too sober for this story," he explained, "which means you're definitely too sober to be telling it."

Chuckling and uncorking the bottle, he raised it toward Mathias in a toast. "To those who care," he said.

"And to those who think they don't," Mathias chimed in.

Both men took a swig—Mathias making a face as the liquor went down—and Benedict took another, then another, and yet another, the familiar burning down his trachea a comfort.

"How long did this courting-behind-her-father's-back last?" Mathias eventually asked.

"Months," Benedict replied, his eyes glazing over after a few more large gulps. "But I was stupid."

"You mean more than you already are?"

Blinking in surprise, Benedict then chuckled. "You've only had one sip, yet you're so bold already! I'm afraid I'm going to have to cut you off." Mathias grinned into his drink, and Benedict continued with his story. "I had joined a band of ruffians upon getting kicked out of the orphanage, led by none other than Thomas Davies himself."

Mathias nearly choked. "He's from London?"

"He is," he replied. "We'd do stupid things like theft and arson and defacing property. Nothing unusual for orphans, but Davies would up the stakes: instead of causing fire in an alley, we'd set fire to entire homes; instead of stealing a few coins out of purses, we'd take the jewels, gems, and watches right off them at sword or gunpoint; instead of breaking down doors and windows, we'd destroy the entire interior of the home, as well."

Mathias's brows furrowed in disgust. "That's horrible!"

"I told you: stupid. It was a thrill. It was . . . me getting back at the unfairness of the world. Most of our victims were from the Upper Lands, anyway, where they could easily afford to rebuild and purchase new gems and jewels."

Mathias slowly shook his head, and Benedict wondered if he regretted helping him based on what he'd done in the past. Three years ago didn't seem like all that much time for Benedict to change his ways, but . . .

"One day, the Taylors were hosting a masquerade ball. They were one of the stops in a marriage tour of one of the family members. I snuck in. I couldn't pass up the opportunity of dancing with Kate, to see her again." To kiss her again. "But her father foiled that, as always, and it forced me to flee the property as it had done so many times. Once I arrived back at the docks, Davies was ready to leave and cause mischief. I agreed to join, as I was in a somewhat foul mood because of Lord Taylor. After setting sail, I went below deck to change. I had stolen her father's wedding coat in my effort to dance with her, apparently."

The memory of sneaking into the dark room and rummaging through the wardrobe made its presence known in Benedict's mind. He had pulled out a fancy dress coat with numerous golden buttons and had thought nothing of it until Catherine had pointed it out. Trying to play it cool, he had offhandedly stated that they had the same tailor, but he couldn't fool Catherine. She had been entirely too perceptive, pointing out that it was too short.

"I did not know where we were going. Nobody had filled me in on the details. So, it was a shock when we showed up at Kate's. I didn't care if they robbed the place blind or destroyed their furniture; I was angry with Lord Taylor, and a small part of me wanted revenge. But I refused to take part and stayed on the ship. Next thing I knew, the house went up in flames. There were screams and gunshots . . ."

Benedict shut his eyes. He was trembling. Bringing the gin to his lips with difficulty, he took one big chug to help dislodge the lump in his throat. He had to keep going. The floodgates were open, there was no stopping it now.

"They had gone too far. I needed to stop them, but first, I needed to find Kate and get her to safety. I found her in the back garden where I had left her that night. Perhaps she went back inside and mingled and simply ran out when the fire started. Or perhaps she never went back inside. I don't know. I'll never know. But there she was, being stabbed, being . . ."

He took another swig, and another. A shaken breath escaped him afterward. He hated reliving that moment in his mind, and he especially hated reliving it while not drunk enough.

"She was being raped by one of the new members," he continued, a quiver in his voice which he quickly drowned with more liquor. "I pulled him off her and we fought. He had no idea what fear and adrenaline and anger make once combined. He ran off with a broken nose and missing teeth. I ran to Kate, but it was too late. She . . ." Was that bile at the back of his throat? "She died in my arms."

“I’m so sorry,” Mathias whispered, his crossed arms falling to his sides.

“I returned to the ship, but Davies wouldn't let me back on. He said that if I didn’t have it in me to keep up with them, then I couldn’t be one of them. And they left me.”

Mathias pushed off against the table and picked up the bottle of whiskey that he had sat by his feet, raising it in the air, his eyes on the ceiling—past the ceiling. “May she be at peace in her resting place.”

Benedict raised the near-empty bottle of gin and finished it off. He wiped his mouth with the back of his bandaged hand, stifling a belch that tasted like a broken heart—which tasted like death, if he had to be honest with himself—before he spoke again. “Now don’t tell me your story with Miss Dirk is anything compared to mine.”

Mathias let escape a hollow laugh that was short-lived as he shook his head. “No, far from it. And now my problems seem trivial in comparison.”

“Well?” Benedict started. “Get on with it!”

Clearing his throat, Mathias looked everywhere but at Benedict. “As I mentioned, Mister Dirk taught Garfield a thing or two in the fields of science and alchemy.”

There he was, dropping formalities again. This time, though, Benedict was sure that it was because of the alcohol, despite Mathias only having had three sips.

"Garfield was enamored with Miss Dirk's eldest sister, and Miss Dirk was jealous. It was cute, at first, but it became a hassle the longer it went on. Impressively, she went on to learn as much as she could in both science and medicine at such a young age in an effort to impress Garfield, and, by extension, me."

Oh, this was getting juicy. Benedict wondered if it would explain why Mathias hadn't given her the time of day when she had dropped off the bowl of steaming water. He glanced down to the bowl with its bloodied water and found Mathias doing the same when Benedict's attention came back up.

"They were set to wed when Miss Dirk's eldest sister fell gravely ill and passed. Instead of mourning, Miss Dirk, who had never once given up on Garfield, tried to get him to notice her, and eventually succeeded a few months down the road. Unfortunately, at that same time, I . . . had fallen for her as well. But I promised myself that I would not infringe. And I never did. I intend to keep my promise, even in his death."

Benedict tsked, partially because it was an idiotic thing to do and say, but also because he was out of alcohol to prevent him from saying such a thing. "I'm sure your friend won't mind.

He's up there with his fiancée now, right? What would it matter if you court Miss Dirk now?"

Mathias frowned. "Says the man who is probably in the same predicament with a certain woman by the name of Kitch?"

It was Benedict's turn to frown. Mathias said nothing more, but his smug expression showed he was standing by his words. Benedict wanted to wipe that smirk off his face.

"So, what do we do now?" Mathias asked, changing the subject for both their sakes. "What do we do about the infusions, the pirates who are after me, and the pirate you're after?"

His head was slightly fuzzy, but he was far less drunk than others who would have swallowed the same amount. He wasn't sure, however, if it was the fuzziness that gave him his idea or not. "I think I need to beat him at his own game."

"And how do you propose we do that?"

"We?" he said, brows raised in surprise. "Are you willingly going to become a temporary pirate?"

"Absolutely not," Mathias scoffed. "But if I don't go with you, you'll end up hurt again. Worse, this time. So, I'll join you as your surgeon."

Benedict grinned, delighted. "Deal," he said. "I suppose that first, I'll need a crew."

"Where do you propose we find one?"

"I can help you with that," came a soft voice as the door opened.

Mathias quickly averted his eyes as Ella stepped in with Benedict's dry clothes. "Miss Dirk, I don't think—" he started.

"How long have you been listening in?" Benedict interrupted, side-eyeing her.

"Long enough," she said, quietly padding her way over to Mathias. "Doctor Darley," she tried, leaning over to get into his line of sight. When she did, he spun around and grabbed a random flagon and beaker from the table, pretending to study the liquids inside. "Doctor Darley, please hear me out—"

"Miss Dirk, I believe it is inappropriate for you to be down here without your father—" Mathias tried.

"I want to help, Mathias!" she said firmly, causing Mathias to look over his shoulder, blinking in shock at her tone. "I'm not an innocent child anymore. I truly wish to help. For Garfield, Maisie, and for . . . for you."

"How do you propose to help, Miss Dirk?" Benedict asked, as Mathias appeared severely uncomfortable.

"Come with me," she said with a mischievous grin. "And bring lots of money."

CHAPTER 22

Benedict was tired of walking. They hadn't even been trekking that long, but he was tired of it. In fact, he was just tired in general. When was the last time he had slept?

There was only a little limp in his step—thanks in part to Mathias for patching him up, but also thanks to the alcohol numbing his senses. He was sweating. Dampness covered his forehead, which should have felt fine against the frigid temperature, but his flushed face from the effort of his hobble was just making it worse.

They arrived at their destination—the streetlamp by the post office—where the flickering gas-lit fire in the glass globe cast dancing shadows about the street. Benedict leaned against the iron post with a relieved whoosh of breath, using the solid object to hold most of his weight, alleviating the throbbing in his leg.

A tiny figure approached, wool cloak swaying with their movement, and a red velvet scarf wrapped around their head and mouth, concealing their identity. Nothing made them recognizable, save for the delighted twinkle in their eyes as their gaze landed on Mathias.

"All right, Miss Dirk," Benedict said. "Lead the way."

She nodded and obeyed, glancing over her shoulder every now and again, adjusting her speed based on how fast Benedict could limp without having to stop to catch his breath.

He and Mathias were easily able to leave the Dirks' abode as they had been guests, but Ella had needed to sneak out. At first, Benedict wondered if her concealment had been slightly overdramatic, but as they followed, he couldn't help but think that this wasn't her first time.

They approached a pub, a dingy little watering hole that reeked of bodily fluids—Benedict didn't care to find out which specific ones—and that looked to be held up by the patrons themselves. Ruffians were known to lurk inside such places, ready and waiting for adventure or a good fight, but Ella led them past the shabby building entirely.

"Where is she going?" Mathias whispered to him, barely audible amid the crunch of ice and snow beneath their steps.

Benedict knew no more than he did. He continued to follow Ella.

Unlike the mess that was the pub—and every other deteriorating building in the Lands Below—the establishment Ella paused in front of immediately elicited a negative reaction from Mathias.

"No," he said, stopping dead in his tracks.

"Come on, silly," Ella purred over her shoulder. "Do you want a crew, yes or no?"

"You have no idea what you're getting into," he replied, shaking his head and taking a step back.

The building was better kept than the others along the street, but still discreet enough to not stand out too much and draw attention to itself. Despite the thin curtains covering each of the multiple windows of the two-story building, Benedict could still distinguish the silhouettes framed by candlelight, a smirk tugging at his lips. He suddenly understood exactly why Mathias was protesting.

Turning around, Ella closed the distance between herself and Mathias as she pulled the red scarf away from her mouth, revealing beautifully painted lips. A twinge of pain in his chest made him wonder if he was homesick and longing to return to London—to Kitch—or if he simply needed more alcohol.

Ella gently took one of Mathias's hands in hers, spreading her fingers in between his own. "I told you," she said gently, "I'm not a child anymore."

Playfully tugging his hand, she took a step, testing the waters to see if he would follow. Mathias barely moved, but the step he took was enough to spread a grin of excitement on her ruby lips. She continued to coax the reluctant surgeon until they found themselves inside.

It was nothing like the brothel back in London. This one was shabbier, draftier, but cozy.

"Why are we here?" Mathias whined, regret and anxiety flickering in his eyes. Ella giggled.

"Your friend needs a crew, and I know of someone who can get him one . . . for a price. Stay here," she instructed, releasing Mathias's hand and stepping up to the front desk.

She leaned in, whispering something to the olive-skinned attendant, whose beautiful honey-hued eyes bore right through Benedict before she stepped away behind the red velvet curtains that matched Ella's scarf. Turning around and giving Mathias a mischievously seductive smile, Ella followed the desk attendant, vanishing from sight. Mathias wiped his sweaty hands against his trousers.

"This is a bad idea. I—" he started, before finally tearing his gaze away from where Ella last stood to Benedict next to him. "Why didn't you stop me?"

"Truthfully, I want to see where this goes," he said, pointing back and forth in between Mathias and the curtain—to Ella—earning a frown of disapproval from Mathias. "But in all honesty, we're in desperate need of a crew if we are to pull this off."

A sigh escaped the surgeon. "I suppose you're right. But still . . ."

The velvet curtains danced before being cast aside, and a tall woman stepped out, her height accentuated further by the heels of her boots and her straight and strict posture. Keen brown eyes intently fell on both Benedict and Mathias before scanning the rest of the patrons, the aged silver strands in her black updo glistening in the dim lights about the room. Her gaze returned to both men before her full cherry-colored lips parted to speak.

"Follow me," she said dryly, before stepping back past the velvet veil.

Benedict and Mathias looked at each other. Mathias might not have been able to see it, but a brothel made sense. If the madam here was anything like the one Kitch worked for, then she had eyes, ears, and sway all over the village and more. She could easily know of a crew of the right people.

Determined, and with nothing left to lose, Benedict moved forward, limping away to follow. He didn't hear the familiar slap of Mathias's boots following until he had stepped past the curtain—Mathias was obviously still reluctant.

Benedict followed the woman down the hall, her red skirts in various shades complementing one another in their swaying dance as she sashayed past moans and grunts beyond closed doors.

Escorted up a staircase at the end of the hall, they stepped into a cozy room with a long leather couch that curled around a large oval table intricately carved from walnut.

Ella was present and already seated to the left—her cloak removed and no longer concealing her revealing corset and baby-blue skirts—surrounded by comfy cushions, silky veils, and soft feathers, while a beautiful young woman with orange ringlet curls sat on the opposite side. They both got to their feet and approached. The redhead slid her hand into Benedict's, leading him to take a seat, while Ella did the same to the very reluctant Mathias.

The woman they had followed made her way to the center of the couch and delicately sat as a brunette appeared from behind sheer curtains with alcohol and three glasses.

"I am Madam Bonifrey," the woman spoke as the brunette poured the drinks. "And you must be Benedict Keenan, hailing all the way from London."

Raising a brow, he replied, "You are correct." He wondered if this was from Ella or her intel. Benedict's courtesan snuggled up next to him, aimlessly trailing her fingers up and down his arm and leg. Casting Mathias a sidelong glance, he watched Ella mirror the redhead's actions, the surgeon squirming uncomfortably.

"I hear you are in search of a crew," Madam Bonifrey added.

"Again, correct."

"And what is the reason for seeking my help rather than going to the pub and recruiting there?"

Benedict turned his head and locked eyes with Ella as she continued to trail her fingers over Mathias. In her silence, he understood why she had brought them to the brothel, of all places—and not just because she apparently secretly worked here.

She wasn't doing it for him . . . it was all for Mathias.

Turning his attention back to Madam Bonifrey, he replied, "Anyone can hire those drunkards. But I need a crew of experts. I also need intel, and since you apparently see all, hear all, and know all, you are the perfect person to seek help from."

Madam Bonifrey appeared both smug and proud of Benedict's words. "Ah, but good information is pricey. You best hope that the good doctor has enough for what you need to know."

Brows furrowed, Mathias seemed to highly reconsider. Benedict did not doubt the high price for the intel, and was counting on Mathias to agree, as he had absolutely no money on him—here nor in London. Reluctantly, Mathias finally nodded, which sent relief flooding through Benedict.

A smile of delight found its way to her cherry lips, and Madam Bonifrey extended her hand, taking a glass from the brunette, who then sat and curled up next to her. Raising her glass in the air for a toast, Ella and the redhead grabbed and handed both men their drinks. Imitating Madam Bonifrey, they joined in on the toast.

"To business!"

CHAPTER 23

Benedict had witnessed enough deals go south by dirty cheats poisoning drinks that he couldn't be too careful.

It wasn't that he didn't trust Madam Bonifrey as a businesswoman protecting her assets; it was that he didn't trust her as a stranger dangling knowledge over his head for a price. Those were the ones to watch out for.

He purposely waited for her to swallow her drink—which she did—before knocking back his own just as quickly, allowing the heat to coat his throat and warm his insides.

Mathias hesitated before drinking his. Opting for a single sip, it quickly turned into desperate gulps as Ella coaxed him on by lifting the bottom of the glass with an index finger. Once empty, Mathias pulled the glass away from his lips, gasping and wrinkling his nose as the alcohol went down.

Benedict's courtesan tried to get a little more touchy-feely, going from trailing her delicate fingers to using her entire hands, running them over his chest. When she crept down to his stomach, he snatched her wrist, holding it steady, resulting in a gasp from the startled red-head. He couldn't afford to be too much more distracted than he already was. He needed what still remained of his wits for this information, and having drowned his sorrows in gin not too long ago, he knew he had to be careful.

"What do you know about a pirate by the name of Thomas Davies?" he asked. "Spare me the details of his life story. I already know those. What I want to know is what he's doing on this side of the Atlantic."

"Ah, yes," she mused. "Captain Thomas Davies of the Gilded Cannon Rovers. My intel says he's been here two years, but I think longer."

"Why do you think that?" asked Mathias, stuttering some.

Benedict wondered if the stammer happened due to Ella distracting him or if it was because of the alcohol. He had seen firsthand how much of a lightweight the surgeon was while aboard the *Amaroq*. Since he had already taken a few sips of whiskey before coming to the brothel, it was highly probable that this last drink was getting to him. He'd probably lose the surgeon soon.

"There have been whispers of a monster. Barely audible."

Benedict frowned. Monster? Was she referring to the cybernetic arms? "What do you mean by 'monster'?"

"I mean what I said," she replied with a shrug. "The whispers are barely distinguishable, which is why I said that I think he's been here longer. The time that he has definitely been here, however, he's been nothing short of a burden and plight, both to the Upper Lands and the Lands Below."

He didn't doubt that one bit, based on their earlier interaction. Davies had seemed pretty well-known by the constables, and it wasn't every day that airships fell from above the Upper Lands.

"What's in the sky above Upper Elgin?" he then asked.

The corners of her cherry lips tugged into a smile, and her gaze twinkled in delight, as if he had just gained favor in her eyes. Turning to her courtesan, she whispered something in her ear before the brunette stood up and poured a second round of drinks. Mathias groaned, leaning forward with his elbows against his knees, covering his face in his hands. He was fighting the good fight, Benedict had to admit.

Ella stood up and stepped around the couch. Leaning in, she slid her hands over Mathias's shoulders and softly pulled him back. He was visibly tense, a protest playing on his lips until she began gently kneading the knots in his muscles. Momentarily shutting his eyes, he gave in, the objection melting into a moan as his head rolled to the side.

Madam Bonifrey's courtesan handed Benedict his glass, and he thanked her with a polite nod before she turned to Mathias. At first, it appeared like the surgeon was going to pass, but drunken dignity seemingly got the best of him, and he accepted dutifully. The brunette handed Madam Bonifrey her own glass before nestling back down next to her.

Bringing her glass to her lips, Madam Bonifrey expertly downed its contents. Benedict had been waiting for that visual confirmation again, making sure that their drinks weren't poisoned by judging the brothel manager's actions. She hardly seemed fazed, so he quickly knocked back his drink just as skillfully. Mathias had a harder time.

Ella had come back from around the couch, sitting next to Mathias, helping—or forcing, rather—by tilting his glass. When Mathias choked, alcohol sputtering out down his chin and onto his clothes, Benedict drew the line.

"Miss Dirk," he started with a frown, as his courtesan took his empty glass, "I believe our friend has had enough."

It had been obvious aboard the *Amaroq* that Mathias wasn't much of a drinker. He definitely needed to gain tolerance for it, and Benedict was more than willing to help with a few dozen more drinking sessions, but this was the wrong way to go about it.

Rigid, eyes wide as if a scolded child, guilt flashed through Ella's expression as she looked at Benedict while Mathias clumsily used his sleeve to wipe his chin. Slowly, she turned her attention to Madam Bonifrey as if either seeking further instructions or validation of her actions. Madam Bonifrey raised her chin. Benedict wasn't entirely too sure what that action meant, but obediently, Ella took the rest of the alcohol away from Mathias, placing it on the table before helping him clean the spill.

Turning his attention back to the brothel manager, he nodded for her to go on with her information. "I believe that round of drinks means you have an answer to my question?"

A smug smile on her lips, she said, "And what makes you think there is anything above the Upper Lands?"

"Call it a hunch," he said, before a groan escaped Mathias. Glancing in Mathias's direction, he saw him cradling his head in his hands while Ella's delicate fingers wiped some stray strands of his hair off his forehead. "Mathias," he said, hiding the concern in his voice, "you're looking a little rough around the edges. Maybe you should get some rest."

"Nonsense!" he slurred, which caused Ella to giggle. He smiled at her half fondly but mostly in a drunken stupor. "I'm not . . ." he started, but seemed to have lost his train of thought when Ella leaned in, planting kisses along his jawline. "I'm . . ." he tried again, then that was it. He said nothing more, his attention now completely on Ella.

Benedict frowned. Sure, he had teased Mathias, curious about how things were going to unfold with Ella after listening to his little story, but this wasn't right. Mathias would have never consented to her actions were he able to think rationally—were he sober—and Ella was taking full advantage of that. Parting his lips to say something, Madam Bonifrey beat him to it.

"I agree," she piped in. "Ella, darling, please take the good doctor to a room so that he can rest."

Ella helped Mathias to his wobbly feet, and he swayed into her with a groan, his hands back to his head. Benedict was impressed; she was a lot sturdier than she looked, helping Mathias with ease, slowly making their way out of the room.

"Miss Dirk," Benedict called out after her. Pausing and turning her attention toward him, he continued. "I trust you will do what is right and allow him to sleep," he said, eyes slightly narrowed. Deep down, it was a threat that he hoped she caught and understood. There would be no taking advantage of the drunken surgeon under his watch.

Nodding with a faltering smile, she turned her attention back to her charge, and they both disappeared.

Benedict shut his eyes, inhaling and exhaling deeply. He wasn't drunk, but dividing his attention three different ways seemed to require more effort than usual. The redhead brought one of his hands to her ruby lips, placing soft kisses against his knuckles, which caused him to snap his eyes open and look at her with a gentle smile.

"There are rumors of airships circling the Great Lakes," Madam Bonifrey finally offered.

"Why?" he asked.

She shrugged, but that smug smile returned to her lips, meaning that she knew more than she was letting on. "My intel tells me they have a poison in their possession. I've heard whispers of it being called Drapyltin."

That poison, if Benedict had to guess, must have been Mathias's infusion. And the fact that they were circling the Great Lakes probably meant that they wanted to test it. The redhead scooted into his lap, and Benedict furrowed his brows. It was getting harder for him to concentrate, his train of thought in constant danger of derailing. "What are the possibilities of it getting into the water system?" he asked, as his courtesan began grinding in his lap.

"In gas form? Pretty slim."

"What would it take to turn it into a liquid?" he asked.

"Cold," she replied. "One would need to cool it below its highest temperature to get it to turn into a liquid."

"Cold enough to freeze the Great Lakes?"

"One would hope not."

Ella returned silently, alone, sliding back onto the couch. The expression in her gaze—and the speed of her return—told him she had heeded his silent threat. His attention diverted back to the redhead's hips, mesmerized, as she continued to grind. He trailed his fingers up and down her thighs before blinking away the fog. What was going on? It usually took a hell of a lot more alcohol than that to affect him . . .

He watched Madam Bonifrey for a moment. If she had drugged the drinks, she wasn't showing any signs whatsoever.

"What were we drinking?" he asked, to which Madam Bonifrey gave a satisfied smile.

"One of my favorites, given to me by my old friend Henriod. House special. Secret recipes even *I'm* not privy to," she said with a coy smirk.

"It's good," he acknowledged.

"Want to try something better?" she asked, licking her lips.

"Better, you say?"

Her courtesan stood and walked to the back room, disappearing. Madam Bonifrey crossed one leg over the other, every bit proper and poised as she folded her hands in her lap. "I don't share my personal stash often, Mister Keenan, but I can't help but like you, and that's a dangerous thing."

"How so?" he asked.

"I'm risking everything as a favor to you." Benedict raised a brow as Madam Bonifrey produced a letter from nearby, waving it in the air so that he could see. "I have here a letter from one by the name of . . . Madam Kitch."

His heart skipped a beat. Kitch? How was that possible? Grabbing the redhead by the waist to hold her steady, his attention was on the letter as she unfolded it. The brunette returned with a dark bottle and two fresh glasses, but his focus, as fuzzy as it was, never wavered from that letter.

"She's a wordsmith, that Madam Kitch," she said admirably. "Long story short, she has requested that I keep my eyes and ears on you."

"How did she know I would be here?" he asked. He never told her his exact destination—which hadn't even been Elgin to begin with.

"As renowned as I am, trust me when I tell you she's impressed even me, and that's hard to do. She's definitely a keeper."

"That she is," he mused, his gaze still on the letter. He always knew Kitch to be resourceful, but this was weirdly accurate and coincidental. He'd need to have a discussion with her upon his return—after killing Thomas Davies first, of course.

Madam Bonifrey's courtesan poured their drinks from the dark bottle. The liquid was just as dark and smelled of various spices, which filled the room.

"I have opened two of my rooms for both yourself and the good doctor. Consider it good faith," she added, folding the letter up and making it disappear once more.

Taking the offered glass, he brought it to his nose, inhaling the strong fragrance. He couldn't quite put his finger on one of the ingredients, but it smelled off from the rest. He wasn't sure if the spices were masking the full scent or if the taste of the previous drink still played on his taste buds, affecting them differently.

Madam Bonifrey raised her glass, and Benedict did the same. "To a new alliance with Madam Kitch," she toasted, before bringing the drink to her lips.

"To Kitch," he repeated, watching her drink first before following suit. It went down smoothly, but there was that taste, that smell, that he just couldn't quite place. "It's incredible," he said, inspecting his empty glass. "What's in it?"

"Oh, Mister Keenan," she purred. "That is a secret that will follow me to my grave."

“That’s a shame,” he said, handing the redhead his glass, which she placed on the table. “Now, about my crew . . .”

“I have not forgotten,” she stated. “I know just the crew. Worth every penny and then some. I shall contact them at sunrise. How about you get some rest? I will keep you informed over breakfast in the morning.”

Benedict nodded before a wave of dizziness washed over him, confusing him, making him light-headed. Despite drinking half a bottle of gin before arriving at the brothel, he hadn’t had enough alcohol to be affected in such a way. He could usually handle so much more. He looked at Madam Bonifrey, watching her interact with her courtesan. She drank exactly what he did and still had her wits about her. Strange. His gaze then traveled to Ella, who sat in silence, one leg crossed over the other, an amused smirk tugging her lips. What did she know?

The redhead removed herself from his lap, and he stood up slowly, his world spinning, threatening to throw him off axis. He parted his lips to speak, but nothing came out.

“Alice, please show him to his room,” she ordered.

“Yes, Madam,” the redhead replied, entwining her fingers in his and leading him out.

Something was wrong. He almost asked for Ella instead, but did he truly trust her more than anyone else? But as soon as the thought made its way to the forefront of his mind, it disappeared just as quickly.

He blanked out down the hall. What happened? How did he get there? Benedict stopped; his vision doubled. Leaning against the wall, he grabbed his head with his free hand.

"What the hell?"

Alice paused, a soft smile on her lips. She was beautiful. Had he known that? Who was she? Did he introduce himself? He couldn't remember. His eyes fell on their hands, fingers interlaced. That *had* to mean that he introduced himself, right?

"Come, just a few more doors," she said.

Raising her hand, he gently kissed her fingers before grabbing her by the waist, pulling her close before he blanked out again.

He couldn't remember how, but he eventually made it to his room. Rolling around on the bed with Alice in heated passion, he paused, looking around. Where was he? What was he doing? Was he drunk? Who was the woman beneath him? He frowned, but then couldn't remember why he was frowning. His vision shifted again; he was seeing double, and the redhead's face looked more and more like Kitch.

"Kitch?" he slurred, but Kitch—or was it Alice—softly shushed him. No. No, he would never do this with Kitch. "Stop," he said, sitting up, completely dizzy and bringing his hands to his head. "Leave me."

"Are you sure?" Alice asked, concerned.

"Just go."

Benedict fell back onto the bed. He might have fallen asleep. Or perhaps he didn't. He didn't know where he was, what time it was, or what he had been doing. All he knew is that a noise startled him, and his body sent uncomfortable jolts through his entire being.

"I said leave me," he mumbled with a slight slur.

"Come now, Captain Keenan," said a woman with a Caribbean accent. "Yuh would nuh talk dis way tuh yuh crew."

His eyes shot open. He knew that voice. He shot straight out of bed, his eyes on Ajani with her sword in hand, aimed straight at him.

"You . . .!" he said, then swayed. Grabbing his head, he tumbled into the nightstand, knocking over the lantern, which shattered on the ground.

"Aye," she said with a grin. "Dis a gon' be too easy," she added.

He took a swing at her, but it was a poor attempt as he clumsily sidestepped, falling onto the bed. Something hard hit him in the back of the head, effectively knocking him out.

CHAPTER 24

Benedict's head hurt, and it wasn't the alcohol talking.

What happened? Where was he? He tried to remember, but he couldn't recall anything past the spicy-tasting amber liquid, and even that was iffy.

His head felt stuffed full of cotton. A groan escaped him, but the gag in his mouth partially muffled it. His body was giving him mixed signals: numbness, cramps, jolts of pain . . .

The discomfort in his lower back was from his bound wrists digging into his skin. He splayed his fingers, feeling a wooden surface beneath them. He wasn't entirely too sure if his environment was doing the rocking or his mind.

Wherever he was, it was dark. Not even a sliver of light was visible. Blinking a few times to make sure that his eyes really were open, he still couldn't see. Had he gone blind? He tried listening, tried to hear something, anything. He zoned in—wincing as his head protested the focus—and heard voices, though he couldn't distinguish what was being said.

Struggling, he sat up and hit his head on something above, falling backward with a cry as his head pulsed like it was going to crack open, but nothing escaped beyond a muffled mumble. When the pain finally subsided, the white-hot heat allowing thoughts to return, he raised his feet only to hit something at the top. Either the ceiling here was incredibly low, or he was enclosed somewhere. It was a good thing that he wasn't claustrophobic.

Pulling his legs into his chest until his feet were flat up against the strange ceiling, he kicked hard. Nothing happened. He kicked again and again, but he was getting nowhere, and his leg wound was starting to burn. Dropping his legs back down, he began flailing. He wanted out.

Suddenly, the ceiling vanished, sending bright light flooding in. Benedict clamped his eyes shut in shock, the pain behind them excruciating. This was it. This was what was going to kill him. An image of Kitch at his grave crossed his dizzy mind, where the tombstone read: *Rest in Peace Benedict Keenan. Died from his brain imploding.*

"Glad tuh see yuh a finally awake." Ajani looked down at him, and a flash from the brothel shoved its way into his memories. He glared up at her. What was she doing? What was Davies up to? And was binding, gagging, and locking him inside of a crate really necessary? "Di Captain be cautious," she explained, as if reading his mind. "Come, he wishes tuh see yuh."

She was anything but delicate in her handling of him, roughly grabbing him by the collar of his shirt and pulling him to his feet.

Benedict's *everything* hurt now, and walking straight was a chore. His head still wanted to explode, his wounds screamed for mercy, and he still saw double, causing him to swagger and stumble.

A few grubby pirates pulled him out from below deck. He squinted in the light—it was past sunrise—as they shoved him along. He hadn't realized how stale and muggy it was below deck until he was in the crisp, cold temperatures of the area. Shivering uncomfortably, he finally arrived before Thomas Davies at the helm.

"So nice of you to join us, Keenan!" he said. Hands still shackled behind his back and mouth still gagged, Benedict could only glare in seething hatred. "Now, I'm gonna remove the gag. There's no point yelling for help; we're far from civilization."

Benedict cast a quick glance over the edge of the ship, only to see nothing but clouds. Davies spoke the truth. Ajani yanked the gag out, and Benedict coughed some before flexing his jaw open and shut. He could have done with having his hands untied to rub the soreness out, but he knew that he'd take advantage of being free to put up a good fight, and he knew Davies expected it too.

"Where's Madam Bonifrey?" he croaked, still glaring daggers.

"Back at her whorehouse, a whole lot richer," Thomas snickered.

That witch! Did she sell him out? "Where's Mathias?" he demanded, glancing about the airship, his heart skipping a beat when he did not see him. Was he still at the brothel?

"He's alive," Thomas replied, "and your cooperation will keep him that way."

Benedict growled. He hated not having the upper hand. "What do you want from me?" he snarled, his shivering making him less vicious than he wanted to be.

"What do *I* want from *you*?" Davies laughed. "You're the one who wanted a crew!"

Benedict's eyes went wide in shock and realization. It couldn't be. There was no way Madam Bonifrey considered Davies—especially after they had talked about him—as his crew . . . did she?

"You see, I was hiring too, and I wasn't going to stop until you joined me, Keenan. We used to be a team, you and I."

Team? He was the one who left Benedict that night. He was the one responsible for the Taylor mansion going up in flames. He was indirectly responsible for Catherine's death, but Benedict still blamed him anyway. Team? They were never a team.

"I won't work for you," Benedict spat.

"You will, or the good doctor will be the one to suffer."

What would they do to Mathias if he didn't comply? Was he even on the ship? "Let me see him," Benedict demanded.

"No," was Davies's simple reply.

"Let me see him," Benedict ordered again, "or you get no work from me."

"That's not how this works, Keenan," Davies said. "But if you want proof that he is aboard and very much alive . . ." Thomas turned to one of his crewmen, a muscular fellow in stripes. "Shoot him in the leg," he instructed.

Benedict's breath caught in his throat. Davies wouldn't really shoot Mathias just to prove a point, would he? "Stop," he said, but the pirate continued below deck as Ajani stuffed the gag back into Benedict's mouth.

His heart raced in fear, and the seconds it took for the pirate to reach his destination stretched indefinitely—feeling like hours, days, weeks, months, years—before a gunshot echoed off every surface of the airship, followed by a loud cry of pain.

Benedict cried out, lunging for the lower deck to get to Mathias, but Ajani yanked him back. He roared against the gag, but muffled mumbles were all that escaped him. Mathias didn't deserve it. He didn't deserve any of it.

"Relax," Thomas drawled, unaffected by what had just happened. "He's a doctor, he can treat himself."

The headache that Benedict had all but forgotten about returned in such full force, he thought he was going to be sick. His legs gave out from under him, and he found himself on his throbbing knees. He leaned forward until his forehead rested on the frozen planks of the deck, and he had to admit that despite his shivering, it felt pretty good.

Thomas's spindly cybernetic fingers grasped a handful of Benedict's hair by his scalp, pulling his head up to look at him. Benedict wanted to cry out in pain, but nothing escaped him. He couldn't ease the pain with his wrists bound behind his back, so all he could do was lean into Davies's grip, eyes watering from the acute stinging of his scalp being pulled.

"This is the way it's going to be, Keenan. Don't underestimate me. I'll give you time to think about it, but there is really nothing to think about." Davies released Benedict's hair, and he practically sighed in relief despite the throbbing. "The answer will be yes, or else," he added.

Two pirates pulled Benedict away, dragging him down below deck, stuffing him back into the crate. They left him with nothing but the darkness, his thoughts, and a splitting headache.

CHAPTER 25

Sudden light awoke Benedict, though not quite as bright as the last time. His entire body tingled, both from numbness and the temperature. He had eventually rolled over onto his shoulder before falling asleep, his fingers and lower back unable to handle his bindings any longer.

Pulled from the crate, it was not by Ajani like the last time, but by a random pirate with a crooked nose and missing teeth. It took Benedict a moment for his muscles to cooperate before being rudely shoved forward, and thankfully, he somewhat knew where he was going, making his way above deck without too much trouble.

Judging by the dim light in the sky, it was either evening or morning. He had lost track of time in the crate, busy keeping score of every wrongdoing Thomas Davies had done. Each additional notch on Benedict's list added fuel to the fire and made him need to torture the sky pirate even more before killing him. He didn't care if he had to use a spoon—he'd get his revenge for both Catherine and Mathias.

He found his way to the helm and into Davies's presence once more. The closer he got, the more he had to contain his fury, for Mathias's sake. He couldn't tell if the trembling was from anger or from the cold. After they pulled the gag out, he stretched his numb jaw by opening and closing his mouth while glaring murderously at Davies.

"Are you ready to do some work?" he asked.

Benedict didn't answer. Thomas's eyes traveled to the crewmen that had dragged Benedict before him, and the pirate gave a slight nod before grabbing one of Benedict's ankles and shackling it to a thick iron chain. If Benedict could've glared at Davies any harder, he would have. The crewman then released his wrists from their binds, and Benedict immediately began rubbing them, finally looking away from the man he loathed to study his wrists. The restraints had been pretty tight, marked by deep red crevices.

"You'll start from the bottom up in the command chain," Davies informed him as another pirate shoved a mop into Benedict's hands. He barely had time to fumble with the handle when he caught the bucket being thrust at him with both arms, the cold, grubby water sloshing all over him. "And you'll stay nearby, where I can keep an eye on you. I know you, Keenan," he added, tapping next to his red cybernetic eye with a spindly finger. "Once I can trust you, I know you'll move up in ranks quickly. You're clever, and I need that on my side. Feel free to advise. I want to know what your thoughts are. Just make sure you address me as Captain. Is that clear?"

Benedict didn't answer.

"Keenan," Davies prompted, disappointment in his voice, "How many gunshots do you think the good doctor can handle because of you before he dies?"

Benedict glared daggers, but eventually said, "Yes, Captain." He couldn't afford to cause any more of Mathias's injuries.

"Good lad. Now get to work."

While he cleaned, he couldn't keep his mind off Mathias. How were they treating him? Was he shackled up and shoved into a crate as well? Did they at least give him the medical supplies needed to patch himself up after shooting him to prove a point? It was cruel torture for both the surgeon and to himself. His mind then shifted to Madam Bonifrey and her betrayal.

What he couldn't quite figure out was how she had kept her wits about her the entire time. Her courtesan had poured the alcohol right in front of them, from the same bottle, and never switched the cups around. Somehow, they tainted his drink. He had been drinking for a few years now—there was no way that he would have gotten drunk that quickly.

Turning his attention to the clear skies past the edge of the ship as it slowed, his gaze fell to the lake below.

"Lake Huron," Ajani said as she stepped to his side. "Second largest a di Great Lakes, an' named fah di Huron people inhabiting di region."

Benedict watched her for a moment, long enough to make sure that she would not attack him in any way. He had noticed her watching him as she spoke with some of the other pirates on deck. It almost seemed like she couldn't trust him—and frankly, he didn't blame her. He didn't quite trust her either. It was a pity that she was on the wrong side of his personal vendetta, however. She held her own in a fight, and that thoroughly impressed him. He'd have loved to grab a drink with her.

Benedict finally turned his attention back to the lake. "What are we doing at Lake Huron?"

"You'll see soon enough," came Thomas's voice.

A flicker caught Benedict's attention above them as the captain pressed a few buttons on the console next to the wheel. Benedict watched the flickering, not quite sure what he was looking at, until mirrored panels moved, revealing a gigantic cannon embedded in the rocks of the hidden floating land. His eyes widened as he connected the cannon to the airships crashing above the outskirts of Upper Elgin. Tilted just right, the mirrored panels imitated the sky instead of the lakes, hiding the massive weapon from view, even on a cloudless day.

He couldn't quite make out the carved designs on the oxidized copper barrel, but the fact that he could see carvings at all just proved how large the cannon was.

Davies pressed a few more buttons, and the bore lit up deep inside the barrel. He watched it for a moment, inspecting, calculating, then pressed a button to shut it off. "Get the good doctor," he told one of his crewmen, who nodded and disappeared.

What did they want with Mathias? How was Mathias even related to this at all?

The pirate soon emerged from below deck with a limping surgeon, who both frowned at the way he was being treated and winced from the pain he was in. Benedict's gaze fell to Mathias's bandaged leg—a piss-poor attempt at a wrap around the wound and trouser leg. Based on that, he knew that they never unbound his wrists from behind his back. There was no way it was Mathias's handiwork. The fire in his belly rekindled. His hands formed into fists before he heard a voice.

"Down, Keenan," Davies said. "Remember the deal."

"I don't recall agreeing to this deal," Benedict spat, eyes still on Mathias.

Ajani approached the surgeon, holding up a familiar trinket. Resting his weight on his good leg, Mathias's eyes were on the infusion as it swayed back and forth, a fearful expression on his features.

"Doctor!" Thomas said from his position at the helm. "I trust you know what this is?"

Looking up to the pirate captain, Mathias's gaze then shot to the cannon above. The fear in his eyes turned to terror, and he took a few steps back, but the pirate that had fetched him rudely shoved him forward, resulting in a cry of pain. Benedict lunged forward to help, only to stumble as the shackle around his ankle yanked him back, dropping him to his knees.

Davies briefly turned to Benedict. "What a perfect example of failed discipline," he drawled. Getting back to his feet with a glare, Benedict adjusted his footing to be more comfortable in the shackle before shifting his attention back to Mathias. "I need you, Good Doctor, to show us how to use it," Davies said.

Mathias blinked. "Me?"

"Aye. You."

"But I . . . I don't know how! I'm a surgeon, not an alchemist."

"Surely, your friend told you how to use it."

Mathias didn't answer, and Benedict, with an exhale of defeat, knew that meant that he did. The captain knew as well and gave a smug grin.

"You know what this means, don't you, Doctor?"

Mathias frowned. "But we don't know the side effects. We don't know the dosage. We don't know—"

"Scientific rubbish," Davies said. "Test it on Keenan, if you must," he added with a shrug.

Benedict blinked in surprise at being offered as the sacrificial guinea pig, but what Mathias said next caught him off guard.

"No," he said defiantly.

Mathias's answer filled Benedict with a sense of pride, but at the same time, it also filled him with dread. Mathias had no idea who he was dealing with and what kind of dangerous games Davies knew how to play. He was gambling enough for the both of them; he didn't need the surgeon to add to the stakes.

Thomas narrowed his eyes. "I'd watch your tone, Doctor. There is no way to get out of this. Either test it on Keenan, or test it on yourself."

Benedict snapped his attention to the captain. That was madness! "What if he doesn't recover?" Benedict asked, alarmed.

"All part of the research," Davies casually replied.

Benedict was taken aback, even though he'd known that the man had such a disregard for human life. After all, he was partly responsible for what had happened to Catherine. Davies's words triggered the fury deep inside, the rage he tried to contain to keep Mathias out of danger, and Benedict growled, lunging at the captain.

His shackled leg did not follow, and a sharp pain in his ankle flashed hot through his body. Thomas spun around to face him at the sound of the chain going taut, delivering a punch with his cybernetic barrel of an arm straight to Benedict's stomach.

The wind was knocked straight out of him, and he flew backward from the strength of the blow, landing against the exterior wall to the captain's quarters and slumping to the ground. He coughed and winced from the pain, gasping for air, fireworks dancing in his field of vision.

Davies spun back around, angry. "Well?" he called out to Mathias. "What will it be?"

Mathias glared at the captain before his attention fell back to the trinket, still swinging back and forth in between Ajani's fingers. "If I refuse?" he asked.

"Matt," Benedict tried, struggling to get back to his feet. He didn't like the way Mathias was challenging Davies. He knew the gears in the surgeon's head were spinning, and it wasn't a good thing.

Davies looked past Mathias and gave a faint nod. Benedict's body stiffened, and when he saw a pirate coming at Mathias from behind, Benedict froze in panic.

Brow raised, Mathias partially turned to see what was going on, only to get slashed in the side by the pirate's knife. The whimper that escaped him sent Benedict into a fury.

"Matt!" He scrambled to reach the surgeon, but the chain at his ankle stopped him once more, knocking him flat on his stomach.

Mathias stumbled, then crumbled as the applied weight to his injured leg overcame him, causing him to land on deck with a thud. His face contorted in pain, and his hands still bound behind his back were not helping matters any.

Red soaked through his wool coat from the cut, and he gritted his teeth, trembling from the pain as he struggled to stand back up.

He was acting so tough and brave . . . it was heartbreaking. There was nothing Benedict could do but helplessly watch. So, when Mathias, hunched over and swallowing hard, looked up at Ajani and nodded, dread washed over him.

"No!" Benedict shouted, resulting in a kick to the ribs from the captain. Despite crumbling back to his knees in pain, he couldn't take his eyes off Mathias.

Ajani produced a key from somewhere in her coat and unlocked the shackles at Mathias's wrists. Wincing, he rubbed at the raw skin before reaching for the infusion with a visibly shaking hand.

"Matt, no!" Benedict shouted, stretching as far as he could go while chained up, flinching when Davies turned back around with a glare.

Back in the jails of London, Benedict had learned to dislocate his thumb to get out of wrist bars. He called it his parlor trick; he'd taught it to the orphans. What he wouldn't give to be able to dislocate his ankle the same way.

"*Mathias*!"

Still trembling, Mathias ignored him as he inspected the trinket and the smoky content inside. When he brought his thumb to the cork stopper, Benedict's blood ran colder than the temperature on deck. Mathias then met his gaze before bringing the infusion to his nose and popping the stopper out. He shut his eyes and inhaled deeply.

Benedict blacked out for a moment. He didn't remember shouting so loud and long that his throat became raw. He didn't remember Mathias doubling over in a coughing fit, collapsing to his knees from the pain of his wounds. What Benedict *could* remember and see was Mathias's body racked with tremors that slowly died out.

Everyone watched in silence, with nothing but the sound of the airship's motor and the waves of Lake Huron below to be heard. Mathias didn't move. Dread washed over Benedict. Was

Mathias dead? Just how potent was the small amount of infusion? His apprehension turned to anger, and he gritted his teeth, fists clenched. Thomas Davies would pay for the loss of Catherine and Mathias.

"He breathes," came Ajani's voice, and Benedict all but forgot about his rage, his breath caught in his throat.

"Doctor!" Davies called out, but Mathias didn't reply or react. "Doctor, raise your hand if you can hear and understand me." It took a moment, but Mathias, at a snail's pace, eventually raised his hand. Surprised by this turn of events, Benedict could only stare. The captain tried again once Mathias's hand dropped back down to his side, limp. "Stand on one foot," he ordered.

At languid speed, Mathias got to his feet and stood straight, as if the gash in his side didn't even bother him. He even stood on the foot of his wounded leg without so much as flinching. Evidently, this Drapyltin turned Mathias into an empty shell who couldn't even feel pain. His eyes were devoid of life.

The crew all began smiling at the display. "Spin in a circle!" one called out. "Jump up and down!" another one said. "Flap your arms like a bird!" said a third. And Mathias, still slow, did so as they laughed and applauded, hooting and hollering at the show before them.

Ajani made her way up to the helm, stepping over Benedict's sprawled-out body with her long legs. "He a bit slow," she said, standing next to Davies.

"It's being adjusted," he said to her before yelling, "Give him a gun!"

Benedict didn't know how much more torture he could take—and especially didn't know how much more *Mathias* could take.

Grinning like a madman as a pirate offered his gun, Davies called out to Mathias. "Doctor, take the gun."

Everything slowed. Benedict didn't even realize that he had been holding his breath until his lungs burned, screaming for air. "Please don't do this," he said, but his plea fell on deaf ears.

Mathias took the gun, blankly awaiting his next order.

"Shoot the man to your left."

The pirate to Mathias's left jumped back, his face dropping in shock. And while Davies chuckled about it, Benedict shouted, "Matt, no! Don't do it!"

"I'm giving the orders around here, Doctor, and I say shoot him!" Davies snarled, before narrowing his eyes at Benedict.

Some of the crew held the victim in place. The pirate struggled as Mathias raised his arm, but he just couldn't get away. Mathias pulled the trigger, and the gunshot echoed loudly aboard the ship, hitting the pirate in the shoulder.

"*Mathias*!" Benedict yelled as loudly as he could. Mathias had to stop. He didn't know what he was doing. Benedict didn't want him having blood on his hands—not this kind of blood—and he especially didn't want Mathias to regret it for the rest of his life if he were to snap out of it. If that was even remotely possible.

"Horrible aim," Ajani pointed out, unimpressed.

"Let's see if we can fix that. Doctor!" Benedict looked up at the absolutely evil grin spreading across the captain's lips. "Aim for his heart."

Still held in place, the pirate whimpered in both pain and fear. Mathias's empty shell slowly raised the gun and shuffled his feet forward, like a zombie, aiming the barrel of the gun right above the man's breast.

"Mathias stop! For the love of—" Benedict started, "you *heal* people!"

At that, Mathias slowly lowered the gun, either slightly confused or having a moment of relapse. The grin on the captain's face faltered. "Remember who gives the orders around here, Doctor!" he called out. "Aim for his heart and shoot him!"

Benedict tried to call out his name again, but it was too late. Mathias raised the gun and pulled the trigger, shooting the pirate point-blank. The crew released him, and his lifeless body crumbled to the ground.

With a smug smile of satisfaction, Thomas turned to Ajani. "It's being adjusted to make them faster, but otherwise it's pretty satisfactory, wouldn't you say?" He then turned to Benedict. "Best get your mop and bucket ready, Keenan. I want all the blood gone by dinnertime. Am I clear?"

Benedict didn't answer. He was fuming. His fingernails scratched at the wooden planks of the deck as they formed into fists. What had he done to Mathias? What if Mathias never reverted back and was this empty shell for the rest of his life? Davies had mentioned that it was being adjusted to make the bodies faster, so did that mean they were going to use the cannons to poison the water? He'd have a never-ending army of ruthless, mind-controlled slaves. Mathias would have never wanted that, which was probably why he used it on himself instead.

Lunging at the captain, he dodged the oncoming swing from the barrel arm, only to have his ankle pulled out from under him. Falling hard on his shoulder, he sat up and turned to look at the chain connected to his shackle. Something wasn't right; he should have had more length. His attention fell on Ajani, who held the chain in her hand. She was the one who had pulled him back.

"Don't you remember what happened the last time you did this?" Thomas asked. "Remember, you'll get more liberties once I can trust you."

"I never agreed to work for you."

"This, again?" He sighed. "I already told you that you have no choice." Davies looked back at Mathias down below. "Doctor! Shoot yourself in the other leg—"

"No! Matt, stop!"

But before anything could happen, Benedict heard the gunshot. He couldn't take it anymore, and his head dropped against his chest in defeat. He was completely helpless. Benedict had never been in a situation where there wasn't at least one slim, crazy chance for him to win.

"Pathetic," Davies spat, kicking Benedict in the gut while he was down, then turning back to the edge of the deck. "Have the good doctor patched up." The crew obeyed, and Thomas turned to Benedict. "Remember: spotless before dinner. Best not waste any time moping around."

CHAPTER 26

Benedict made the deck as spotless as he could, but he couldn't stop thinking about what he'd borne witness to. The mind control replayed so vividly in his head that he often found himself frozen in place, unable to breathe—and it wasn't because of the frigid temperature. Every time he blinked back to reality, he found Ajani keeping an eye on him as she spoke with various crew members. Shaking his head to clear it, he got back to work, only to have the event replay in his mind once again.

Mathias would be devastated if he ever regained control. And two gunshots to the legs? He knew Davies wouldn't stop there. Eventually, one of those shots would cause Mathias to go into shock, or it would kill him—if it hadn't already.

He would need to keep his every word and action in check like never before. He needed to do this for Mathias.

Dinner was bland, but that was fine—Benedict had no appetite. While the steaming stew could've warmed him up as he sat on deck, chained near the captain's cabin and covered in a wool blanket, he absentmindedly stirred the food instead, his thoughts on Madam Bonifrey. Did she even know what she had sold them into? He wanted that greedy woman to get what was coming to her. As for Ella? He sincerely hoped that she wasn't in on it, for her sake, and especially for Mathias's sake.

His thoughts shifted to Mathias. He hadn't seen the surgeon since that afternoon. He wasn't the praying type, but since the mind-control incident, Benedict had silently pleaded to all those that others deemed holy that Mathias would pull out in one piece.

Hinges creaked as the door to the captain's quarters opened, and a pair of boots thudded toward where he sat, stopping nearby. He recognized those boots and the long legs that came with them. His eyes narrowed.

"Captain have a job fi yuh."

Benedict bit his tongue. He really wanted to tell her to shove it, that he hadn't agreed to do anything for Davies. But for Mathias's sake and safety, he couldn't. And so he didn't, but the metallic taste in his mouth only proved the restraint it took.

Following Ajani's legs up to her face, he didn't say a word but gave her his full attention.

"Di captain say yuh good at sneaking."

Benedict shut his eyes and sighed. Internally, he groaned. He had a feeling that Davies was going to make him do something that he would regret, and he'd have no choice but to comply, or they'd torture Mathias again. Opening his eyes, Benedict got to his feet and followed Ajani into the captain's quarters.

Davies sat at the head of a wide table, poring over a prominent blue map laid over all the others, its curling corners held down by rocks and gears and whatever else was heavy enough to keep it in place.

"I told you that if you were good and obeyed, you'd get liberties." Thomas grinned.

This did not relieve Benedict's concerns. After all, he despised the man and was still planning to somehow exact revenge for Catherine and Mathias. His mental tally list continued to grow each time Davies was unsavory.

However, Benedict was also highly suspicious of Davies's words. He'd get liberties if he was good. Had he not acted out that afternoon? Had the captain already forgotten about it?

"Here is what we need you to do," the captain said. "Inside this military building, there is a case."

The hairs on Benedict's neck stood up, and he swallowed hard. He couldn't believe that they wanted him to sneak inside a guarded military building. Were they crazy? This wasn't some random noble's mansion.

His eyes fell on the blue map, which didn't look like a map at all, with its white lines and rectangles and squares.

"What's in the case?" Benedict finally asked.

"None yuh concern," Ajani replied.

"It's inside this room here," Thomas said, ignoring everyone else as he pointed to an area of the blue map with spindly metal fingers. Benedict furrowed his brows, confused. How did Davies deem that a room at all? "The best way to sneak in would be to go through this tunnel here," the captain added, dragging his finger down to a circle outside of the box with all the lines. "That will bring you to the cleaning room, where you can then apply your skills however you like." Benedict's eyes never left the mess of white lines. "From there, you'll need to go down the hall and down these stairs. The lab is in the basement."

Ajani then went on to physically describe the size and color of the case, but Benedict was stuck on the map-not-a-map. He blinked a few times, tilting his head some, but he just couldn't see what they could.

"Is something wrong, Keenan?" asked Thomas.

"What . . ." he started, pointing to the blue map, "is all of this?"

Ajani smirked in amusement. "It a did call a blueprint. Like a map fi di buildings."

The captain traced the exterior of the building, then all the floors and rooms, and suddenly the map-not-a-map made sense. He could picture what the captain had been saying.

As the captain rolled the blueprint back up, Benedict caught the next map underneath. It was one he knew how to read all too well, of a location that seemed oddly familiar. He noticed a bunch of areas marked off, one in particular with the word *home base* scribbled at the top.

Furrowing his brows, he studied it until Ajani stepped between him and the map. Realization sunk in that it was probably something he shouldn't have seen. Quickly feigning being deep in thought, he tried to make it seem like her movement didn't affect him at all.

"Is the tunnel the only way in?" he asked, glancing up at the captain as if he had a brilliant idea. "Are there any chances of open windows?"

"Not at this temperature," Davies mused. "And if you want to use doors, I have one warning for you: if you so much as think about alerting the military, you will severely regret it, starting with the good doctor. I won't just have him shot this time—I will have him dismembered. Am I clear?"

Glaring at the captain, his loathing for the man bubbled in his core, ready to explode like a dangerous volcano. "Crystal," he replied through gritted teeth, seething, before adding, "Speaking of Doctor Darley, I request to see him, Captain."

"Request denied."

Benedict's stomach dropped. He just *had* to see Mathias. Unfortunately, he knew Davies was going to make things as difficult as possible, and that he wouldn't be able to bribe or threaten his way around the situation. Swallowing down his anger, he said as calmly as he could, "I need to make sure that he's all right."

"He's none of your concern," Thomas said.

Benedict shut his eyes. "Just let me see him," he said with a sigh before opening his eyes once more. "I can take her with me," he added, pointing to Ajani, who blinked in surprise. "As reassurance."

Thomas eyed him suspiciously. "What are you playing at, Keenan? If this is another one of your—"

"Don't make me beg," he cut in darkly, his hands clenched into fists. "I never beg, and you know this, Captain."

Thomas continued to watch him for a moment before finally speaking. "You're right, I've never known you to beg. But it's not too far beneath you and your orphan ways."

Benedict's eyes narrowed at the insult. Thomas Davies never knew what it was like growing up as an orphan. Sure, he had been a rebel, disowning his parents and indulging in disrespectful behavior, all in the name of feeling more in control in his life. But he never lived life as a street urchin the way Benedict did. The way Kitch did.

Benedict never begged, and he taught that to the other kids at the orphanage too. There were ways to get what one needed without lowering one's standards. Unfortunately, Davies seemed immune to these other ways. Immune and tyrannical.

But he couldn't let the captain affect him. For Mathias's sake and safety, his fists loosened, and he turned to walk away in defeat.

"Ajani, darlin', take Mister Keenan here to see the good doctor." Benedict paused, glancing over his shoulder. "If he gets even slightly out of hand . . . shoot them both," he added, narrowing his eyes in warning.

"Aye, Captain," she replied, stepping past Benedict and leaving the quarters to unchain him.

"It's as I said, Keenan," Thomas spoke, without looking at Benedict. "Liberties."

Watching the cyborg for a moment longer, he nodded in thanks before following Ajani. He still didn't fully understand Davies's game, but if these *liberties* could get him and Mathias off the airship, then he'd have to shift to a whole different strategy—and that was how he played best.

The infirmary below deck wasn't much: dark and damp despite the cold and containing nothing but a bed and a few cases of medical supplies and tools. In fact, it had Benedict fooled, at first, into thinking it wasn't an infirmary at all.

Mathias lay on the bed with a hand over his eyes, his chest slowly moving up and down beneath the wool blanket. Good—he was still alive. Wiping his sweaty palms on his trousers, Benedict parted his lips to call out to him, but anxiety kept his voice from escaping. What if he was still under the influence of the infusion? What if he never came to?

Ajani banged loudly on the wall with the side of her fist, causing Mathias to jump, startled. He was awake! He was reacting! Benedict heaved a sigh of relief and found it shaky.

"Matt!"

Mathias snapped his head toward the voice, eyes wide in surprise before they rapidly squeezed shut as he grabbed his head with a pained hiss.

The mind-controlled surgeon definitely hadn't moved that fast. The heaviness that weighed on Benedict lifted, leaving him practically light-headed. For a moment, he didn't know what to do. What could he do? He was no doctor.

Carelessly shoving past Ajani, Benedict was at Mathias's side in three long strides.

"You've snapped out of it!" he whispered; the relief only lasting seconds before shifting to worry once more. "How do you feel? Are you all right? Do you remember anything?"

Mathias winced, then peeked out through one eye. "I'm—I don't know," he croaked. "I remember very little . . ."

His heart sank as every single moment flashed in his memories all at once. He *wished* he couldn't remember. It was going to take a lot of alcohol to properly forget about it. But just how much *did* Mathias remember? "Do you remember . . ." He swallowed hard, unable to continue. He didn't want to be the one to tell Mathias that he had killed someone while brainwashed. Mathias seemed like the type that would eat himself up over it.

As if knowing exactly what Benedict was going to say, Mathias spoke while shutting his eyes. "I don't remember pulling the trigger," he said quietly, "but they were pretty quick to tell me when I regained control."

"I'm so sorry," he whispered, clenching his fists.

It was all his fault. Mathias wouldn't have killed anyone if they hadn't been sold to Davies, and they wouldn't have been sold if Benedict hadn't saved Mathias from the wreckage to begin with. But he'd needed the reward money.

His fists relaxed as he watched Mathias. It didn't matter; he was glad that he rescued the surgeon. He'd turned out to be a really nice guy, and Benedict had grown fond of him.

"That was so foolish of you," he eventually scolded, folding his arms over his chest. "Did you even think of the consequences? You could have died or permanently become a lifeless shell!"

Frowning in disapproval of being lectured, Mathias's expression turned into a grimace of pain, and his hands swiftly returned to hold his head. Benedict's arms dropped to his side as he watched, helpless.

After a few deep breaths, Mathias finally replied, "Yes, I did think through the consequences of my actions. Honestly, whatever was going to happen to me was insignificant in comparison to what could have happened to everyone else."

Deep down, Benedict knew that was the reason Mathias had done what he did. He knew that there was absolutely nothing that he could do to change it. A clearing of the throat pulled him from his thoughts. He glanced over his shoulder at Ajani, then turned back to Mathias, changing the subject.

"How are your legs?" he asked. "And your side?"

"Excruciatingly painful."

"Were you able to patch yourself up?"

"Not yet," Mathias admitted. "I can't . . . I can't think straight."

Benedict's eyebrows gathered in, and he lifted a hand to scrub over his scraggly, unshaven face. He deeply regretted being unable to prevent the course of actions from earlier, despite trying his best. His ankle throbbed and stung in response to his thoughts, as if reminding himself how much he really did try.

But mostly, at that moment, he regretted knowing nothing about patching up bullet wounds and sword gashes. Swallowing the lump in his throat, he turned to the supplies and began digging through them. Maybe there were instructions. Maybe there was an easy way.

"What yuh up tuh, Keenan?" Ajani asked, narrowing her eyes, suspicious.

"Trying to . . ." he trailed off, pausing in his actions. What was he trying to do? He didn't even know. Rubbing at his chest, he noticed the difficulty he was having with breathing, like his lungs could not fill completely. He was panicking, and Benedict never panicked.

"Ben," Mathias tried.

"I need to . . ." Rummaging about once more, he pulled out medical objects that he didn't recognize. His hands trembled. "I . . ."

"Ben," Mathias tried again.

He threw everything onto the floor and pulled the supply case from the shelf, frantically searching for who-the-hell-knew-what. He sure as hell didn't know. Helpless. He was completely helpless, much the same as he had been when Catherine died in his arms.

He heard Ajani yell something at the same time as Mathias. Snapping his attention to the sound of their voices, he found Mathias standing in front of him, eyes shut, with one hand outstretched to halt Ajani, who had her gun drawn. Eyes wide and heart threatening to pound out of his chest, he remembered Thomas had instructed Ajani to shoot them both if things got hectic—and he was definitely making things hectic.

His gaze found Mathias, who slowly opened his eyes after wincing in pain. Casting Benedict a weakened smile, he placed a trembling hand on his shoulder.

"It's all right, Ben," he said calmly, quietly. "The medic aboard did his job. And while it's not up to my personal standards, it's satisfactory enough until I can do it myself."

This didn't make Benedict feel any better, but it was something that he would just need to accept. Nodding in understanding, he then caught Mathias, who had finally collapsed.

Helping him back onto the bed as he cried out in pain, he helped to make sure that none of the wounds reopened. He found that he could, at the very least, manage that much.

Making sure that Mathias was as comfortable as possible, he quickly composed himself, hands closed into fists. He needed to get Mathias off this damnable ship and to safety. Spinning, he spitefully glared at Ajani before shoving his way past her to prepare for his job.

CHAPTER 27

Hands in his pockets, Benedict casually made his way toward the military structure, the vapor of his breath dancing in the crisp temperature as he whistled an old London tune he remembered from childhood. He took in everything he could in the cover of night—every alley to run down, every large object to hide in or around, every bench and loose brick to help him climb.

A particular feeling had been developing in the pit of his stomach since leaving Mathias, a feeling beyond panic and anxious knots. He was taking Davies's threat of dismemberment seriously and needed to make sure that he did not screw up or get caught for Mathias's sake, but sneaking into a guarded military establishment was nothing like sneaking onto Lord Taylor's property. He only had one chance.

He studied the comings and goings of the military guards, scientists, and alchemists for a bit before giving the building a wide berth, encircling it, getting as good a view as he could from all angles before making his way toward the tunnel.

The way in, he found out, wasn't a tunnel at all as Davies had claimed, but a sewage pipe. The part of him that wondered if Davies *had* known wished the cyborg to die a very slow and painful death. And the part of him that wondered if Davies *hadn't* known wished him a very painful death as well, but maybe just a little swifter.

As he approached, the knots in his stomach shifted to nauseous churning from the stench. The pipe was going to be cozy, and whatever was oozing out of it did not interest Benedict in the slightest. He sincerely hoped that it wasn't toxic.

Wrinkling his nose in disgust, he found the flow uncomfortably lukewarm as he got down on his hands and knees. It almost reminded him of the sludge aboard the *Nine*. Trying hard not to gag, he lowered his whole body into the fluid and crawled his way into the pipe, using nothing but his elbows, following it down until he came upon a drainage gate above.

Turning onto his back excruciatingly slowly to not give away his location with sloshing sounds, he listened intently while peeking through the steel grate to see if he could detect anything. Unable to see or hear much, he then tested the grate, realizing that he could easily lift it. Pushing it over some, he slowly sat up and glanced around the room.

It seemed to be some sort of mixture of a supply room and laundry room, filled with mops and brooms, buckets and bottles, and a full rack of lab coats, which suited him just perfectly as he climbed out of the sewage, eager to shed his sopping, fetid duds.

Remaining as quiet as possible, he did another take around the windowless room—his eyes pausing momentarily on stacked cupboards—before he deemed himself safe and alone.

Peeling off his heavily soaked and filthy winter layers, he rushed to the cupboards, opening all the ones without padlocks in a search for not only clean clothes, but ones that would fit. He rummaged about and ended up with a cotton shirt from one cupboard, trousers from another, and a pair of boots two sizes too small. He hid behind the rack and wiped himself down with one of the coats after ditching his dirty clothes. Quickly dressing, he winced from the uncomfortably tight footwear as he donned a clean lab coat. Taming his hair, he then grabbed a cotton mask and placed it over his face, hiding his beard.

He could still smell the fumes from the sewer pipe, and he couldn't figure out if his body reeked or if the nauseous smell was unfortunately stuck in his nose. If it was coming from his body, he was going to have to be extra careful to not be noticed—if he could even manage that. The stench was pretty potent. Opening the only door and peeking out down the empty corridor, he spotted a disinterested guard at the end of the hall.

His heart pounded so loudly as he waited for the guard to turn around that he was sure the entire building could hear it. He couldn't succeed at sneaking into a guarded military building. There was no way. He was going to get caught, and Mathias was going to suffer. He was going to need a few drinks to forget about this. Hell, he could really go for a drink *right now*.

No. He couldn't think that way. Not with Mathias's safety on the line. Inhaling and exhaling deeply, he forced his mind to think positively. He could sneak in and out of shops, and on and off ships. He had even escaped from jail on the regular. Benedict imagined the establishment as the Taylor mansion, only with heightened security. The guards were Lord Taylor, and this case was Catherine.

Benedict shook his head, forcing the idea to dissipate from his mind. It would never work. Once the guard turned around, Benedict beelined down the hall in the opposite direction, wincing from the throbbing squeeze around his feet.

Reaching the correct door, he quickly opened it to find the staircase that led to the basement. Unfortunately, as he rushed down the stairs, he slowly came to a halt. Something he hadn't accounted for: the door mechanism requiring either a keycard or alchemy to activate . . . neither of which he had.

Glancing about for a way around it, the door suddenly flung open, surprising both Benedict and the scientist in question. His heart skipping a beat, Benedict felt like they had caught him red-handed.

"I didn't mean to startle!" Benedict quickly said, recovering faster than the scientist.

"No worries," the man finally replied, attempting to step past Benedict.

This was his zone of genius, and he had already locked on to the location of the key out of habit. Purposely bumping into the man, he abruptly apologized as he easily snatched the card from the man's lab coat pocket and grabbed for the already-opened door at the same time.

Right before a forced apology—one well-practiced from having pulled this off hundreds of times—the man sniffed at the air with a look of disgust. "What is that god-awful smell?" he asked, wrinkling his nose.

Damn. The smell wasn't just in his nose. He wasn't prepared for this, but he had to think quick.

"The sewer is backed up," he replied, before mentally scolding himself. That was the worst comeback ever!

"Again?" the scientist said, incredulous, before shaking his head in disbelief and waving goodnight, then turning back around and continuing on his way.

Benedict stared for a moment. He couldn't believe that had actually worked in his favor. Heart racing, he could only imagine what that kind of blunder would have cost Mathias had he gotten caught.

Slowly, he walked past tarped-off rooms, briefly peeking inside without being seen. He found maybe half a dozen scientist and alchemists total inside the different areas, and thankfully, none of them were where he needed to be.

Slipping between the tarped flaps at the end of the area, he entered the room, his heart sinking as he stopped. There, upon one of the counters, were three large, enclosed glass boxes—one of them containing a thick black case—glowing from alchemy. Glancing about, Benedict tried to find a lever or switch or something to turn off the protective alchemy but found none. So how was he supposed to get the case?

Running his fingers along the edge of the countertop, he tried to feel for something—anything—hidden but came up short. A slight growl of frustration vibrated its way past his throat. He was running out of time! Just as he was about to give up and move to the next counter for a solution to his problem, he spotted something out of the corner of his eye and did a double take back to a small area on the front of the farthest counter. There, a small slit was barely visible. Glancing down at the front of the counter before him, he noticed the same slit.

Kneeling, he ran an index finger over the narrow opening before swiftly rummaging in his lab coat pocket for the stolen keycard. Pulling it out, he inspected it, noticing the tiny ridges along one edge, as if it acted like an actual key. Carefully placing the card in the matching hole, it clicked and lit up blue before loudly releasing steamed pressure. Benedict held his breath, eyes wide. If anything was going to give him away, that would. He waited for a moment, still kneeling behind the counter, listening intently for voices or footsteps indicating someone was coming to investigate, but nobody came, and there was no noise out of the ordinary. Quickly glancing up to the countertop, he found the box was no longer glowing. Perfect.

Standing back to his full height, he carefully lifted the clear box and grabbed the case. And that was it—he had managed to reach the fictional Catherine from the imaginary, made-up version in his head of Lord Taylor's mansion. Shaking his head over the fact that he compared his beautiful Catherine to a case, he grabbed the keycard and took a step to leave when his eyes fell on another unlit box with a similar case to the one in his hands, the next counter over.

Uh-oh.

Davies and Ajani never mentioned there being other cases. Glancing back and forth in between them, he needed to make a decision, and he needed to make it quickly. Spinning around, he looked at the box that he had retrieved the case from. Alchemy guarded it, which Benedict gathered meant that it was important. And nothing could have been *that* ridiculously simple, could it?

That was it then. That was his decision.

Turning back around, he walked up to the tarp opening while removing his lab coat. Casually slinging it and the case over his shoulder, hiding the object from view, he peeked past the tarp, spotting an alchemist stepping out from a room and heading for the door.

Slipping out of the back room, he rushed to match his strides with those of the alchemist to remain hidden, his footsteps drowned out by the other's shuffling. The alchemist traced a symbol over the keycard slit to exit. Benedict snuck behind the man fast enough to barely catch the door, preventing it from shutting. As painful as it was in his tight footwear, he tiptoed up the stairs at the same speed as the other man.

How was sneaking in and out of a guarded military building this easy? In fact, it was so simple that Benedict wondered if he could simply walk out the front door. He had a keycard, after all . . .

Once at the top of the stairs, the alchemist opened the door and stepped out, sniffing at the air and glancing behind him as he did so with an expression of disgust, nearly jumping out of his skin when he saw Benedict.

"Sorry, I didn't see you there," the alchemist said, holding the door open for Benedict.

"Thank you," he said as he quickly slipped by, holding his breath. He wasn't in the clear just yet.

"What's that smell?"

Benedict refrained from rolling his eyes. "The sewer is backed up," he tried again. After all, it had worked once before.

"Not again," the alchemist sighed. "Well, have a good night!"

Benedict nodded politely, and they went their separate ways. He marched right to the front door, keycard tightly in hand, hoping he wouldn't make a fool of himself and that the card would let him out. He was almost there, almost free . . .

As he slid the keycard into the slit on the keypad, the mechanisms shifted, allowing him to push the door open.

"Hey!" the alchemist called out, and Benedict froze, his heart skipping a beat. Slowly, he turned, glancing over his shoulder. "Nice boots!" the man called out. "I have a pair just like them!"

He only raised his free hand and waved in response before turning back around and stepping out into the crispness of the night. He didn't dare strike up a conversation, nor did he want to stay and find out if the boots on his feet actually belonged to the alchemist.

He tore his mask off as he continued down the street, his heart beating so fast that he thought it was going to break free from his rib cage. When the coast was clear, he took the first chance that he could to duck down a dark alley and scale a building with ease, finally catching his breath once he reached the roof.

He never wanted to do that again. Ever. It was risky enough breaking out of jail, but breaking in and out of a military building was on a level that he didn't dare care to repeat.

But there he was, safe, sound, and undetected. Now, it was time to find out what the case contained.

He tried various ways to unlock the tiny mechanism holding it shut, but no matter what he did, it would not budge. Lifting it up to his ear, he gently shook it, hearing nothing but the faint rattle of glass. Benedict raised a brow. What did Davies need with something that contained glass?

He shivered from the cold. He sure wasn't going to figure it out while freezing to death up there on the roof. The lab coat did little for warmth as Benedict clumsily made his way across the rooftops due to his throbbing feet, then toward the airship hidden on the outskirts of the village.

Stepping past the sky pirates that were on watch duty, he made his way to the captain's quarters, where a single candle was flickering inside. Knocking softly in case Davies was sleeping, a grumble greeted him.

"Come in."

Benedict opened the door to find Davies poring over some maps. He stepped inside and immediately closed the door behind him, shutting his eyes and reveling in the heat coming from a nearby pot filled with steaming coal.

"Ah, Keenan," Thomas started, and Benedict's eyes shot open as his body continued to thaw. "Good man," he added, getting to his feet and holding out his metal hand.

Benedict was silent as he handed the man the case, biting his tongue to prevent himself from saying anything that would get Mathias hurt. He did, however, glare at the captain. He didn't know if Davies could understand the meaning behind the glare—the pure hatred and the additional *don't-you-dare-make-me-do-that-again*—but Benedict was definitely adding a notch to his revenge list for having been made to do what he had done.

"Now get out of here," Davies ordered, unimpressed. "You're stinking up my quarters."

Narrowing his eyes further, Benedict simply turned around and walked out, heading to clean himself up.

CHAPTER 28

"Keenan," Thomas Davies said, stepping out of his quarters.

Benedict paused in scrubbing the deck, his knees sore from having crawled all over to get it clean, and his fingertips so frozen from the cold water and frosty morning temperatures that they threatened to fall off.

He did not turn his attention toward the captain, nor did he acknowledge him in any other way. The hatred he had for the cyborg was already deep, but he was still particularly bitter about having snuck into and stolen from the military, even days later.

"Keenan, I have another job for you."

Honestly, he wasn't interested, especially if it involved sneaking around military buildings. He'd had his fair share for the next forever. Finally turning to face Davies, he watched him through narrowed eyes. "Yes?" he drawled.

"We're approaching Lake Ontario to repair the damaged cannon, and I want you to be the one to fix it."

Raising a brow, Benedict slowly stood up. "You want *me* to fix it?" he repeated for clarification.

"Aye. I told you, Keenan; if you were quiet and did what you were told, you'd get liberties. Why do you think we have not chained you up as of late?"

Glancing down at his ankle, free from the chain, he had to admit that it felt good to not have to constantly drag that thing around with him. When he cleaned up the sludge stench from the sewer pipe after his mission, Benedict had returned to his usual spot in the corner of the captain's quarters, beneath the overhang. He hadn't voluntarily chained himself up, but no one else came to do it either. He had taken that as a good sign and would not press his luck.

But he wasn't going to thank the captain for leaving him unchained. Davies didn't deserve that. He was still the bully Benedict always remembered him to be, just more conniving and controlling. And so, all he did was nod before turning back to his chores.

Unfamiliar movement caught his attention on the main deck, and to his surprise, Benedict spotted Mathias weakly dragging his feet from below deck. Panic seizing him, he spun his attention back to Thomas, hoping the captain hadn't spotted the surgeon.

There Thomas stood, with both his regular and cyborg eyes on Benedict and a coy smile upturned in the corner of his lips. He knew. The captain motioned with his head for Benedict to join his friend before turning and heading back inside his quarters. Caught off guard, Benedict did nothing but blink in surprise until he heard an unhealthy cough.

Rushing down to the main deck, he approached Mathias. He was both relieved to see the surgeon, yet nervous. Worried. Mathias's skin was pale, with tiny beads of sweat scattered across his forehead. His gaunt cheeks seemed sunken, and his mop of black hair was disheveled, some of it plastered against his forehead and neck.

"Are you all right?" he asked, as Mathias carefully sat his weakened body down on a small crate.

Mathias nodded faintly. "I was able to dress my wounds to my satisfaction," he replied.

"That's not what I asked," Benedict said, and Mathias slowly shut his eyes with a long exhale.

"I'm fine," he replied, opening his eyes again, but Benedict knew that to be a lie. "I must say that I have grown a bit bored, but . . . the cold air is doing me some good right now."

"It's really not," he scolded, removing his wool coat and placing it around Mathias's shoulders. "We need to get you to a doctor."

"The medic on board said I'll live—"

"I mean an actual doctor, Matt," he cut in with a frown, which shifted to a look of concern when Mathias raised a shaking hand, palm out, to stop him.

Silence was thick between both men for a moment. Benedict couldn't stand to see him in such a poor state. He needed to do something, but he had already proven himself helpless—quite pathetically, in fact.

"How have you been?" Mathias finally asked, drawing Benedict's attention back to him.

Benedict watched him for a moment before sighing. Pulling up another crate, he sat next to Mathias, bringing him up to speed on the happenings in hushed tones.

"Be careful," Mathias warned. "Don't sabotage your newfound liberties."

"Don't worry," he replied. "I'll be careful." Glancing up, he spotted Ajani watching him as she spoke to another sky pirate, as she always seemed to do. He *had* to be cautious or risk being snitched on.

Shivering from the cold, he rapidly rubbed his numb hands together, then brought them to his mouth, breathing on them to warm them up.

Mathias watched him and gave a weak smile. "The cold here is bitter, and frostbite happens quickly. Keep your extremities warm: fingers, ears, toes, and nose."

Wiggling his toes in his winter boots to judge their temperature, his eyes followed Mathias's over the edge of the ship as both men fell silent once more. Warming up the palms of his hands from the friction of rubbing them together, he then tested his ears and nose. They were definitely cold. He'd have to go to the galley and warm up.

"It's snowing," Mathias casually pointed out.

Benedict snorted, watching the clouds below. "No, it's not."

"It is!" Mathias insisted. "Those are snow clouds." Benedict cast him an incredulous side-eyed glance, and Mathias feigned insult. "What, you don't believe me?"

"You're pretty good at making stuff up," he retorted, and Mathias chuckled softly.

"Trust me, I've lived here long enough to know."

A warm smile made its way to his lips in the peaceful moment that followed, and it was almost enough to heat him to the core. Almost, until the focus on that warmth reminded his body that he was no longer wearing his wool coat. The nature and fresh air were extraordinary, and he understood why Mathias would live here for as long as he had, but he didn't think he'd ever get used to the cold.

A clearing of the throat pulled Benedict and Mathias from their individual thoughts. They both turned their attention to Ajani, who watched them while leaning against the mast with her arms crossed, then looked at each other. Mathias let out a shuddered sigh. "I guess I'll let you return to your duties."

And just like that, his peaceful moment came to a crashing halt. Nodding in forced agreement, his heart ached for Mathias, who struggled to stand. Jumping to his feet, he offered his hand. Mathias stared at it for a moment before accepting and grasping it. His hand was clammy and hot, a sign of his current feverish disposition. Slipping Benedict's coat off his shoulders and handing it back to him, he then limped below deck, teeth chattering loudly.

"Take care of yourself, Mathias," he mumbled as he put his coat on. He really needed to figure out how to safely get Mathias off the airship.

He didn't know how long he would need to be good to gain a few more liberties, but when that time came, he was going to enjoy turning the tables and exacting his revenge for both Catherine and Mathias. With one final narrowed glance in Ajani's direction, he then returned to scrubbing the deck.

It didn't take long for them to arrive at the shores of Lake Ontario, nor for the sighting of a group of rogues nearby to spread across the ship like wildfire. Abandoning his chores, Benedict approached the gunwale and looked out into the distance. They wouldn't be able to get to the cannon with the rogues around unless Davies decided to take them on. If that happened, the military would get involved, and they still wouldn't be able to get to the cannon.

He ruminated over possible scenarios and figured out a possibility of drawing them out and away from the massive weapon.

"What are your thoughts, Keenan?"

Snapping his startled attention over his shoulder, he saw Davies approach, pausing next to him. Benedict looked back out across the lake. He really didn't want to tell the captain about the scenario going through his mind. The longer he could postpone fixing the cannon, the better off the world would be. He needed to prevent the mind control that happened to Mathias from happening to anyone else.

But he could only keep silent for so long. Davies knew of his skills—he witnessed them in the past. Thomas knew better.

"I think we can draw them away," Thomas said, almost on cue. "What say you?" Internally sighing, Benedict nodded in agreement.

Stepping away, he bellowed orders to his crew and instructed Ajani onto another ship in his small fleet. Pirates ran about to their stations, calling out when they were ready.

They changed course by turning the ship's bow into the wind, and Benedict rushed down the steps, helping with the sails. It wasn't his job—he was the one who made the ship look spotless—but he wanted to hear and see how the battle was going to take place and study the captain for weaknesses.

He was also keeping an eye out for Mathias in case he came above deck, as unlikely as that was.

Breaking off to encircle the rogues, Ajani, aboard a sloop-of-war and followed by two regular sloops and a handful of small cutters, pulled away for the chase. A tactic to get the rogues to follow—and sure enough, they bit.

Two of the larger rogue airships went after Ajani, and Benedict gripped the rope for the sail, awaiting the order, practically holding his breath in anticipation.

"Two ships flanking the *Nightingale*, Captain!" came a call from the crow's nest.

And that's when the captain called out the charge.

Releasing the rope, the ship lurched forward and flew across the sky, the steam motor chugging along double time. Cannons fired in the distance as the approaching flanking rogues tried to take down Ajani's ship, which continued to outsail them before suddenly veering to the right.

"Portside cannons ready, Captain!" called out a pirate.

"On my mark," Thomas roared. "Steady!"

They were gaining great speed when the captain suddenly jerked the wheel to the right, skidding into position. "Fire the cannons!"

A barrage of cannon fire and smoke thundered, expertly taking out a few of the rogue ships, catching them off guard. Ajani pulled the same tactic to the two that chased the *Nightingale*.

Davies ordered to give chase once more. The odds were infinitely better—four rogue ships left—as their game of cat and mouse continued. The cutters split off, taking down one of the rogue ships after surrounding it.

Quickly glancing out to check on Ajani's progress as the captain ordered a new attack, his eyes narrowed. Something was wrong. Suddenly, Benedict stumbled forward as the rope yanked from his hands, burning his palms. Distracted, he had missed an order from the captain. Hissing in pain while some pirates on deck shouted at him, Benedict abandoned his station as they attempted to regain control of the situation, rushing to the helm.

"They're not going to make it—" He suddenly broke off.

Why did he even care? With Ajani out of his way, it would be easier to take down Davies when the time came. But it was too late; he had already said it, and the captain took heed.

"Keenan, get to a blasted station," he warned, after ordering his crew to catch up to the *Nightingale*, leaving the other rogue ship in the capable hands of the cutters.

His tactical mind working overtime, he ignored the captain. An airship was attempting to tether to the *Nightingale*. It followed closely, remaining parallel to the sloop-of-war as the other one chased it, occasionally damaging it with cannonballs.

"Go right," Benedict suddenly said.

"What—" the captain started, confused.

"Take her portside."

"Keenan—" Thomas said in a low growl.

"Go after the larger ship, or you'll lose Ajani!" Benedict snapped. "Leave the tethering ship to me," he then added, swiping Davies's sword and gun before the captain even realized what was happening.

Rushing down to the main deck as the captain yelled out for him, he shoved the gun and sword through his belt as a makeshift holster and sheath, then grabbed one of the grappling hooks, shoving the shank down the bore of the grappling cannon's barrel.

A pirate on deck tried to stop him, but he put his hands out defensively before he bellowed up to the captain, "Spin around now!"

Raising one of his arms up in the air, he made a circle motion to tell the captain to spin the ship around, then aimed the grappling cannon at the rogue ship. They were higher in the sky than the rogue ship, so he wouldn't be able to tether to the side, but he could probably do a lot of damage by aiming at the rigid balloon, both yanking it away and causing it to crash. It was going to be an incredibly stupid move, but in theory, it should work—as long as Davies cooperated.

Turning around, he gave an exasperated look to the captain. They were running out of time for this to work.

Thomas shook his head but did as instructed, and as the back end of the ship swerved, Benedict fired the grappling hook.

Hooks plunging into the metal top fin, the barbs gripped tightly in place. Clenching his jaw tight, Benedict growled in annoyance at his failed shot. That wouldn't be enough to bring down the entire ship, and his window of opportunity was shrinking down to nothing. He needed to stop that rogue ship. Grabbing one of the loose hooks, he connected the bend to the rope . . . and jumped.

Rope-burned hands stinging in protest as he zipped down the line, he quickly calculated his next moves: his landing, his descent down the airship balloon, and his steps to reach the tethers to cut the *Nightingale* free. Just as he noted the location of each rogue on the main deck, he suddenly felt the rope snap before going slack.

The only noise that escaped him was a gasp as the inertia that continued to propel him forward slowly gave way to gravity, pulling him down toward inevitable death. Heart in his throat, Benedict only had a moment of panic, one that he swiftly recuperated from. This wasn't his first stupid move or his first fall.

Determination strengthening his will, he extended his arm, jabbing his hook into the rigid balloon. Unfortunately, it did absolutely nothing but scratch the surface. Gritting his teeth, he tried again, this time hooking onto the rigging and zipping as far down as he could before he let go, crashing into a rogue.

Rolling and stumbling, he stabbed at the man with his hook, connecting with the rogue's hand, resulting in a cry of pain before they both came to a stop.

Dizzy, Benedict jumped to his feet and spun around, desperately blinking away his unsteady vision as three men rushed at him. Grabbing Davies's sword and gun from their makeshift home through his belt, he shot at one of them, hitting them in the shoulder as he defensively lashed out at the second man and completely missed the third one as he pulled the trigger over his own shoulder.

A stray bullet whistled in front of his eyes as he took a step back, his sword connecting with another blade. That could have been disastrous, but Benedict quickly decided that he'd rather not think about it. Slashing out at his opponent and connecting, a deep gash revealing itself from shoulder to midriff, he shot the oncoming attacker in the gut.

He didn't want to think of the body count. He couldn't. But every time his attack connected, his mind mockingly hissed *Coldbath* at him, with a flickered image of an unimpressed Kitch.

Quickly glancing about, he found one of the tethered ropes and lunged for it, cutting it with his blade, breaking Ajani's sloop-of-war free from that one line. The sound of a war cry caused him to spin around with his sword raised, the metal clashing loudly as he defended himself. Kicking at the rogue, he pulled the trigger as the body stumbled back, then ran for the next tether, cutting it before the rogues aboard the *Nightingale* could return.

Some tried to jump back onto the rogue airship but missed, plummeting to the Lands Below. A sudden explosion of debris coming from Thomas's cannons startled Benedict as he shielded himself, but the resulting blow worked in his favor by taking out two of the rogues.

Cutting the last two tethers, he watched as the crew of the *Nightingale* gained the upper hand before he rushed below deck to secure the rogue airship.

"Hands up," he said to the last few people aboard—a sad and sorry lot that reminded him of his time aboard the *Nine*. As they raised their hands in defeat, Benedict heard footsteps quickly approaching from above deck.

Stepping back to conceal himself as much as possible, he readied Davies's gun as a figure rushed below deck. Benedict aimed his gun at the same time as the figure, only to find himself looking down the barrel of Ajani's gun. For a moment, they remained frozen, staring at one another before Ajani finally pointed away from Benedict, toward the rogues.

"Yuh can eedah join di crew or suffah deadly consequences. Choose wisely," she said, and Benedict watched them comply as she led them above deck.

He followed, bringing up the rear, but then pulled away, parking himself along the stairs to the upper deck, lost in thought.

Why had he helped Ajani? What was it that sparked him to do so? Was it because he needed something different to do? Was it because he was growing accustomed to being among sky pirates? He was a little disgusted with himself—yet it felt good to pull that off. Dare he realize that he'd actually . . . enjoyed it?

"Keenan." Benedict blinked, pulled from his thoughts, to find Davies standing at the base of the stairs. He hadn't noticed him boarding the rogue airship. "Cheer up!" he added, snatching his weapons back. "You've just earned yourself a ship!" Benedict frowned, confused, before the captain continued. "You wanted a crew, Keenan, and now you're part of one. Don't pretend like this isn't what you wanted."

It wasn't at all what he wanted. He only wanted a crew to play Davies's game and exact his revenge. Deep down, he still wanted Davies to pay. But he also found himself enjoying not having to obey any of society's rules.

His eyes fell on Ajani as she presided over the rogues that valued their lives. He could have let her die. He could have allowed the rogues to take out some of Davies's crew. Having fewer pirates to deal with would have helped him. And yet . . .

"Come!" Davies said, pulling Benedict from his thoughts once more. "Let us return to the *Condor*."

"I thought you said that I earned myself a ship?"

"I did!" the captain said, sheathing his sword and holstering his gun. "But just because you earned it doesn't mean that you have unlimited liberties. Remember: I'm still your captain, and I still have control over what happens to the good doctor. Now, let's go."

Davies was right: he did still have Mathias. Benedict had to keep playing Davies's game just a little longer, even if it was killing him on the inside.

What Benedict particularly regretted, however, was the fact that he had taken Davies's weapons with such ease, yet hadn't even thought to use them on the captain. He knew that was a weakness he would never be allowed to exploit ever again.

CHAPTER 29

Carefully inspecting every single tooth for defects on the bronze gears and scrutinizing every coil loop, relay switch, metal fuse wire, and driver component from the control panel, Benedict then set them down on the floor in a specific order so he could properly put them back later on.

Working in silence alongside another pirate in the small alcove while two others did their jobs on the outside platform, he studied each part, desperate for a way to sabotage the repairs without being too obvious. Whatever Davies was planning—however he was going to use the Drapyltin—Benedict couldn't allow it. Nobody deserved to be controlled like a puppet the way Mathias had been.

In between each part pulled from the control panel, his mind went back over the last battle.

He hated being forced to do all these jobs for Davies, but that last part—rushing to save Ajani and the *Nightingale*—hadn't been forced at all. That had been all him. He hadn't done it for Catherine or for Mathias or Kitch, and he definitely hadn't done it for Davies. He'd done it for himself. And he had done a pretty decent job if he did say so himself.

It was early evening when the captain returned. To not draw the attention of the military—and especially to not draw suspicion to the cannon—Thomas and his crew had scattered after dropping Benedict and the three other pirates off, sailing along the edges of the lake and nearby villages and towns.

Davies's return had relieved him only slightly. He had refused to leave Mathias, concerned that Davies would take off with him and mistreat him, which resulted in a guffaw from Davies who put his mind at *ease* in the worst way possible, telling him that the surgeon would have been mistreated were Benedict there or not. Benedict had mentally added another tick mark to his revenge list, only slightly reassuring himself with the fact that Davies should at least return for the other three crew members.

He remained inside the alcove as Thomas tested the cannon, watching as multiple sample tubes of infusions fed through the tubes at the top. Where had Davies managed to get that much Drapyltin? Davies had mentioned something to Ajani about working on the infusions to make the victims' movements quicker . . . were these samples the new and improved version?

They powered the cannon back down, and as the pirate collected his tools, a brilliant idea came to Benedict. Gathering his own gear, he purposely left the flaps and straps open to the leather kit. When he turned to leave, the tools clumsily fell to the ground in an awful cacophony that loudly echoed off the walls.

The pirate sneered at Benedict's misfortune before leaving the alcove. Benedict waited a moment, putting some distance between him and the pirate.

Heart racing, he lunged for the control panel with screwdriver in hand, swiftly removing the panel. He tried to focus on any tiny sound in case someone walked back in, but it was difficult beyond the pounding of his heart in his ears.

Yanking on one of the metal wires, he dislocated a coil and a few gears, which fell to the bottom of the control panel. Rapidly screwing it back up, he then picked up the tools, shoving them back into the leather kit before casually exiting the alcove and embarking back onto the airship.

"Excellent job, Keenan," Davies said as Benedict passed him when dropping off the tools. He didn't answer, keeping to his act, but on the inside, he grinned like a maniac at the sabotage.

Davies would soon find out exactly how excellent of a job he'd really done. "Permission granted to visit with the good doctor."

Benedict spun back around, blinking in surprise. Had he heard right? A frown made its way to his features as Davies turned to walk away. It was unlike him to be so generous, but Benedict wasn't going to argue. He was going to take that liberty and run with it.

It was cold below deck, but not frigid. Benedict grabbed some stew from the galley and made his way down the dark passageways illuminated every so often by infused lanterns.

The sound of heavy breathing grew louder and more labored as he approached the makeshift infirmary, concern churning in the pit of his stomach with each step, ready to boil over at any moment.

"We need to get you to a hospital," he said upon finding Mathias sitting up against the icy wall, drenched in sweat and half passed out.

There was a stench in the air, and Benedict wrinkled his nose as he set the bowls down. His attention fell to the bandage at Mathias's side, visible beneath his open shirt, and the fear of an infection crossed his mind.

"I'll be all right," Mathias said, barely even able to whisper.

"No, you won't. You're as white as a sheet," he said, turning around. "We need to dock—"

"Ben, no."

The pathetic croak made him glance over his shoulder, and it was all Benedict could do to keep himself calm. He couldn't stand to see Mathias like that. "I didn't save your life just for you to die kidnapped by sky pirates." Mathias didn't reply. "I'm going to get you some help," he confirmed as he walked away.

His pace sped up down the passageways until he was at an all-out rush up the stairs to the captain's quarters, pounding loudly against the closed door.

"Davies!" he called out, then quickly reworded. "Captain! We need to dock at the nearest hospital."

The thumps from Thomas's footsteps quickly approached before the door swung open. Davies looked Benedict up and down with both his regular and cybernetic eyes, as if searching for the reason they had to make an urgent stop, before frowning when he came up empty-handed. "This better be good," he growled.

"We need to take Mathias to the hospital," he replied.

The captain glanced over Benedict's shoulder, searching for the surgeon, before looking back at Benedict. "He's a doctor, he can fix himself—"

"He's a surgeon," Benedict corrected through clenched teeth, "and surgeons don't fix illness."

That last part had caught the captain's attention, and his eyes hardened. "What kind of illness?"

Benedict threw his hands up, exasperated. "I'm not a doctor!"

With a grumble, Thomas shoved his way past, thumping heavily on his way below deck. "Get Duffey down here, now!" he bellowed.

Benedict followed closely behind, only to rush past Davies to where Mathias now lay curled up, shivering. Grabbing the wool blanket from the bed, he placed it atop of Mathias, tucking the edges beneath him.

"You called, Captain?" the medic said as he approached.

"What's wrong with him?" he asked, pointing a spiny metal finger in the surgeon's direction.

Duffey said nothing as he stepped into the room and approached Mathias as if he wasn't even aware of his condition. Had nobody noticed how pale and clammy the surgeon was when he had come up for air?

Helping the medic sit Mathias up, Benedict otherwise stood by, as helpless as ever, as Duffey checked the surgeon over. "He's got a fever," he confirmed.

"Is it contagious?" Thomas inquired.

"Can we just get him to a hospital?" Benedict asked.

"I'll need to run a few tests—" Duffey started, completely ignoring Benedict.

But he would have none of it. Mathias needed help, and he was going to make sure it happened. "You're going to bring him to a hospital at once," he demanded, turning to face the captain, fists clenched.

Davies glared menacingly. "Now you listen here, Keenan. I give the orders around here, and if you—"

"What are you going to do, shoot him again?" he asked, returning the glare with equal intensity. "He's going to die if we don't do something!"

"Keenan," Davies warned, but Benedict interrupted him.

"If you want me to continue to work for you, you'll dock at the closest hospital. No, *the best* hospital," he ordered through gritted teeth. "As long as he's still alive, I'm yours, remember? But if Mathias doesn't pull through, I swear I am coming after you."

Davies watched Benedict for a long moment before finally releasing an enormous belly laugh. A frown made its way to Benedict's face. He didn't find any of it very funny.

"You can't come after me and the entire crew, Keenan, but I admire the fact that you'd even consider trying," he said, becoming serious once more. "But you're right. Don't think your cooperation lately hasn't gone unnoticed. I'll consider your request," he said, before adding to Duffey, "Block off access to the infirmary until we get him off the ship, then disinfect *everything*." Nose wrinkled in disgust, Thomas turned around and walked away.

"A *good* hospital!" Benedict called out after him. "One of the best!"

The captain grumbled something, waving him off as he disappeared. Duffey fetched some supplies to help bring the shivering Mathias's fever down.

"You're not dying, Mathias," he said as he leaned against the wall. He didn't even know if Mathias was conscious or not, and it tugged at his heart. "You hear me? Not on my watch. We may be kidnapped, but I'm going to get us out of here."

Helping Duffey pick Mathias up and lay him on the bed, Benedict watched in silence as the medic performed a few tests. Mathias had helped him plenty; this was the least that he could do.

It was the shuffling that woke Benedict hours later. Blinking away the sleep in his eyes, he peeked down between the railing to the main deck, where a couple of pirates—Duffey included—laid Mathias, wrapped up in a couple of wool blankets, into a secured dinghy. His heart skipped a beat when they began lowering the small boat.

Panicked, he rushed out of his makeshift bed beneath the stairs to the captain's quarters, jumped over the rail, and landed onto the main deck in a tucked roll before jumping to his feet and skidding to a halt at the edge of the ship. Were they seriously going to drop him off without him present? Where were they even dropping him off? He didn't see them anchored anywhere.

He went to jump the edge of the ship to join Mathias when a hand grabbed him by the collar and yanked back.

"Nuh so fast," Ajani said.

"I have to go with him!" Benedict insisted.

"No, you don't," Thomas said from behind.

"I told you—" Benedict started, grabbing Ajani's wrist, trying to get her to let go.

"That you won't cooperate with him injured, ill, or dead. I know," the captain drawled, cutting him off. "So, we're at a *good*, non-militarized hospital off Lake Erie, where they will take *excellent* care of him, and he will survive. You, on the other hand, don't need to be present when this happens, so I suggest that you back down before I shoot you."

Benedict froze. So, they were just going to abandon Mathias?

The airship sailed dangerously close to the hospital; the dinghy lowered all the way, almost dragging on the ground in front of the building. Once it was low enough, two pirates cut the ropes and the small boat landed with only a minor bump as the *Condor* sailed off.

Hospital personnel scrambled outside to see what the commotion was. Some rushed to Mathias—and intense relief washed over Benedict at the sight—while others pointed to the airship as it pulled away.

"You just left him!" he yelled as he spun back around, enraged.

"He's alive and will get better. That was your deal, remember? You mentioned nothing about staying with him in your pathetic bargain."

Benedict growled, but the captain was right. He hated that Davies used that information against him. Finally pulling free from Ajani's grip, he stormed off back to his makeshift bed.

With Mathias off the ship, he didn't have to play nice anymore, starting immediately.

CHAPTER 30

The dice clattered inside the wooden bowl before both players flipped their dish onto the lid of the barrel that acted as a table. While his opponent glanced at his own hand, Benedict studied the physique and weapons of the pirates on deck out of the corner of his eye, wondering if he could swipe them just as easily as he had taken the captain's weapons when he went to save Ajani.

They had set anchor somewhere in the Lands Below. Where and why, Benedict was no longer interested. All he cared about was how he was going to exact his revenge on Davies. The payback for Catherine's death had waited long enough, and it was now burning hot and dangerous, with Mathias's torture thrown into the mix.

Unfortunately, the captain had been right when telling Benedict that it was impossible to go after him with the entire crew so close by. But if he could take some of them out from a vantage point he was more familiar with—like from the rooftops in town—then his chances would increase. So, when he had been told to remain aboard while Davies, Ajani, and a handful of the crew disembarked, his mind went into overdrive.

"Four fives," his rival bid with a sly grin, revealing his missing teeth.

Casting a quick glance beneath his bowl, Benedict placed his own bid. "Eight fives."

"Liar," his adversary said, his smile shifting into a scowl.

As he flipped over his bowl, his opponent occupied with counting the dice, he swiftly glanced around at the few other pirates on deck. Some continued their chores, though at a much slower pace, leisurely enjoying that they didn't have to hustle for their captain. Others were taking a well-deserved break, much like his dice rival was. He watched their movements, looking for any sign that they weren't "leisurely" strolling about, but were instead on some sort of patrol. He had to test that theory.

"You got me," he lazily admitted to his adversary. "One five and a wild makes four with your hand."

Allowing the pirate to rub his deliberate loss in his face, Benedict stretched his frozen legs as he stood from his seat, testing if he could safely walk away from the game.

"Hold up, Keenan," said his opponent. "I'm not done with you yet."

"I need to thaw out," he admitted, slowly pulling away, "or you'll be facing a frozen corpse next game."

Ignoring his rival's mocking jeers about being unacclimated to the cold, he immediately took notice of no less than four pirates monitoring his every move. His gut instinct had been right.

He made his way below deck, where seven pirates suspiciously stood around. "Where's the fun, boys?" he casually asked, heading for the galley.

The heat from the cast-iron stove felt amazing against his frozen skin, until his cheeks, ears, and fingers prickled uncomfortably. Damn the winter. Grabbing a roll of bread from a nearby basket, he loitered in the kitchen area for a moment while his captors continued to be terrible at being stealthy.

Once he made his way back to the main deck, most of the pirates that had been "leisurely working" were gathered around the stairs.

"What's going on?" he asked, taking a bite of his loaf.

"Just waiting around," one of the scrawnier pirates replied.

Nodding sagely, Benedict languidly made his way to the edge of the ship, looking out at the beautiful frozen scenery, the snow glittering beneath the sun. As he did, one of the larger pirates paused next to him, arms crossed. Watching him from the corner of his eye, he took another bite.

"If I didn't know any better," Benedict said with his mouth full, "I'd say you were keeping an eye on me."

"You'd be right," the large pirate replied.

Swallowing his mouthful, he turned his attention to the large man, four other pirates approaching in his peripheral vision. "Why?" he innocently asked.

"Because according to the captain, you're smart. Troublemaker smart."

"I'm flattered!" he replied, taking another bite before offering the rest of the roll to the pirate, who knocked it out of his hand. The bread roll bounced off the edge of the ship, tumbling out. "Well, that wasn't very nice," Benedict said with a tsk, turning to face the surrounding pirates. He casually sat up against the edge. "Here," he said. "Let me go get it."

He flipped backward off the edge of the ship. Reaching out, he gripped the netting against the hull to stop himself before he could hit the ground. Once he had his bearings and gathered up from down, he released the net, tucking and rolling as he landed in the snow, then jumped to his feet, darting off as the pirates yelled after him.

Glancing over his shoulder, he continued running, zigzagging away from their gunshots as a few pirates jumped off the ship in pursuit.

Hiding in the bushes and behind tree trunks, he tried to lose them, but the vapor from his breath—rapid from the race to find an escape—in the crisp, frigid air would certainly give him away, as well as his tracks through the snow.

Placing a hand over his nose and mouth to prevent the vapor from releasing into the air, he fell to his knees, desperately trying to slow his breathing, which was hard to do as he was limiting his air intake. His internal urge to prevent suffocation was growing stronger, but he couldn't give in. He couldn't afford to get caught. He had to stop the cannons, find Mathias, and kill Davies—in whatever order happened first. He didn't care.

His fingers clasped tighter around his face, and he focused on inhaling and exhaling to a slow four count rather than an internal scream as his body fought for air.

Finally, he calmed down in time as the pirates got excessively close, following his footsteps through the snow.

One of them tested the itchy conifers, stabbing through the bushes inches away from Benedict. He didn't have any weapons to fight back, so he timed the next jab just right and grabbed the sword from the pirate, slitting his throat in one swift movement.

Kitch would have a conniption, were she to find out what he had just done, but Benedict was over it. Coldbath had reserved a cell with his name on it for a few days now, he was sure of it, and it was only a matter of *when* they would lock him up for his crimes.

Pulling the pirate into the bushes, he held the body against him with his free hand over the pirate's mouth to prevent the gurgle from alerting the others.

Placing the corpse down at his feet, hidden from view as much as possible, Benedict's movements were slow, calculated, and as silent as he could make them. Grabbing the body's gun as he stood back up painfully slowly, he now had a sword and a gun to fight back if he needed to.

The others continued their search but became alerted by the missing pirate. Benedict swallowed hard. It looked like he was going to have to fight his way out, after all.

Aiming the gun straight at one of the approaching pirates' chest, Benedict pulled the trigger, and the body went down instantly. As predicted, however, the two others bull-rushed the bushes.

Jumping out from his hiding spot, he pulled the trigger at the stocky bald man while blocking the sword blow with the blade in his other hand, missing his shot. Kicking him in the stomach and dodging a scruffy pirate, he shot the bald pirate's foot and butted him hard in the face with the hilt of the sword, effectively breaking his nose.

A sharp, hot pain suddenly seared into Benedict's sword arm, and he stumbled backward, wincing from the gunshot as the scruffy pirate lunged at him. A cry of pain escaped him as he raised his arm, barely blocking the hit with his sword. The sword fell from his hand, suddenly absurdly heavy, as he took another step back. He quickly aimed with his good arm, pulling the trigger, emptying the gun into the man's chest.

A cry of pain escaped him as he stumbled forward, falling to one knee, his side set afire by a fresh wound. Whipping his head around, he glared at the bald man on the ground with blood oozing from his broken nose.

His gun was empty. The bald man discarded his gun off to the side, which meant his foe's weapon was empty as well. Gritting his teeth from the pain, he got back up to his feet and marched up to the pirate, angrily hitting the broken-nosed pirate in the back of the head with the butt of his gun, knocking him out.

Gunshots echoed in the distance, and Benedict knew more pirates were coming for him. Dropping the gun, he limped as fast as he could toward the nearby town, hands on his side. If his footprints were going to give him away, the best thing he could do was mix them with other footprints.

Glancing behind himself every now and again to be sure he wasn't being followed, he finally dove into an alley, his back resting against the brick siding of the building.

His arm wound was intensely painful, but it was the burning sensation from the injury at his waist that was taking over his focus. Biting his tongue to keep himself quiet, he pulled his blood-soaked hands away. He was going to need a surgeon, but he didn't even know where he was.

Pushing off the wall with a wince, his frozen body protesting in agony, he continued toward the thick of town, unsure if he was going to bleed to death or freeze to death first.

Breathing on his frozen digits and rubbing them together as he blindly walked, he concluded that he wasn't going to make it. His teeth chattered louder than anything he had ever heard in his life, and aside from the acute pain from the gunshot wounds, the rest of his body was going numb. He needed a hospital. He needed . . .

He couldn't think straight anymore. Stumbling into the open street, he was so hyperfocused on trying not to die that he almost bumped into a woman in a red dress as she exited her carriage. Barely able to whisper an apology, he continued, hunched over, legs shaking.

He was so absorbed in his pain that he barely registered his name being called. He paused, dazed and confused, before he heard his name again and turned to see someone rushing toward him.

That was it. They found him. He was done for.

But as the person approached, he caught a flash of a red dress and heard his name screamed out in a panic as he blacked out.

CHAPTER 31

Benedict awoke to soft chatter taking place at the other end of the room. Kitch was deep in discussion with someone—he could only guess one of the other courtesans.

He must have fallen asleep in her room again, after a drunken night of tomfoolery. Usually, she would have abruptly woken him up and rushed him out of her room before receiving anyone, unless he was so plastered that he couldn't move. When had he even gotten drunk?

Not that he *couldn't* move; he was just so comfy and warm beneath the perfumed blankets that he didn't *want* to move. The faint aroma of spices permeating the air was a pleasant addition, too, though a bit different from Kitch's usual tastes.

The spices were a bit *too* unusual for Kitch. In fact, it was impossible for him to be hearing her voice, because he wasn't in London. His heart skipping a beat and his eyes flying open, he found himself staring at an unfamiliar plaster ceiling. Where was he?

He shot up in the bed of silks and furs, only to yelp as his side erupted in flames. A woman sprang to her feet from her chaise next to the fireplace and rushed toward him.

"Ben! It's all right, you're safe. Lie back down," she ordered.

Mouth agape, he stared at the black-haired woman, afraid that she would disappear if he so much as blinked. Was his mind playing tricks on him?

As she helped him lie back down, he tentatively lifted a shaking hand, reaching out for her face. Kitch. It was actually Kitch, in the flesh and blood.

No. No, it couldn't be. He must have been dreaming.

When he gently cupped her cheek with his trembling hand, Kitch paused in her actions, raising her blue eyes to meet his own, her concern shifting to a gentle smile.

"Kitch," he whispered.

Maybe she was real. But if she wasn't, he didn't mind this dream at all.

Benedict winced as the throbbing heat in his arm and side grew stronger. That couldn't be part of his dream, could it? He really had been shot, hadn't he? There was no time to think any further on the subject because the other figure approached just then.

If he was dreaming, it had just turned into a nightmare. He quickly sat back up to protect Kitch from Madam Bonifrey, but the pain was too great, and he fell back down.

"Ben!" Kitch shrieked.

"Did you drink anything that she gave you?" he croaked, grabbing her by the shoulders, gritting his teeth against the pain.

"It's all right," Kitch stated. "She explained what happened. I've . . . had words with her," she added, frowning over her shoulder at the madam.

Madam Bonifrey cleared her throat, hiding her shame as she straightened her posture. "I apologize for my greed," she said.

"We'll discuss that later," Kitch shot back in irritation before her attention fell back to Benedict.

She ran a hand over his scruffy-bearded cheek, and he leaned into her touch, placing a hand over hers.

It was really her. Kitch was there with him, all the way from London.

"How are you feeling?" she asked.

"Like I've been shot," he croaked, and his body screamed to prove a point.

"We know that much. We had a surgeon stitch you up. What the bloody hell happened?" she asked, brows knitted with concern.

"Well, after someone sold us out to Thomas Davies," he started, casting a glare in the brothel madam's direction, "it kind of became a long story."

"Davies?" Kitch said. "You mean . . ."

He nodded in response. "All the way from London, with cybernetics. Huge, clunky, dangerous—" He then stiffened. Were Davies and Ajani searching for him? Had they followed the trail of blood? "They're probably coming for me," he hissed.

"Captain Davies won't be back," Madam Bonifrey replied. "He left two days ago."

"Two . . .?" He blinked in confusion, looking back and forth in between Kitch and the brothel owner. How was it possible that Davies had set sail two days ago without returning for him—and downright killing him for deserting? "How long was I out?"

"Two days," Kitch confirmed. "What on earth happened?"

He'd been unconscious for two days. In that time, Davies could have done anything. "I have to—" he started.

Struggling to get out of bed, he stumbled to the ornate door. Kitch scurried in front of him, standing firmly in front of the door, palms against his chest, to prevent him from leaving.

"Ben, please! You really need to lie back down; you've been through hell."

"I need to stop the cannons," he said urgently. "I need to get to Mathias, I—"

Kitch frowned, shaking her head, confused. "Stop, you're not making any sense."

Grabbing her wrists, he tried to move her out of the way, but white-hot pain shot through his entire form, his knees threatening to give out from beneath him.

Kitch pulled him back toward the bed, and when an extra hand touched his bare shoulder—Madam Bonifrey—he immediately jolted away from her touch, still disgusted that she had sold him to Davies.

Benedict stumbled into the wall with his injured arm, and his wound scalded intensely as his body gave out. He slid to the ground, darkness dancing in his vision. Kitch immediately dropped to her knees at his side.

"I'm going to fetch the surgeon," Madam Bonifrey said as she whooshed past him, shutting the door behind her.

"Ben, what on earth is going on?" Kitch scolded once they were finally alone.

It took a moment for the pain to subside enough to allow him to formulate a thought. "Davies is going to fire on the Great Lakes. Some kind of mind-controlling poison."

He whispered so low that Kitch had to lean in just to hear him. He didn't trust anyone but her to overhear what he had to say, especially not Madam Bonifrey. Not after what she had done. He needed Kitch to trust him, believe him. She couldn't keep pressing the matter. And if she truly had moved up to a position of power like Madam Bonifrey had claimed when she waved the letter about, then he needed her to understand that the walls had ears, and she'd need to figure out the rest on her own. Maybe he was being paranoid. He hoped he *wasn't* being paranoid.

Kitch was so close to him, it hurt. Far from the searing pain of his gunshot wounds, it instead tugged at his heart, squeezing it so tight as if in a vise. He'd promised he'd return to her, but his heart threatened to shatter beyond repair a second time whenever he thought back to her sob when he left her that night, and how it could have been the last thing he ever heard from her as he froze to death. Or bled out. Or both.

Her gaze locked on his, and she slowly nodded in understanding, determined. "Let's get you back in bed," she whispered.

His back against the wall for support, he pushed up on shaky legs as Kitch helped him by wrapping his good arm around her shoulders. Oh, how he'd missed her. Once he was stable, he kept his arm around her, using his other hand to gently lift her chin to stare into her blue eyes, lost in their beauty.

She swallowed hard before she spoke. "I've been so worried about you ever since I found out that you never made it to your destination."

"What, are you spying on me?" he asked with a smirk.

"You basically dared me to," she quipped back, and Benedict chuckled.

"I'm glad you're here," he said with a wince as he pulled her in for a hug, resting his chin on top of her head.

"I'm glad you're alive." She sighed, content.

The door opened, and Kitch pulled away as the surgeon stepped in, immediately beelining for Benedict, the brothel madam in tow.

The surgeon helped him to the bed before inspecting Benedict's wounds while Kitch stood by, brows knit with concern, and Madam Bonifrey returned to her tea by the fire.

"The stitches are fine," the surgeon said, "but I must insist that you rest."

"Thank you, Doctor," Kitch replied, before she turned and headed for Madam Bonifrey.

The surgeon asked him questions as he patched the wounds back up, but Benedict's attention was on Kitch as she leaned in and whispered in the brothel manager's ear. His stomach dropped. For a split moment, he actually second-guessed his trust in Kitch.

As she headed for the door, he spoke up. "Where are you going?"

"To fetch you some clothes."

His body stiffened. "You're leaving me alone with *her*?"

"Yes," was her simple reply. "I told you; she apologized. We'll talk about this later." Kitch stepped out, barely making a sound as she gently closed the door.

"Mister Keenan, please," the surgeon insisted. "I need your full cooperation."

"Right," he said, blinking back to the matter at hand. "Sorry."

"You need to stay warm. I suggest that you either take a hot bath or go sit by the fire. Even a nice cup of something hot to drink can work—"

"No!" Benedict said immediately. There was no chance of him drinking anything belonging to Madam Bonifrey.

"I can pour you some tea, if you like," Madam Bonifrey said. "It'll warm you right up."

"Hell no," he emphasized, glaring at the woman, flashes of Mathias, Ella, his red-headed courtesan, and Ajani partially reminding him what had happened the last time he drank anything that she had offered him.

"I must insist then," the surgeon said, "please go sit by the fire."

He kept glaring at Madam Bonifrey as the surgeon helped him up. Dragging his feet, his legs still shaky, he slowly made his way to the fireplace.

His body already thanked him as he sat in the empty chaise. The surgeon threw some furs and silks around Benedict's shoulders and legs before telling Madam Bonifrey to fetch him again should something else happen.

Benedict refused to look at her as the surgeon left, his eyes focused on the door as he awaited Kitch's return. He hoped nothing had happened to her.

"Let's discuss what happened," Madam Bonifrey said, breaking the awkward silence.

"You mean when you sold me to Davies?" he hissed, finally moving his attention to her.

"Well, yes . . ."

"Then you better start explaining."

His hardened and hateful gaze was on her for the longest time before she finally cleared her throat. "The money was good," she admitted. "I couldn't resist."

Of course she couldn't. And truthfully, he couldn't blame her. Deep down—and depending on the amount—he might have done the same in her position. But the drinks . . .

He continued to watch her for a moment before finally speaking again. "How did you do it?"

"I beg your pardon?" She blinked.

"You drank the same thing from the same bottles as Mathias and I. And I know I can hold my alcohol, so how did you do it? How did you stay coherent?"

Madam Bonifrey sat up straight and cleared her throat again before taking a sip of her tea. "It wasn't the alcohol that was tainted, it was the cups. Your friend was easy, he went down quick.

But you, as you say, you can hold your alcohol. I was almost afraid that it would not work at all, to be honest, so I had my girl taint another glass further. You both surprised and impressed me."

Benedict hissed in discontent. He knew it couldn't have been because of the alcohol. He usually drank way more than that with no effects.

Finishing her tea, she stood up and adjusted her clothing—he guessed to appear more regal.

"For whatever it's worth, I do apologize." Benedict didn't answer. Apology or not, for the right price, he was certain that she would do it again. "I suppose I will leave you to get your rest. Can I get you anything, Mister Keenan?"

"I don't want anything from you."

"Not even one of my girls to keep you company? Alice took a liking to you last time."

He narrowed his eyes in resentment. He didn't trust Madam Bonifrey or anything that came from her, the girls included, no matter how nice they were to look at.

A part of him wondered about Ella. Had she been in on it the whole time? Was Madam Bonifrey using her?

"Suit yourself then," she said when he didn't answer. "These are my personal chambers. I will be in the room down the hall. Let me know if you need anything." Before he could assure her that he certainly would *not*, she stepped out of the room, leaving him to his own devices.

CHAPTER 32

"Ben."

The familiar voice startled him. Heart racing, all of his previous thoughts—Davies, the cannons, Mathias—came flooding back, knocking away the vibrating numbness of his sleep. His eyes fluttered open lazily, following the swishing movements of red skirts before falling on the dying flames in the fireplace. He had dozed off by the fire, cozy as could be.

"You shouldn't sleep in the chair like that," she added, setting down bowls of steaming stew on the table between both chaises before tending to the fire, stoking it with the wrought iron poker to revive it. "It's not good for you. You'll stiffen your neck muscles."

Clearing his throat and adjusting his posture, Benedict rubbed at a sore spot in his neck, just as Kitch had warned about. She sat down and began eating, but Benedict did not move.

His stomach growled loudly—when was the last time he'd even had a decent meal—but he didn't trust the food, he didn't trust the plate. Madam Bonifrey had admitted to tainting the cups, so what else had she tainted?

"I cooked the food myself," she offered, which only comforted him slightly. Sure, Kitch had spent a lot of time in the kitchen as an orphan, but the courtesans at the brothel didn't cook for themselves. Was there such a thing as being out of practice with food-making? "I rinsed off the plates first," she added.

A chuckle escaped him, and he shook his head in amusement before turning his attention to her. "I'm not sure which part of all that should make me feel any better."

Narrowing her eyes, she leaned to the side and playfully swatted at him but was slightly out of reach to connect. Benedict grinned in response.

Kitch returned to her food, and with each bite she took, Benedict's stomach rumbled until he finally gave in and unburied his hands from the covers to grab the other bowl.

The chunks of beef mixed in with the broken-down peas, potatoes, and onions looked delicious, and his mouth watered as he tried to convince himself that everything would be all right, that he wouldn't black out and find himself hit on the back of the head by Ajani again.

His mind went back to Kitch whispering something to Madam Bonifrey. He could still trust the woman he grew up with, couldn't he? She wouldn't do the same thing to him, would she?

Mindlessly stirring the stew, he eventually brought a spoonful to his lips, tentative. It smelled absolutely divine and definitely wasn't helping the gnawing sensation of hunger pangs any. Finally, he took a bite, and it was even better than he imagined it would taste. The peas added their own sweetness to the flavor, but most importantly, there was no strange aftertaste that he couldn't quite place.

"How did you find me?" he asked, after taking a few more bites.

"You stumbled by me, frozen half to death." Her brows knitted with concern. "Don't you remember?"

"That's not what I meant," he said, setting his half-eaten bowl back onto the table and focusing on her. "How did you find me? How did you know I was in Elgin?" It was suspicious—how had she found him when he didn't even know where he was?

"I didn't," she admitted, and he raised a brow at her words. "When I read in the paper that the airship you boarded had gone down . . ."

Her voice quivered at the end as she paused, and it was like Benedict took an arrow to the heart. It truthfully hurt more than his gunshot wounds, and not only because of the numbing unguent the surgeon slathered them with.

She recuperated quickly, however, swallowing hard before continuing. "I was beside myself with grief. You promised me, Benedict Keenan!" He blinked in surprise as she slammed her bowl down next to his, knuckles white from the tight grip on her spoon in anger. "You promised that you'd come back to me! But you're such a *liar*."

He said nothing to defend himself, nothing to change her mind. He *was* a liar and couldn't deny it. But he was also a man of his word—somewhat—when it came to things that would benefit him. Staying alive was definitely one of those things. Besides, he'd tried his damnedest to make good on his promise to return to her. At least he was still alive.

Still alive, and still able to fulfill that promise . . . to an extent.

Her swift breathing settled back to normal as her anger dissipated. When she was calm again, she continued.

"I tracked your original destination and boarded a mail steamship setting sail across the ocean. I even bribed them with a *large* sum to sail faster. I used their broadcaster and put my newly earned skills to the test and reached out to our brothel network to keep an eye or ear out for you."

Suddenly, the *letter* from Kitch that Madam Bonifrey had waved around during their initial meeting made much more sense; it wasn't a letter at all, but a *note* taken from the broadcast. But what were these "newly earned skills" she mentioned?

"I received word of you being locked up in a place called Elgin, but once I arrived, you were no longer there. Seeing as I was in Elgin anyway, I figured that I'd reach out to Madam Bonifrey, whose network is *phenomenal.* You actually stumbled by just as I arrived, thankfully for me, and *luckily* for you."

He watched her long and hard, contemplating the validity of her answer. It made sense, but could he trust her? "You're telling me you just up and left everything you worked for behind? Left your job, the life you built for yourself?"

"Why not?" she asked defiantly. "You did it."

"It's not you who you are," he challenged back. "You're withholding something from me."

She didn't deny it. "You withhold from me all the time."

"What are you hiding?"

"I can't reveal that just yet," she whispered—so low that he almost missed it. "I'm still looking into something."

Fair enough. From her whispers, it seemed she didn't fully trust Madam Bonifrey either, which sent a wave of relief through him. Knowing that the brothel owner had the most reach and most eyes and ears, it wasn't a good idea to speak openly of anything while in her personal room, of all places.

Getting to her feet, Kitch held out her hands for him to take. “Come, let’s get you back in bed for some rest.”

He complied, placing his hands in hers and allowing her to help him to his feet. His body ached, but it was a dull ache—not nearly as bad as when the adrenaline rushes wore off.

He slowly followed Kitch and sat on the edge of the bed, all his movements painfully drawn out. He couldn’t hold back a hiss as he laid on his back. Kitch helped with the blankets, covering him up to get warm and comfy.

“What are your plans?” she asked as she sat next to him.

“I don’t know,” he admitted. “I don’t know where to look for Mathias and don’t know if Davies returned for him in order to draw me back out.”

“I have someone looking for him, don’t worry,” she reassured him.

“I’m slightly concerned about that,” he said. “I don’t trust her.” He mouthed the last part without a sound.

Kitch nodded in understanding. “How do we stop the cannons?” she asked.

“I need an airship. I need a crew,” he said. “Not from her, though,” he added. The last time he needed a crew, she sold him to the very man he wanted to kill. He didn't want to do that again.

Kitch smirked. "I'm working on that."

Benedict raised a brow. "You are? When did you have time for that?"

A giggle escaped her. "What do you think I've been up to all afternoon? Surely, fetching you clothes doesn't take that long."

"It depends on where you got them from."

"Why, only the *best* men's clothing store in the Upper Lands, of course," she said playfully. "Where else would I get them?"

"With what money?"

"With the money you gave me. The same money I used to bribe the mail ship."

"Of course," he chuckled, breaking off to yawn. It seemed she'd found a use for it other than bailing him out of Coldbath, after all.

He shut his eyes and felt her get up and rummage about. It was a shame that if he survived stopping Davies, he was going to be locked up in Coldbath for the rest of his life.

CHAPTER 33

The sunrise cast a lazy orange hue about the room as it glistened off the frost on the windows. Kitch's body slowly rose and fell as she breathed softly, curled up next to him. She looked so peaceful as she slept, as if she kept the weight of the world at bay for a few hours through her dreams.

She was resourceful, that Kitch. Always had been. Not only had she figured out what ship he had boarded, but she had found him on this foreign land across the Atlantic, even when Elgin wasn't his original destination, even when he had spent most of his time flying over the Great Lakes.

He was so grateful for her. She had always been there for him; occasionally getting him out of jail, caring for him and his hangovers, and scolding him when he fell too deep into his downward spirals. Even at the orphanage, she'd share her bread with him and lie for him when he'd get in trouble. Even when he'd picked on her and teased her, even when he'd pulled her hair . . . she'd always forgiven him.

An uncomfortable chill traveled through his body, and he shivered, running his hands over the goosebumps on his forearms.

Slowly crawling out of bed, wincing as he forced his muscles to cooperate, he made his way to the embers in the fireplace, steadily bending over, cautious of his side wound. He rekindled the fire as best he could with the logs at the back of the fireplace that had missed being burned.

The heat broke through the chill of the room, and he remained in front of the fire for a few more minutes, gradually straightening back to his full height. He closed his eyes, allowing the fire to warm him for a moment longer. When he finally opened his eyes, Kitch stood by his side, deep in thought as the flames danced through her eyes.

"Did I wake you?" he asked.

"You did, but it's all right. I have a lot to do today."

"What's on your mind?" he asked, turning to her.

"I can't stop thinking about how I thought I was going to lose you," she whispered. "You just collapsed in front of me and didn't wake up for the longest time . . ."

Benedict softened, and he gently pulled her into him, holding her as tightly as his sore muscles and wounds would allow.

There was that weight of the world again, back on her shoulders, threatening to drag her down as he'd seen it do so many times. But he had also watched her stand strong beneath the weight each time, occasionally with a little wobble, but always quick to shake it off.

"I never want to lose you," she added. "Why do you do this to me? Why do you stress me out so much?"

He chuckled, running his fingers through her silky hair. "It's so easy to do," he teased, kissing the top of her head before pulling away, sitting on the red and gold chaise by the fire before his weakened legs could give out. He ran his hands along the velvety smooth material, settling comfortably against the tufted cushion. Oh, Kitch was definitely going to need one of those in her room. "What are your plans for the day?" he asked.

"You mean besides keeping an eye on you? I plan to follow up on some leads."

"Good. And while you do that," he said, getting back to his feet, "I'll see if I can find anything on—"

"*You*," she said firmly, folding her arms over her chest, "are not going anywhere."

"Kitch," he tried, desperate. He had to find Mathias; he had to find out where Davies was and uncover the state of the Great Lakes. "I can't stay."

"You can, and you will. You can't go without a plan."

A smirk tugged at his lips. "But that's how I work best."

"I agree," she said, blatantly. "And it's also how you get into situations like you did three days ago. You didn't think about what would happen if you got shot, did you? You didn't think about freezing to death or about—"

"No, I didn't," he admitted with a frown. She didn't need to remind him. "But I'm still here, aren't I?"

"Thanks to me!" she sighed, throwing her hands in the air, exasperated.

"I'm glad that it was you," he said gently.

"Oh, Ben . . ."

Tears glossed her eyes, threatening to fall and trail down her cheeks. But she quickly composed herself, as she always did. He admired her for that.

"You've changed."

"We've both changed," she pointed out.

"Yes, but the image in my mind is of this little girl who used to cry when I pulled her hair." He smiled softly. "And she has become this refined, composed . . . noblewoman."

Kitch let out a slight laugh. "I can hardly be considered noble."

"No, it's true," he said. "The way you compose yourself . . ." He trailed off, envisioning Catherine standing before him for a moment before the image eventually dissipated.

The smile that dropped from his face found its way to Kitch's lips. "As a noblewoman, I should charge you more."

He couldn't help but grin at her quip, though it was short-lived as a knock sounded at the door, and a woman's voice piped up from the other side.

"Madam Kitch, there is someone waiting for you in the lobby."

"Thank you," Kitch called out. "I'll be there in a few minutes."

"Madam?" he asked, brow raised.

She only nodded in response, clasping her hands together. "Your clothes are hanging in the pampering room. Please don't leave yet," she added in a pleading whisper, begging him with her eyes.

Benedict stared at her. He couldn't afford to stay. In fact, the fate of thousands of people couldn't afford him to, either. But he couldn't say no to her, especially when she looked at him like that. He had to trust that her network was toiling away on figuring out the same thing. He finally nodded.

As if that was the thing that she had been waiting for, she grabbed his hand and squeezed it tight, mouthing a "thank you" before turning around and leaving the room.

The pampering room was small, with a commode and a basin for washing. He smiled as he inspected the clothes that Kitch had bought for him—with his own money. They were well tailored and crisp, made for a nobleman or alchemist, or one that acted like one of them, like he did.

Turning to the basin, he filled it with water and cleaned up, even spending a very long time shaving off his scruffy beard after finding the straight razor.

He dressed, running his fingers over the broadcloth material of the waistcoat and pants, then the smooth and crisp cotton shirt. Kitch knew his tastes and had wasted no expense.

He was sitting by the fire, pulling on long black boots, when Kitch came back in. "Lord Keenan," she started, curtsying in her striped blue and black dress, "may I request the honor of your presence?"

Benedict chuckled and shook his head in amusement. He was no lord, no king or prince—not even a noble. But he enjoyed her childish behavior and humored her in turn. Getting to his feet, he adjusted the fitting of his clothes before he bowed as much as his sore body would allow, extending a hand for her to take. "Lady Gladstone, it would be my honor if you joined me for . . . tea," he added after a pause, glancing about, unsure of what exactly they should or would be doing as nobles at that very moment.

"Thank you, my lord!" Rising from her curtsy, an amused smile on her ruby red lips, she delicately placed her hand in his.

Bringing her to one of the chaises before the fire, he continued to hold her hand as they sat in unison, Kitch pulling her feet up to lounge properly like the queen she was. "What news do you bring for the country?" he asked, still in character.

Kitch's smile faded. "We found your friend."

Benedict's stomach dropped, and the grip on Kitch's hand involuntarily tightened for a moment. She found Mathias. "Is he all right?" he asked, dropping his act. "Where is he?"

"He is as well as he could be, all things considered," she replied. "And he's in Elgin. We fear it is as you suspected: Captain Davies is using him to lure you out."

"Perfect," he said darkly as he got to his feet. This was it. He would not wait any longer; he was going to make Davies pay.

"Wait!" she cried as he headed for the door. "You don't have a plan!"

Plan? His plan was to kill Davies. Exactly how he was going to go about it, that part he hadn't quite figured out.

"I'll make it up as I go," he said, waving her off.

Opening the door, he was taken aback to find Madam Bonifrey standing on the other side, just as startled. Madam Bonifrey composed herself first.

"I couldn't help but overhear," she started, then cleared her throat. "If you're going back out there, you're going to need weapons and a coat."

It was true; he was at least going to need that much. But his eyes narrowed, watching her with distrust. What was she trying to do now?

Kitch's hand rested on his back as she stood beside him. She looked up and gave him a single nod. He might not trust the brothel owner, but he trusted Kitch.

Benedict turned his attention back to Madam Bonifrey. "Lead the way."

The flashes of memories as he followed Madam Bonifrey through the brothel were uncomfortable, to say the least. It would take a while before he'd be able to trust the establishment and the owner, if ever.

They stepped past some heavy purple velvet curtains into a cramped room. Shelves lined the walls, stocked full of folded sheets and blankets, boxes of various sizes, and plenty of cleaning supplies.

Picking up the hanging lantern against the wall to the right of the doorway, Madam Bonifrey turned the key at the bottom, causing the infused orb inside to float and glow. With a click, she then pulled the key out, revealing the long brass stem and stubby bit of a hidden barrel key.

Handing Benedict the lantern, Madam Bonifrey kicked the floral rug out of the way, revealing a small hole big enough for the key. Cautiously glancing toward the curtains, she then kneeled and inserted the key, turning it with a click.

The mechanism under the floor sprung to life, coils and gears turning and churning as he could hear more and more clicks unlocking the extremely well-protected hidden door. Standing back up, she shoved the key back into the bottom of the lantern and made her way to the door, peeking past the curtains before turning her attention to Benedict.

"Go!" she hissed.

Where was he even going? He cast a suspicious glance at Madam Bonifrey. The fact that she seemed to hide this from even her own staff slightly concerned him.

Reaching for the handle with his good arm, he struggled slightly to open the trapdoor, the wound at his side reminding him of its existence by throbbing slightly.

Peering down into the darkness, he stepped onto the rungs of the ladder before looking back in Madam Bonifrey's direction as she kept a lookout.

Quickly glancing at Kitch, he shot her a meaningful look. He didn't trust the brothel owner in the slightest, and this suspicious activity only increased that feeling tenfold. But Kitch gave him a reassuring smile.

"I'll be right behind you," she whispered.

With a nod, he continued down into the darkness.

Once he was close enough to the bottom, he jumped the rest of the way, stirring up dust from the ground as he winced from the jolt of pain at his side. The trap door above closed, and Kitch and Madam Bonifrey worked their way down. Setting the lantern on the ground, he offered his hand to Kitch, helping her stay upright as she stepped off the ladder. He reluctantly did the same for Madam Bonifrey.

"I'm warning you," he started, eyes narrowed. "If this is a trap . . ."

Waving off his warning, she picked the lantern up. "This way," she instructed, tilting her head down the pitch-black hall.

Eyes still narrowed as he stepped past Madam Bonifrey, Benedict led the way. Stepping into a large room, dozens of infused orbs instantly lit up around a hidden armory, bathing an array of medieval, current, old-fashioned, alchemical, and techy weapons in a bluish light.

Kitch gasped in awe as he whistled, impressed, but Madam Bonifrey hissed at them both. "Keep it down!"

Sheepishly, Benedict sunk his head into his shoulders, but it didn't last long as he slowly inspected the weapons around the room.

"Where do these all come from?" Kitch asked quietly.

"My personal collection started with this lance here," Madam Bonifrey said, her hand lovingly running up the jousting weapon of old. "It was given to me by my first lover in exchange for housing."

Benedict glanced over his shoulder with a raised brow. It was an interesting object to exchange, he had to admit. Turning back to the weapons, he continued his stroll, inspecting each one.

"Each time he'd return from whatever adventure he'd run after, he'd bring me back another, and another, and another . . . then I never saw him again." She fell silent for a moment before continuing, "I later learned of his untimely passing, but strangely, the weapons kept on coming. It turns out that I suddenly had a reputation for being an antique weapons collector. Unfortunately, that also meant that I was more prone to inviting thieves into my home, and then the fires started. My establishment burned down three times before I cut my losses and built a hidden room. Not even my staff knows about it."

All right, he was impressed. It was a smart move on her part and explained the reason behind her actions . . . as long as what she said was true. She was almost as good a storyteller as Mathias. Her story didn't make him trust in her any more than he did beforehand, but he was impressed, nonetheless.

"Condolences on your loss," Kitch said, dropping her gaze.

"Thank you," she replied, before quietly clearing her throat. "If you are going to save the Great Lakes from the Drapyltin, Mister Keenan, I suggest you take as many as you need. Captain Davies will be relentless."

"Not as relentless as I'm going to be," Benedict growled.

Oh, he was definitely going to ruin Davies's day. Maybe even his year. And then he'd kill him. Of course, stopping the cannons would make Mathias happy, and that thought made him happy, so he'd do that too.

He came back around after having gone full circle, inspecting all the weapons. He found his way back to Kitch's side, silently ruminating over which weapon would be best to use and easiest to hide, most comfortable, and lightest to wield with his injuries. Madam Bonifrey stepped into a side room, returning with a wool coat and a shoulder holster with multiple places for weapons.

"Where did you get that?" Kitch asked.

"They belonged to my lover," she explained. "Mister Keenan seems approximately the same size."

Benedict accepted the wool coat and, with difficulty thanks to his gunshot wounds, slid it on. It fit just right. "Your assumption was correct," he said, twisting his body and waving his arms as best he could without injuring himself.

"What did your lover do?" Kitch asked.

"Your guess is as good as mine," Madam Bonifrey said, her eyes on the coat.

"You never asked?" Benedict said.

"I was young and naive back then," she replied, helping Benedict with the leather holster. "I never wanted to know, really. It would only cause unnecessary worry."

Benedict shot Kitch a meaningful glance, and she looked away. She was always unnecessarily worrying about him, causing her more stress than needed.

As Madam Bonifrey tightened the belts about his shoulders, Benedict's attention fell back to the coat. "Why are you helping me?" he asked.

"Because, Mister Keenan, the world will be in your debt. And I also can't seem to apologize enough for my greed, so I figure that my actions now speak louder than words."

"We appreciate it, Madam," Kitch chimed in, as Benedict studied the brothel owner's face. She seemed sincere enough.

Benedict ended up with two military short swords, one revolver, a short-barreled pocket pistol, and two daggers hidden in his boots. If anything, he was over prepared. Standing before Madam Bonifrey, he extended his hand for a handshake. "Thank you," he finally said.

"It's the least I can do," she replied, ignoring his hand in favor of fussing over the wool coat, straightening the material and holster.

Kitch approached, hugging herself. "I'll stay here and gather some more intel," she started, trying and failing to force a brave smile. "I'll have your crew ready for you, and we'll find your friend."

Benedict turned to Kitch, placing a hand on her cheek, caressing it with a thumb. She was so grown-up. He knew that it had been ages since they were children, but sometimes, he just couldn't see her as anything but. Other times, however, he just wanted to kiss her.

After he forcefully pulled himself away, Madam Bonifrey led him to a gate at the far end of the room. Opening it with difficulty and hissing when it loudly squealed and creaked, she stepped aside to allow Benedict through.

"This will take you to the surface," she instructed.

With a nod and one last look at Kitch, he crawled through and vanished.

CHAPTER 34

The air was extra crisp and frigid in Elgin Below as the sun continued its journey through the sky, and Benedict hated it. Despite the wool coat, he felt the gradual change in temperature as he approached the hidden exit. When he made his way above ground, he thought his eyelashes would fall off and his nostrils would fuse together, and the first breath he took through his mouth felt like he'd inhaled a lit match.

How did Mathias tolerate this piercing cold? How had he been able to grow accustomed to it? It was bitter enough for Benedict to instantly take back every thought he ever had about permanently settling on the beautiful land. No way. He couldn't do it.

Ducking into his coat in a rather poor attempt to keep the cold at bay, he dug into the coin purse Madam Bonifrey had slid into his pocket, pulling out a coin for the bundled boy selling newspapers on the corner of the street.

Sitting on a bench near a couple of men in front of a shop, he did what he did best: listen in on the goings-on.

Elgin was a big place, so he had to be smart about where he'd find Davies and Mathias. If they had docked, it was very likely that they'd be in the Lands Below, seeing as how unwelcome sky pirates were in the Upper Lands. But if they hadn't docked, they'd be above the Upper Lands, and nobody seemed to acknowledge that was even a possibility.

Unfortunately, it was early; the pubs weren't yet open for his usual eavesdropping tactic, and the gossip circles were unhelpful in their discussions of tools and wares, shaving, and ice fishing. Even the paper he'd bought contained nothing of interest, and so he continued on.

Eventually, he hissed his discontent. He hadn't heard anything back from Kitch or Madam Bonifrey's network, which concerned him—if they couldn't find Mathias, how was he supposed to?

Time was running out to stop the cannons. He was still waiting on the crew Kitch had promised him, but if he could just somehow get to the cannon above the falls, he might be able to sabotage that one too. But something was off . . .

The lull of early morning village life was missing the thundering rumble of the falls in the distance. No wonder he hadn't recognized where he was when he had stumbled—disoriented, frozen, and in pain—into the village during his escape from Davies's crew.

Glancing about, he noted that the rising mist created from the sheer power of the falls was nowhere to be found to let him know which direction to go to find the falls.

Spinning around at the familiar sound of a steam carriage chugging along, he rushed up to the driver, putting his tourist charm on.

"Pardon me, my good man," he started, forcing his London accent to thicken, "I've heard stories of the falls in their winter splendor, but I can't seem to find them." The driver pointed him straight ahead, and Benedict tipped his head in thanks. "Much obliged!"

He kept to the alleyways in case Davies's crew meandered about, and sure enough, two pirates turned the corner of the street, making their way toward the falls in hushed conversation.

Testing his frozen fingertips against the bricks along the back of the building, he scaled all of two steps before a searing jolt, like lightning from the bullet wound in his arm, ramped into blinding agony. He found himself back on the ground faster than he could blink. Biting into his knuckle to keep quiet, he waited until the pain settled back to a dull throb before peeking out to get his eyes back on the two pirates.

His attention diverted, however, as an all-too-familiar voice cried out in anger.

"Release me!"

Benedict's heart sank as Mathias struggled to break free from his two captors a little farther down. Hands closing to fists as the dormant volcano of rage inside of him threatened to erupt once more, he rushed through the back alleys, pausing only once he ran out of cover.

Back against the wall, he peeked out past the edge of the building as they led Mathias over the frozen water.

Following was going to be hard; there was nothing left to hide behind or beneath, and his footprints through the snow would give him away. How was he going to get near enough to hear what they were saying? How was he going to save Mathias?

A familiar figure approached on the ice from the other direction, and Benedict bristled. "Davies," he growled. And was that the stolen military case in his spindly hand?

If he could get farther from the edge of the village before advancing, then maybe that would work. Moving away from the building in a parallel manner, the frozen snow crunched so obnoxiously loudly beneath his feet that he was certain it echoed across the falls and gave him away. Heart thumping anxiously with each step, his attention remained locked on both Mathias and Davies.

Having moved down the blanketed field enough to be relatively out of sight, Benedict lowered himself to the ground and edged along with his elbows—excruciatingly slowly thanks to his wounds—to flank from the side.

He cursed the winter. He wished he was back in London. Cold? That was nothing compared to this. He resented the beauty of the magical wonderland that accompanied such bitter temperatures: the natural ice sculptures, thick icicles, and snow-and-ice-coated trees and bushes that framed the falls. Formed by the mist, everything sparkled and glistened in the sun.

Catherine would have *loved* it.

Davies and Mathias walked across the thick ice, deep in argument, followed by four other sky pirates keeping guard. He couldn't hear what they were saying, but he could only imagine. He needed to get closer . . .

Continuing to crawl forward as quietly as the crunching snow would allow, he eventually arrived on the ice. He still hadn't seen Ajani yet, and he sincerely hoped that he wouldn't, but he knew that wherever Davies was, his fleet quartermaster wasn't too far behind.

A creak sounded beneath him, and Benedict stiffened in fear; it hadn't come from the snow, but from the ice. The falls weren't *actually* completely frozen over—the water continued to run beneath the solid surface.

He didn't like that. It meant that the top layer wasn't even and that it might break at any point. And there Mathias was, standing at the edge of the falls. It was dangerous. Benedict had to get to him before it was too late.

Another creak sounded, this time from behind him. Swiftly pulling a dagger from his knee-high boot, he rolled onto his back just in time to deflect the long blade of a familiar-looking sword.

CHAPTER 35

This wasn't the first time Benedict had found himself looking up past Ajani's infinitely long legs.

Unfortunately, having spent as much time with her as he had, he no longer entertained the thought of having a drink with her. In fact, he'd be happy to never see her again, let alone have to fight her. He wasn't in the mood for this. He had better and more important things to do.

"Di captain wan' yuh head," she informed him.

"I rather like my head where it is."

It was a shame they had to do this. Deep down, he really enjoyed listening to her accent when she spoke, and he admired her skills and impressively tactical mind as a fleet quartermaster.

Ajani pulled her sword away, immediately shifting it, stabbing downward at him. He swiftly moved his legs out of the way, and the blade embedded itself deep into the ice. She was out for blood.

Quick to counter, he kicked upward at her face, narrowly missing as she dodged backward. His other foot kicked out at the lodged sword, hoping to break the blade. It didn't.

Ajani slashed out at him once more as he scrambled to his feet, using a second cutlass from around her waist. He parried the attack with his dagger and had just enough time to grab his own sword before she slashed out at him again.

She was relentless, and it actually scared him. She was such a good fighter that a tiny sliver of doubt crept through his mind, whispering negativity, attempting to permanently disarm him.

He wouldn't survive. Ajani would bring his head to Davies. He was done for.

Benedict blocked with his dagger, but Ajani held strong, gripping her weapon with both hands, applying more pressure. A flash of Kitch popped into his mind. Mathias. No, he couldn't let Ajani win.

No, he would not die today.

Gritting his teeth, he pressed his sword hand against his dagger hand to keep Ajani's sharp weapon from making contact with his face, then pressed the mechanism near the hilt with his thumb. The single blade separated into three, and Ajani blinked in surprise.

Taking the opportunity, he twisted the trident dagger, entrapping her blade, and pulled down as he slashed out at her throat with his sword. She dodged with flexible ease and kicked, swinging her foot out at his temple.

There was that damned boot blade again, sticking out past her toes, hidden in the sole. Jumping back, jaw clenched, he recalled the unwanted close shave he had received, and his thumb throbbed in remembrance of connecting with the hidden blade.

Ajani grabbed the hilt of her other cutlass, yanking it from the ice. It didn't budge.

"Ha!" he cried out victoriously, then charged at her with his sword, but she was quick to parry his attack with her other blade.

He had her on the defensive, though, which was where he preferred having her. She was far too agile for his liking, so him being on the defensive was a recipe for disaster. Their blades clashed loudly, and the ice beneath their feet vibrated from the sound. He didn't like that one bit.

"You're not my target, love," he said. He wanted Davies's life, not hers.

"I know," she replied, charging at him after a successful parry.

Great. Now he was on the defensive, exactly where he didn't want to be. Dodging and blocking blow after blow, he forcefully took a step back each time.

Eventually, his foot settled against the stuck blade. Sidestepping to not trip over it, he thrust his trident dagger out as she slashed at him, entrapping the blade.

Stumbling backward from a kick to the chest, he barely recuperated before she lunged forward again. Benedict jumped to the side and swung his own blade to the sound of something terrifying: the ice cracking beneath their weight. Ajani blocked with her blade and expertly spun around to attack, but the cracking sound grew louder, and suddenly, the ice at their feet shifted.

Eyes wide, they both instantly stuck out their arms to avoid losing their balance as the ice crumbled around them, some of the freezing water sloshing onto the surface of the drift ice they stood on.

Ajani lunged, and the weight of the ice shifted dangerously. Benedict suddenly found himself lower than the fleet quartermaster on account of the uneven weight to one side of the floating ice piece. He swung and parried her, pushing away and backing up until they were even once more.

"A yuh afraid?" she asked.

"Hardly," he quipped back.

She lunged out once more, but Benedict slipped as he went to dodge, falling flat onto his back with a hiss of pain. Ajani spun around, but her footing caused a solid piece of ice along the edge to break away, and her leg fell into the frigid waters.

She shrieked in fear and surprise and shock all at once, continuing to fall backward into the water, her balance completely lost.

Rolling over onto his stomach, he snatched her hand as she was half submerged. What the hell was he doing? He could easily get to Davies with Ajani out of the way, but there he was, just like with the *Nightingale*, coming to her aid.

"Come on!" he said, grabbing at her other flailing hand as he got to his knees. "Stop moving!" he warned. "I'm losing my grip!"

The throbbing wound in his arm was feeling like a fire again—out of control, singeing him from the inside with each pull to help Ajani out of the water. But she wouldn't stop, and it forced Benedict to let go.

She sank, completely submerged, fear in her eyes as another large piece of drift ice crashed into his, covering her from view. Panic seized him—fear of ending up like Ajani—as the piece he was on broke in half. Scooting to the center of his new section, he breathed a sigh of relief when he didn't tip over.

Watching the surface for Ajani to break through, he then paused. Why did he care? Why was he suddenly so soft? Would this mean he'd hesitate when it came to killing Davies? Mathias's panicked cry grabbed his attention, and he turned to find Mathias on his knees, frantically picking something up, with the captain aiming his gun at the surgeon's head.

No, he'd definitely kill Davies.

He glanced about at the wintery landscape around him. He needed to reach the intact surface of the falls to get to Mathias. Slowly standing so that he didn't flip the drift ice over, he jumped onto the large single mass of pack ice next to him, arms out for balance, until he made it to more stable ice.

His body wanted to collapse, but he couldn't afford to as he forced himself to make a run for Mathias.

Thomas turned his gun in Benedict's direction, and gunshots echoed in the air. Benedict zigzagged to dodge the bullets despite not being able to see them, tripping on a frozen chunk of ice sticking out of the ground.

Landing hard on his knees, he slid forward on the ice, the obliterating pain making him forget how to breathe. As the pain dampened, he looked up to see the captain's four goons headed right for him.

"Get up, get up, get up," he urged himself, slowly getting to his feet on shaking legs. He was so done with everything. Damn the ice, damn the winter, and damn the whole situation!

His knees ached, but he couldn't focus on that; he needed to get past the four sky pirates.

As they charged, Benedict slashed out at the dark pirate with gray hair and kicked the pale lanky one in the groin. As the lanky man garbled a cry and doubled over, Benedict dropped his dagger and grabbed a handful of the man's raven hair, pulling him up and using him as a shield just in time as the gray-haired pirate gutted the lanky man.

Shoving the corpse into the gray-haired man, Benedict then spun around, struggling because of the height difference, and blocked a blow from the sword of a shorter pirate.

Pulling his gun from its holster, he shot the oncoming fourth pirate in the stomach—a golden-skinned man. The pirate collapsed, and Benedict dodged both a slash from the shorter pirate and a stab from the gray-haired man.

Blocking another swing, his sword went flying as he cried out in pain from a rather blunt blow to his fingers with the butt of a weapon.

Swiftly pulling his second dagger from his other boot, he blocked the attack as he pulled the trigger. The gray-haired man went down. Turning, he then aimed at the shorter pirate's head, eyes focused and intent.

The shorter man skidded to a halt before stumbling backward on the ice. Benedict pulled the trigger without mercy. He then set his attention on the captain and Mathias.

"Davies!" he roared, allowing the rage to consume him.

This was it. This was the moment he'd kill him once and for all, avenging Catherine and Mathias and himself. No more fooling around. It was time.

CHAPTER 36

Benedict marched across the solid surface of icy Niagara Falls. He was freezing, he was hurting, and he was furious.

He didn't have a plan. What would he do if Thomas fired his gun again? There was nothing to hide behind, and the closer he got to the sky pirate, the more unlikely it was that he could dodge the bullets.

Kitch would have scolded him. Mathias would have blanched at the thought. Making things up as he went was how he worked best, but the only thing Benedict could do was allow the fiery rage to consume him—allow the molten anger to roll through him, pulsing through his veins, vibrating through his entire being. That festering fury and wrath was all he had, and that was going to have to be good enough.

Thomas aimed the gun back at Mathias, jamming it against his head. Mathias squeezed his eyes shut, pausing in his frantic actions. The vials in his hands and scattered over the ice from the dropped case resting near his knees could only be one thing—Drapyltin.

"I'm disappointed in you, Keenan," Thomas said.

"I've heard that my whole life," he replied. "It's somewhat lost its effect on me."

"Witty remarks won't prevent me from killing the good doctor," Thomas pointed out with a forced grin.

"Leave him out of this. This is between you and me."

"You took your liberties and ran. I don't take too kindly to abuse of my generosity."

"What generosity?" Benedict snarled. "Kidnapping me because I'm good at what I do, and refusing to take no for an answer, therefore forcing me to interact on your terms? That isn't generous."

"I never forced you. There was always a choice."

"Compliance under threat of death is not exactly a *choice*, it's an inescapable decision to avoid a power-hungry attempt at adding excitement and drama to the life of someone who craves it because they lacked proper attention and supervision growing up."

Thomas narrowed his eyes dangerously at Benedict's words. "Says the orphan," he spat, pulling the trigger on Mathias.

The gun clicked, empty. Mathias cried out in surprise, dropping the vials in his hands in favor of uselessly shielding his head and scampering away. Benedict's stomach had dropped with the spiteful trigger squeeze, and he jumped, startled by the short, sharp sound of the gun's hammer striking the cap. Empty or not, Benedict felt something snap inside of him: the match lighting his fuel.

"Always the bully," he said before lashing out at the captain, unsheathing a sword.

Davies grinned in amusement, easily blocking it, sending sparks flying as the steel blade made contact with the huge, clunky cylinder from his cybernetic arm. Spindly fingers clenched tightly, Thomas swung his fist, but Benedict saw the punch coming.

That mechanical fist had caught him before, and he was not interested in a painful repeat result. Whipping out his trident dagger, he released the mechanism, catching the tip of the middle blade inside the cylindrical opening that was Davies's wrist, trapping his arm, then kicking at the captain's knee.

Thomas blocked with his thick barrel before flinging his other arm, pulling the stuck dagger straight out of Benedict's hand.

While relieving himself of the trident dagger kept the cyborg occupied, Benedict swiftly pulled the gun from its holster and pulled the trigger. The bullet, unfortunately, bounced off the cybernetics. Thomas cackled as he swung his cylindrical arm out at Benedict, who failed the dodge.

Flying from the force of the hit, Benedict landed on his backside, losing the weapons in his hands and sliding into the empty case, scattering the vials across the ice and dangerously close to the edge of the waterfall.

There was no time to react as Thomas darted at him with a wild swing of his arm. With a gasp, Benedict flinched and extended his arms out in self-defense, catching the captain's arm with both hands.

The sting against his frozen palms was so intense, he was certain that something broke. But he didn't have time to check. He was on the defensive again and desperately needed to get Davies out of his position of power.

Releasing Thomas's arm, Benedict grabbed the trapped blade by the hilt, yanking hard to get his trident dagger free, but lost it again as the cyborg pulled his arm back and aimed the cylindrical arm at Benedict.

Eyes wide in surprise as he stared down the barrel of Davies's built-in cannon gun, he kicked up at the arm, sending the bullets flying over the falls instead of into his head. Using both legs, he kicked Thomas in the stomach, using the captain's solid mass to push off and away, sliding on his back. The clink from a vial caused his body to stiffen in fear, knowing how close to the edge of the falls he was.

Rolling onto his stomach, he reached out for one of the vials, dangerously balanced on a protruding chunk of ice, but fumbled. The vial bounced from his fingers, tumbling down the waterfall, shattering.

Benedict's heart froze as solid as the ice he was lying on as flashes of a brainwashed surgeon barreled to the forefront of his mind.

The Drapyltin, which was now a liquid thanks to the frigid temperatures, had more than likely contaminated the ice, which would eventually melt and travel through the water and start a chain reaction from there. Was one vial enough to affect people the way it had affected Mathias? Was this the Drapyltin that would speed up the mind control? How diluted would it become?

"Ben!"

Mathias's urgent cry pulled Benedict from his thoughts, and he scrambled to his feet as Thomas stomped forward. The all-too-familiar cracking sound from the surface caused him to look at Mathias, concerned. That sound wasn't good.

"Mathias!" he yelled. "Get off the ice!"

Standing on the very edge of the waterfall with the captain fast approaching, there was not much else Benedict could do. Jumping backward to escape was an absolute no with the sharp ice mounds and icicles at the bottom. Gritting his teeth angrily, he dug into his pocket, pulling the gun back out and shooting at Davies.

Of course, Thomas blocked the bullet with his clunky cannon arm. Shooting the cyborg again, the blocked bullet ricocheted off, hitting his other arm, damaging one of the internal infusion wires.

The blue liquid spluttered out, and suddenly, Thomas couldn't move his arm. He roared in anger and surprise. "What have you *done*?!"

Benedict wasn't going to stick around to find out. Sidestepping away from the captain and the edge of the waterfall, he took careful aim and shattered the infused wire in Thomas's other arm as well, disabling both cybernetic arms.

Another crack in the ice made Benedict glance about for Mathias, but his attention shifted back to Thomas as he slowly began to move his spindly fingers.

It was now or never. Benedict aimed his gun at the captain's head.

"Oh?" Thomas chuckled. "What's this now, Keenan?"

"This is for everything you've ever said to me." Benedict took a few steps toward Thomas, who started to sweat. "And for everything you've ever done to Mathias." Placing the barrel of the gun against the middle of Davies's forehead, the cyborg was quivering, his breathing growing heavy. "And this . . ." Benedict's grip trembled as the memories flooded him, mixing with his rage. "This is for Kate."

As he pulled the trigger, Davies swiftly knocked his cannon arm into the gun, causing the bullet to graze the side of his bald head instead, while his metal hand tightly gripped Benedict by the throat.

Benedict dropped his weapons in favor of trying to break free from the crushing grip.

"These are heavier than I thought without the infusions," Davies remarked, still huffing and puffing from the effort before grinning. "Word to the wise, Keenan: when you have the chance to kill someone, just do it."

"That goes . . ." Benedict struggled to breathe, ". . . for you, as well."

Davies raised a brow before Mathias hit him over the side of the head with the thick case of infusions. The sky pirate released Benedict as he stumbled sideways, tumbling down the edge of the solid waterfall, getting impaled by one of the jagged edges on the way down.

The ice cracked and broke apart in a lightning bolt pattern, and Benedict, gasping for breath, grabbed Mathias by the arm.

"Run!" he croaked.

They dashed for the riverbank of the massive waterfall as the strong current broke free from the frozen surface, driving some of the ice into a single mass that shattered others, carrying it along.

Benedict was sore and exhausted, which was slowing him down. Feeling the ice breaking beneath his feet, the panic gave him an extra little boost of speed, but it wasn't enough. A sudden torrent broke the ice, and the raw power of the waterfall rushed on by.

Leaping as a last resort, he crashed into Mathias, both men painfully tumbling into the crunchy snow and ice.

Lying on his back, writhing in pain, his mind was blank to everything but his agonizing twitching and spasming muscles. As the pain slowly dulled, he couldn't tell if anything was broken, but he was sure there was a sprain somewhere, some stitches might have come undone, and there were definitely plenty of bruises.

Trying to catch his breath, he found Mathias sprawled out next to him in much the same situation. "Are you all right?" he asked, barely able to get the sound out past the rushing waters. Mathias only gave a faint nod in reply.

Benedict was thankful that he could save Mathias. He was grateful that the surgeon was alive, that he wasn't as ill as the last time he had seen him. He'd have asked him how he felt, but their celebration would have been short-lived.

"I failed," Benedict said. A vial—maybe more—had still managed to contaminate the water. As the largest freshwater system in the world, things were going to get bad.

“How?” Mathias huffed, still catching his breath.

“One of the vials. It—”

“They were sterile.”

Benedict blinked. “Sterile?”

“Yes.” Mathias struggled to sit up. “I realized it after I spilled the contents. As I was picking them up, I noticed tiny ice crystals forming on the inside. That only occurs in sterile infusions.”

A sigh of relief flooded over him as his eyes looked to the sky, his body losing its stiffness at the wonderful news. “Who switched them?” he asked.

“You did.”

His attention swiftly shifted back to Mathias, brows knit in confusion. “What?”

Mathias nodded. “Captain Davies said that you fetched the wrong case, and he wanted me to ‘fix it.’”

A shaky chuckle escaped his lips. *Of course* he stole the wrong case. Davies and Ajani had failed to mention that there was more than one, and they’d *especially* failed to tell him to *not* grab the one that was under lock and key.

Mathias suddenly frowned, his eyes upward, and Benedict followed his gaze. The mirrors over Lake Erie were retracting, and the massive etched cannon in the sky powered up.

“Are those sterile?” Benedict asked, painfully sitting up.

"I don't know," Mathias answered with concern in his voice.

"Then I guess we better stop it before we find out the hard way," he groaned. Struggling to get to his feet, his side wound screamed at him. He knew he'd opened it up again.

"How do you suggest we do that?" Mathias asked.

"Making it up as I go is my specialty." He grinned, but it slowly disappeared as a crew of at least twenty ships approached.

"Need ah ride, Captain?" came a very familiar lilt, which caused his hairs to stand on end.

Slowly looking up, he spotted Ajani, wrapped in a thick wool blanket, as she let down the roped ladder of the cutter. He'd thought her dead. She had gone under in the frigid water, trapped beneath the ice. "I had tuh follow his orders, Captain. I was his hostage."

Benedict narrowed his eyes. There was no way Davies would have let her be fleet quartermaster as a hostage.

"Now, wid him dead, I am free. I owe yuh a debt . . . and mi life and service."

"Her story checks out!" came another woman's voice, and Benedict's heart filled with adoration as familiar black hair and blue eyes popped over the edge of the ship.

"Kitch!" he exclaimed in delight, grabbing onto the ladder and climbing faster than he'd ever thought possible considering his physical state. Once aboard, he grinned broadly as she leaped into his arms. He held her tightly, never wanting to let her go.

Lifting his hands, he cupped her cheeks, absolutely melting over her ruby smile. "I brought you your crew—" she started.

"I hate tuh break di reunion shawt, Captain, but we have a cannon tuh deactivate," Ajani cut in.

Benedict pulled away from Kitch, his eyes hard on Ajani with distrust. Kitch placed a hand against his chest to stop him. "Wait, Ben." His eyes fell to Kitch as she looked up at him. "Davies had her family. He shipped them off to somewhere only he knew about to guarantee obedience. Thankfully, my intel found them in London, safe and sound."

He looked back to Ajani, his gaze softer. If anyone knew about that experience, it was him. He had lived it firsthand with Mathias aboard the *Condor*. Though he felt empathy for her, he still didn't fully trust her. Unfortunately, he was going to need all the help he could get, and that meant she was now involved. "You and I are going to have a long talk about your impending demotion when this is over," he said to Ajani.

"Aye, Captain," she replied, dropping her gaze, saddened, despite continuing to stand tall and proud, wrapped in the wool blanket.

"In the meantime, I need you to do what you do best."

Her gaze snapped back at him, and she nodded solemnly. "Aye, Captain!" she said, with a little more pride.

"And none of that, please," he said, grimacing. He didn't want to be reminded of Davies. "'Yes, sir' is fine."

"Yes, sir," she replied, a smirk on her lips.

Benedict turned his attention back to Kitch. "I need to know what you know."

"I know that none of the other cannons have been activated so far, so all we have to do is focus on this one."

"Perfect." Turning to the few men aboard the airship, he gave his orders. "Head for the cannon!" To Ajani, he added, "I want a few ships to follow, but I need the rest of the fleet to form a blockade to stop anyone from getting in."

"Aye, Captain! I mean—yes, sir!"

Benedict leaned in to Kitch. "I need a team to dismantle the other cannons, but I don't trust her to lead the fleet," he muttered, nodding his head in Ajani's direction.

"I told you, her story checks out."

"We'll discuss that later."

"I can do it," she then said.

"Absolutely not," he dismissed. "I need you here with me as my eyes and ears."

"Then who do you suggest?"

He didn't know. He didn't know how to break up the crew to get everyone where he needed them to be and still perform all tasks without risk of backstabbing. He needed to keep Kitch near him, and he needed to keep Ajani close in case she was planning a coup. But who could he trust to take the fleet to the other cannons without worrying about them failing or turning on him and activating them?

"I'll do it," Mathias said. Benedict turned his head to the surgeon, blinking in surprise. "I won't be one of your pirates, but I will volunteer to be the surgeon on board and watch them."

He was torn. Mathias had been through so much already, but he was the only other person he could trust.

"Are you sure?" he asked, and Mathias nodded. His heart swelled with pride, but it also clenched with worry. He extended his hand anyway, and Mathias clasped his own hand over the offered one. "Take a big ship," Benedict instructed as they shook hands. "And be careful."

CHAPTER 37

They readied the six small cannons along the hull of the cutter as Benedict's narrowed gaze focused on the weapon of destruction before them.

He found it difficult to judge the size of the massive cannon due to the reflective mirrors. Approaching it too closely or too far could have vastly different consequences. All he could do was guess based on his repairs—and sabotage—of the one over Lake Ontario. That was as good as it was going to get, and it was a little like making it up as he went, he had to admit.

At the helm, his hands were tight on the smooth mahogany wheel handles. Kitch, who stood by his side, occasionally placed a hand atop of his. Her hands were so warm—mostly hidden inside a soft fur muff—and her touch relaxed him while also boosting his confidence.

Each time doubt crossed his mind, her warmth melted it away like the springtime sun.

"We need to shoot the mirrors," he instructed his crew. "But be cautious not to hit the cannon. We don't want it to accidentally fire." Carefully sailing into place, he alerted his crew. "Steady!"

His crew. That was definitely something he could get used to. While the cutter he was currently sailing was no galleon, he found the freedom it provided was just as liberating to his soul and mind as it was to his heart.

"All guns ready, Captain!"

With a large inhale, Benedict then bellowed as loudly as he could: "*Fire*!"

The small cannons exploded, hurling their heavy load at the massive weapon, and the airship shook slightly from the force of the blasts. But a previously invisible honeycomb-shaped shield strangely deflected what would have been a direct hit, its panels shattering to nothingness as they were hit.

Benedict clenched his jaw as the outlines vanished. Infused shields were weak alchemical protection systems—he'd learned that the hard way thanks to Lord Taylor—but they were cleverly designed: they gave the defenders time to prepare an offensive strike, as artillery could rarely pass through by hitting the same spot twice until more panels were destroyed.

His irritation, as he called out for a reload, shifted to surprise as a familiar head peeked out from the control room alcove. He recognized the figure as the one who had sheltered him and Mathias while they were on the run.

Mister Dirk stepped out onto the platform, clutching something small in one of his hands, moving the other one about like a mime would. Seemingly satisfied, his eyes fell on Benedict.

"I can't let you go on with this, Mister Keenan," he said, a little too casually for Benedict's comfort. Was he in the same situation as Ajani? Was Ella safe?

"It's Captain, now," he countered, before continuing, "Mister Dirk, you don't have to do this. Davies is dead."

"Hm," he replied, not at all relieved like Benedict thought he'd be. "Thomas Davies actually works for me, not the other way around."

Benedict blinked in surprise before hissing his discontent. How long had that been a thing? Mathias had trusted him; just how much had he unintentionally revealed to the old man?

"All guns ready, Captain!" one of his crewmen hollered.

He raised a hand palm out, a silent instruction to hold steady as he focused on Mister Dirk. "What are you up to?" he asked. "You *are* aware of what Drapyltin does, aren't you?"

"Of course I know what it does," he said offhandedly. "I fixed it because *somebody* stole the sterile study samples."

There was that blame again. Benedict shoved that trivial circumstance aside in his mind for the more significant matter at hand. "Fixed it how?" he asked, wary.

"I made it better!" he said with a smile, pulling a vial out of his pocket. "Deadlier! The ones you were meant to steal rev up the effects. When Davies sent me samples, I realized they were the wrong ones and that it was too late to go back for the correct ones, but I succeeded in creating the recipe on my own, then came here to switch them out myself since I have incompetent assistants."

"Mister Dirk . . ." He really wished Mathias was with him, as he knew the scientist the best. Benedict didn't know enough to be able to properly talk the madman out of anything. "Why are you doing this?"

"This world has collapsed into a state of disrepair," he replied. "Ever since the lands split, it has just grown worse."

Benedict knew this all too well. Life had dealt him a horrible hand from the beginning, but Benedict had played it like a pro with his head held high. When the world split and the nobles and alchemists *literally* looked down on him, he had to start playing dirty, and a little more often each time.

But not once did Benedict ever think about burning the world to the ground. He adapted and molded his way around the wrenches life threw, working his way to the top—despite his occasional downward spirals. He loathed the gap between social classes and desperately wanted to be on top, but had never poisoned anyone—except himself, with alcohol—to get there.

"The world needs to be reset, and I'll be the one to do it," Mister Dirk added.

"You'll die with it," Benedict pointed out.

"My family will be safe; we've taken the antidote. And I have enough to give to whomever I please." He shrugged, then peeked inside the alcove. "Bring him out," he calmly instructed.

Two large pirates appeared, shoving a battered, bruised, and *very-much-alive* Thomas Davies to his knees onto the iron grate platform next to Mister Dirk.

An instant frown made its way to his features as the fire inside him rekindled. Kitch gasped. Davies was still alive. How was it possible? Benedict had watched him get impaled.

"Open it up," Mister Dirk gently ordered one of his goons. Some of the shield panels in front of him phased in and out before disappearing completely, and he moved forward on the platform, standing on the very edge.

"This is for you," he pleasantly said to Kitch, opening his other hand, revealing a smooth, smoky gray sphere that he had been clutching tightly.

Kitch raised a brow, and as she went to move, Benedict quickly shot his arm out to keep her in place.

With a shrug, Mister Dirk shifted his gaze from Kitch to the crewman closest to her. "Catch."

Swinging his arm like a pendulum, Mister Dirk tossed it for the crewman to catch, but he released it a little high, causing the small sphere to arch right over him, shattering near Kitch.

She shielded her face, and Benedict grabbed her upper arm and yanked her back as the cloud of infused poison, which the old man had kept from liquefying in his grip, dissipated into the air. She began to cough, as did a handful of the others that had been directly in the cloud's radius.

Benedict froze as his stomach dropped—he knew exactly what that was, and it was a lot more than Mathias had inhaled on his own. At first, he thought the old man had horrible control and aim. Now he knew Mister Dirk had done it on purpose.

"Kitch!" he cried in a panic, grabbing her by the shoulders and spinning her around to face him. Kitch and the three other crewmen stood still, empty shells as Mathias had been.

"Attack," Mister Dirk directed.

Suddenly, the bodies moved, but not how Benedict expected. Unlike Mathias's slow and sluggish actions, they snapped their attention up, striking surprisingly quick.

Taking a step back, startled as Kitch lashed out at him, he snatched her wrists as she scratched and clawed like some sort of crazed wild animal, his long arms holding her at bay. She was stronger than normal, and that greatly concerned him. He turned his attention to the rest of his crew as they restrained the ones that had been turned.

"Tie them to the mast!" Benedict yelled. "Bind their wrists!" He looked back at Kitch. "Snap out of it!"

His grip tightened as she tried breaking free, but he wouldn't let go. A part of him was afraid he was hurting her, but the other part of him didn't want her to injure him any further than he already was.

Pulling her arms toward her mouth, she chomped down on his frozen hand, and he cried out in both surprise and pain as he shoved her away from him, blood trailing down his hand. He hoped it wasn't infected. "Gag them!" he ordered, as Kitch lunged back out at him.

Dodging to the side, he stretched his good arm out, grabbing her by the waist and spinning her back into him, facing outward. Quickly snatching her wrist with his injured hand, he crossed it over her other arm, effectively trapping her.

Disturbing high-pitched screeches escaped her as she writhed in his grip. Someone finally came running to his aid with some rope and grabbed one of Kitch's ankles, but she kicked at him with her other foot and continued alternating, making it near impossible to tie her up.

"Kitch, stop!" he growled through clenched teeth.

A second and a third crew member came to help, and Kitch grew increasingly more violent. Benedict squeezed his arms together with all his might, the searing hot pain from his gunshot wounds so intense as it coursed through his own body that he couldn't hold back an anguished roar to match her shrieks once he could finally release her.

The gag only made her more frantic as Benedict scooped her up with trembling hands and slung her over his shoulder as she continued to thrash. The three other mind-controlled men were already bound to the mast, and Benedict swiftly set Kitch down before them, firmly shoving her shoulders between two of them as the rest of the crew made quick work of securing her.

He looked into Kitch's eyes to find them empty, soulless. There was no hint of remorse, pain, or even fear. The other three were just as crazed as she was, controlled by the order that had activated them.

All the sensations and emotions he searched for in her eyes, he was feeling twofold: he felt guilty for tying her up; he feared for her life under such a large amount of Drapyltin, and his whole body screamed, objecting to every tiny movement. But he had to keep going. For Mister Dirk's sake, the antidote better be nearby.

"I'm sorry," he whispered to her before pulling away.

A loud, deep, and resonant boom caused the airship to quiver. Benedict spun around as Davies fell onto the small cutter.

No, not fell—jumped.

Thomas leaked a mixture of blood and a black viscous substance as he slowly rose to his full height, mechanical gears rotating inside of gigantic holes and gashes in his torso.

Benedict's nose wrinkled in disgust. Just how much of himself had Davies given up to be stronger and deadlier?

Davies's non-cyborg eye was just as empty as Kitch's were, and Benedict didn't like that at all. Glancing at Mister Dirk atop the platform, he watched the man grin like the mad scientist he was.

"Kill them all," he instructed, and Davies lunged forward.

Barely leaping off to the side and out of the way in time, Thomas easily mowed the others down like a bull while explosions thundered all around—the military had arrived, and Ajani's portion of the crew was now divided in between those still loyal to Davies and the newcomers.

There was too much going on at once. Benedict couldn't keep up as the massive cannon powered up. With Davies preoccupied by the crew aboard the cutter, Benedict needed to concentrate on the most important thing first: preventing the Drapyltin from poisoning the Great Lakes.

Jaw clenched so tightly he thought his teeth might shatter, he rushed to the cannons. He needed the shield down, or at least a hole big enough to get him into the alcove. Unfortunately, as one of the most demanding jobs on a ship, aiming had to take into account various details far more complex than simply shooting a gun, and he was well aware that he was a terrible shot.

"I need a gunner!" he bellowed over the racket. A crewman with wide shoulders pulled away from the fight to join him. "Knock out as many panels by the entrance as you can," he instructed as he picked up one of the forked staffs that was still smoldering.

The gunner nodded and aimed with ease, firing instantly, shattering one of the invisible shield panels almost dead on before Benedict could even point his small cannon in the right direction. His whole body hurt, and everything felt like it weighed double, even the air. Setting off his cannon, his aim was nowhere near his target. He rolled his eyes, glad Mathias wasn't there to witness his failure, and tried again.

The second one was still off, but closer when the gunner called out to him after firing four of the six cannons.

"Captain!"

Benedict glanced to the alcove just in time to see the outline of the shattered panels disappear. It was enough to get him through. Climbing onto the gunwale, he inhaled and exhaled deeply—counting to three for yet another one of his *made-up-as-I-go* plans—and jumped.

The grate clanked loudly from his landing, vibrating beneath his feet as he gained his balance. He had never given in to vertigo before, but he swallowed hard at the sight of frozen Lake Erie so far beneath him and the floating chunk of land. It was, however, a far more welcomed sight than the gun barrel he stared down once he stood up.

He growled dangerously at the man behind the gun. "Where's the antidote, Dirk?"

"Oh, you won't find any here, I'm afraid."

Benedict shut his eyes as he exhaled in disappointment. Focus. He had to focus. "You have to stop this thing."

"No," he blatantly replied, and Benedict's eyes shot open once more. "No, this world is too divided, and there is nothing left to do but start over." Anger flashed in his eyes. "My beautiful, innocent Maisie didn't deserve to die as they kept the antidote for her illness from me! All because I wasn't good enough for the alchemists! Or the tech users! I—"

Explosions rattled the cannon—the shield was down. Benedict took the opportunity to swipe the gun out from Mister Dirk's hands into his own while he was distracted, then shot him.

He had been sympathetic to the old man's story when Mathias had told him, but now he was feeling a little detached from the whole thing after everything he had gone through and witnessed.

With a wince and a smirk on his face, Mister Dirk fell to his knees, holding his stomach. "It's too late," he croaked.

Anger flaring, hungry for revenge for Kitch's current affliction, Benedict shot the man in the chest before ruthlessly kicking the corpse off the platform. There was a tiny flash of remorse—unlike all others, he hadn't killed Mister Dirk in self-defense or preservation—but it was fleeting.

He had already come to terms with the fact he was headed for Coldbath. All he wanted to do now was turn off the cannon, take Kitch back to London, and drown himself in alcohol until they came to lock him up.

There were so many wires, tubes, gears, buttons, and levers everywhere when he stepped into the alcove that Benedict didn't even know where to start. Trying to deactivate it was nothing like repairing—or sabotaging—it, and this cannon differed vastly from the one at Lake Ontario.

Reaching out to pull the wires, something caught his attention out of the corner of his eye: a case of vials, sitting out in the open, untouched.

Oh, the people he could threaten with that Drapyltin, or the price it could fetch by selling it on the black market . . . The fantasies fluttered through his mind, wrapping his judgment in their silky promises.

He almost fell for it.

A frown slowly scrunched his forehead as he scattered the embellishing lies from his brain like a fine mist.

Those were pirate thoughts.

Yet he continued to stare at the vials, torn, until everything shook violently around him, instantly stirring him from his thoughts as the cave ceiling crumbled in places, threatening to collapse. He had to hurry.

In one swift movement, he suddenly snatched two of the vials and shoved them in his pocket, convincing himself that they were to replace the infusion Mathias's friend had told him to guard with his life—the same infusion Mathias used on himself to prevent anyone else from getting hurt.

Returning to the control panel, he grabbed the wires and yanked them free, cutting power to everything. Another explosion furiously rocked the platform, knocking larger chunks of dirt free from the ceiling and walls.

He didn't want to stick around for the next hit, especially if it meant being buried alive or crushed to death. Spinning around, he darted for the exit as a large slab of destroyed oxidized bronze landed right in front of the doorway. Using his momentum, he dove in between the doorway and the chunk of the massive weapon, tumbling out onto the platform just as the alcove collapsed behind him.

His breath caught in his throat when he started sliding down the shifting platform as the cannon slipped off the floating land. Gritting his teeth, Benedict jumped, catching himself on the ledge of the cutter just as the cannon knocked the grated platform right off, which tumbled down into Lake Erie.

Wincing and grunting, struggling to pull himself up as every inch of his body violently trembled in discomfort and pain, he pulled himself back safely aboard the airship, collapsing onto his bad arm with a cry.

Sword clashes rang and gunshots thundered on deck, which vibrated with each one of Thomas's heavy steps. Davies was still alive. How many of Benedict's new crew had he killed?

How long would he continue to be under the influence?

Staggering while getting to his feet, he turned around to assess the situation, then froze.

The scene before him practically played out in slow motion, and all he could do was watch the doomed sequence as his body refused to cooperate. Darkness threatened his vision and an intense nauseating sensation washed over him as Davies pulled his blade back from Kitch's stomach.

Her eyes were wide, perhaps in surprise or pain or shock. Had she regained consciousness? Would she have screamed out if they hadn't gagged her? Somebody was crying out her name, and it took Benedict a moment before he realized it was him.

The rage inside of him finally caught up to the moment, and he exploded, blindly lunging forward, grabbing a stray sword on deck as he rushed by.

Benedict slammed the blade straight through Thomas's shoulder as he turned around, but it didn't even faze him. Still an empty shell with an order, Davies swung his arm out as if Benedict was nothing but a pesky fly.

The hit connected, sending Benedict flying. Not only was Thomas stronger thanks to the new Drapyltin, but it felt like his arms were re-infused as well.

Quickly picking up a nearby fallen sword and gun, Benedict's swift attempt at a block from the cyborg's oncoming attack resulted in his blade breaking from the clash and force of the hit.

He blinked in surprise but was swift to react as Davies swung his cannon arm downward, rolling away before being crushed, the wood from the deck splintering upon impact.

A ragged gasp escaped him when Thomas's spindly fingers grasped his throat. Releasing the broken hilt, he grabbed the cybernetic hand while his other arm rose, firing the gun right at the sky pirate's chest, but Davies didn't go down. Pinned against the deck, Benedict couldn't escape as Davies readied his cannon arm in Benedict's face.

This was it. This was the unglamorous and highly unsatisfying end of Benedict Keenan. Every emotion traveled through him in an instant, and he winced when the thunder sounded before he realized it wasn't from the arm cannon.

Davies collapsed to the side; Ajani had fired point-blank at his head. Releasing the cyborg's mechanical fingers from around his throat, he took much-needed breaths. Ajani had returned; she'd saved him. Maybe she *could* be trusted. Giving her a quick nod in thanks, he quickly scrambled to his feet and rushed to Kitch, whose head drooped on her shoulders. Her breathing through her nose was rapid and sharp.

She was dying.

"Cut her loose!" he ordered in a panic.

"Captain, dem a still undah di influence—" Ajani started, but he'd have none of it.

"Cut the blasted rope!" he bellowed, before attempting to apply pressure to her wound between the ropes.

She did not cry out. Raising one of his trembling hands, his eyes widened at the amount of blood coating it, but he instantly recovered, swallowing the enormous lump in his throat with a loud gulp. He had to be brave for her.

Yanking the gag from her mouth, she growled for half of a second before falling limp in his arms, released from the ropes tethering her to the mast.

"Kitch . . ." His voice quivered involuntarily as he softly lowered himself to the ground with her cradled in his arms. "Please don't leave me . . . I already lost Kate; I can't lose you too." His bloodied hands applied pressure to her wound once more. "I need a medic!" he cried out to anyone that could hear him.

Footsteps approached, and a man kneeled next to Benedict. "Where's Mathias?"

Slowly pulling his eyes away from Kitch, he stared at Lieutenant Darley for what seemed like forever. At first, he didn't recognize him—his mind a haze with nothing but Kitch at the forefront. But when he remembered the stony-faced man, he simply gave him a desperate, pleading look.

It could have been seconds later, like it could have been hours, but the military pulled him away from the woman as the medical officer dropped to his knees to help. Benedict couldn't hear anything, not even his own cries, as he tried to free himself from their grasp.

"Kitch! *Kitch*!"

CHAPTER 38

He didn't know how long he'd been sitting on the small wooden crate, lost in his memories of the orphan and prostitute, as he silently stared at Kitch's drying blood on his hands.

The military had cuffed him; simple cuffs that he could easily escape from by dislocating his thumb, by using his *parlor tricks*. But restraining him had only intensified the anger—much like with Kitch after she had inhaled the Drapyltin.

He had been lucky that the military was holding him back, struggling to keep him still as he yelled and screamed. Because when the medical officer—wiping blood from his hands with a rag, his clothing stained red—stepped over to Captain Fitzgerald, shaking his head with a flash of regret in his eyes, Benedict's entire body had given out, and they'd had to catch him.

There was lots of dry retching. His chest was so tight, he was convinced his insides were going to come out with the next heave.

He loved Kitch more than he loved anything or anyone else in the world. Always had. He always returned to her first thing whenever he was away for work or in jail. He always missed her when she wasn't next to him. Hell, even when he had decided he was going to marry Catherine, he had also decided to bring Kitch to the Upper Lands with him, to be comfortable and have what they never had growing up.

Now it was too late. He had lost the only two women he loved.

"We've interrogated everyone that was apprehended," someone said as they approached, footsteps thudding against the wooden deck. "You're the last one." Benedict didn't react. After a few beats, they spoke again, more gently this time. "Condolences, Mister Keenan. We did everything that we could."

He didn't reply, but he knew the military had that same duty to help, just as Mathias did as a surgeon; that it didn't matter who was hurt, they had to try to save them. He appreciated their effort, but it didn't make him feel better. It didn't rectify the fact that he would never again look into her beautiful blue eyes or run his fingers through her silky black hair, that he'd never again smell the soft rose pomade when he kissed the top of her head or hear the almost musical titter of her giggles as they shared a joke. And even if it rarely ever happened anymore, he'd never again taste her delicious bread or stew.

"Someone said her name was 'Kitch.' Care to elaborate?"

Benedict continued to stare at his hands, the voices of the orphans calling out to her all those years ago a painful memory, made even more agonizing when those very orphan voices were actually his own as a child.

"Kitch! Come and play!" "Kitch is in the kitchen again!" "It's Kitch's turn to count!"

He could see them both in his mind's eye as children, running around the orphanage and the streets, laughing and smiling without a care in the world. He used to love pulling her knotty hair and making her cry.

The memories made his vision blurry. Was it blurry? He shut his eyes. No . . . it was tears.

"Mister Keenan," Captain Fitzgerald tried, a little louder.

"Captain Keenan," he finally replied, correcting him as he opened his eyes and blinked away the mistiness. "I heard you. Her name was Rosalind Gladstone. Kitch was her nickname."

"You wouldn't happen to know where Doctor Darley is, would you?"

Mathias. In all his rage and shock over Davies, Dirk, and Kitch, he had practically forgotten about the man he had originally rescued from the Atlantic for a reward and had eventually grown fond of. They had shaken hands before Mathias departed, overlooking the plan to dismantle the rest of the cannons. They could have been anywhere by now. Was he even still alive? It hadn't occurred to Benedict that he had practically fed Mathias to the wolves. The surgeon couldn't even fight. What would happen if the crew turned on him?

Benedict's eyes screwed tightly shut as he pinched the bridge of his nose. Great. He might have lost all *three* people he cared about. With a sigh, he shook his head as a reply to the captain.

Two other sets of footsteps approached, and Captain Fitzgerald inhaled and exhaled deeply before continuing. "Are you aware that we must arrest the lot of you and charge you for piracy and crimes against the Crown?"

Benedict nodded again as both men pulled him up by the arms. Captain Fitzgerald patted him down, and Benedict winced when a tiny *clink* sounded from his pocket. Pausing with a raised brow, Captain Fitzgerald reached inside and pulled out the two vials, inspecting them for a moment before handing them off.

"And theft," the captain added to Benedict, before turning to the third man. "Private Cambridge, log this as evidence."

The blond man straightened. "Yes, sir," he said, releasing Benedict's arm to take the vials.

It wasn't as difficult as Benedict thought, to admit to himself that he was just a little disappointed about having the Drapyltin taken from him. One of those vials could have replaced the one Doctor Marsden had given Mathias, yes, but the other one could have been his to do with as he pleased.

The other thing that was surprisingly easy for him to admit to himself was that he had enjoyed his temporary freedom as captain of a crew, as fleeting as it had been. Being a pirate was, dare he say, *fun*.

"I'll talk," Benedict said.

"I beg your pardon?" Captain Fitzgerald asked, confused.

"Release my men. They didn't kill Dirk or Davies; I did," he partially lied. There he was, looking out for Ajani again. "Release them, and I'll tell you everything you want to know."

Captain Fitzgerald stared at him for a moment before casting a quick glance at Darley and Cambridge. He inhaled deeply before he spoke. "Mister Keenan—"

"Captain," he corrected again.

The captain's eyes narrowed at the interruption. "Though we are grateful that you prevented a substantial disaster upon the Great Lakes, you are still pirates wanted by the Crown. However . . ." Benedict felt the lieutenant stiffen some. "I will call off the search. Even *I* know it's fruitless. But know that if your crew ever happens to be in the vicinity of the military, they will be arrested."

Benedict nodded. It was only fair.

As they escorted him to the tethered military zeppelin, he cast a glance over his free shoulder, making sure that none of his crew remained aboard the cutter. It was unfortunate that he didn't know who had been apprehended and who had escaped.

Stepping onto the ship's gangway and aboard the military vessel, he turned around, setting his sights one last time on the cutter. The small airship had served him well, but next time, he'd need something bigger and better.

Benedict didn't really care where he was being taken. He sat quietly on the wooden bench in the cell, his back against the wall and his eyes shut as they sailed to wherever. It was just easier to keep them shut. It prevented them from stinging whenever his thoughts traveled back to Kitch.

"Mister Keenan?"

Benedict peeked through one eye, looking at Private Cambridge on the other side of the iron bars. "Captain," he corrected yet again.

The private ignored him. "What would you like done with Miss Gladstone's body?"

He didn't want to return to London to bury her. There was nothing left for him there, and without him, there was really nobody there for

Kitch. Nobody that cared, anyway. So, what else could he do?

Deeply inhaling and exhaling, he finally parted his lips to speak. “Give her to Madam Bonifrey. She owns a brothel in Elgin Below. She’ll know what to do.”

Private Cambridge blinked in surprise for a moment before glancing down to his paperwork and scribbling with his fountain pen. Benedict detected the faintest rosiness to the man’s cheeks and chuckled to himself as he closed his eyes once more.

Oh, Madam Bonifrey was going to have *fun* with Cambridge.

CHAPTER 39

Benedict Keenan had escaped prison. It was the first time—it had taken months—and it more than likely wouldn't be the last.

He stood at the edge of the riverbank, staring out at the majestic blue water and misty spray of Lake Erie. The cloudless summer morning scenery before him was entirely different from when he'd last seen it covered in snow and ice, though just as majestic.

A figure approached from the side, and he bristled, slightly defensive, until he caught a flash of deep purple.

"She would have liked it here," the woman said over the thunderous roar of the falls.

He turned to Madam Bonifrey, ever the picture of poise, elegance, and grace in her purple silk faille gown and bonnet. A small cherry wood box rested delicately in between her hands, and

Benedict swallowed the lump that instantly formed in his throat.

"Thanks for coming," he said.

She nodded in acknowledgment. "Like I said: she impressed me, and that's hard to do."

He reached for the box in her hands, a slight tremble to his fingers as he lifted the cover back to the ashes resting inside. His eyes stung, and the next exhale he released was shuddered. Gently shutting the lid, he looked back out at Niagara Falls.

He hadn't wanted to return to London to bury her, and not just for selfish reasons entirely his own. While in prison, what-if scenarios often plagued him during his grieving. One of the most prevailing thoughts was what if she would have wanted to be buried back in London?

Even if Kitch's customers, fellow escorts, and brothel manager would pay their respects, slowly, as with every other grave, they would stop coming. Kitch didn't deserve to be forgotten. He would never forget her; how could he? She wouldn't have deserved to have her grave neglected while he was locked up in Coldbath, to have her bones disinterred by gravediggers and her coffin sold for firewood—as often was the case with London's overcrowded churchyards—whether he was behind bars or not.

But he liked to think he knew her tastes and desires a lot more than that. He agreed with

Madam Bonifrey; Kitch would have loved living near the Great Lakes.

Flipping the lid once more as Madam Bonifrey continued to hold the box, he scooped the ashes up with his large hands—the last time he would ever get to touch her—then turned to the falls, his shaking arms extended as if in offering.

And when the warm summer breeze picked up from behind him, he slowly emptied his hands.

The ashes scattered into the air, carried away by the wind. Madam Bonifrey helped him by tilting the box so that he could get to the rest, and when he finished, he felt satisfying closure; yet there was also an immeasurable emptiness deep inside of him.

"Madam?" came another voice from behind.

They both turned to see a pale redhead girl standing next to a tall and gruff older man, who respectfully removed his cap in presence of the madam.

Benedict recognized the escort as the one from when he was first brought to the brothel by Ella. Glancing around, he looked for the youngest Dirk daughter until Madam Bonifrey's hand gently rested atop of his shoulder as she lightly shook her head with slight unease in her brown eyes. She leaned into him.

"I have not seen Ella since her father's death," she said gently before pulling away, her hand slipping from his shoulder and extending outward to introduce the other man. "This is Theodore. He's going to take you somewhere nice."

Nice? Benedict's eyes hardened slightly as he inspected the man before him, with his mussed curls and wisps of gray that increased in number the further down his face Benedict looked, until he reached the scraggly beard that contained more salt than pepper.

"What is your plan?" he cautiously asked, turning his attention back to Madam Bonifrey, who tutted.

"*My* plan is to return to my brothel and go about my business. *This* plan is in execution by a certain fleet quartermaster by the name of Ajani Ballou."

His eyes widened in surprise. Ajani! So she had successfully escaped. Finally acknowledging Theodore with a nod, he turned back to Madam Bonifrey.

"Thank you for taking care of her in my absence."

The smile upon her cherry lips was warm, yet playful. "The young man that nervously delivered the news was absolutely *delightful*." This made him smirk. "It was my pleasure, and I thank you for trusting me enough with her."

"Lead the way," he said, and Theodore happily obliged.

As Benedict boarded the anchored sloop, he took one last look over at the mist coming from the falls. He might never want to return to London, but he'd definitely do his best to return to Elgin—as long as it wasn't during the winter.

Benedict kept to himself during their trip, always on guard, his mind reeling over any attainable vantage point on the airship and every possible item he could use as a weapon on the off chance that the sole three members of the journey turn on him.

The last few rays of sun disappeared past the horizon when they arrived at their destination, and Benedict couldn't decide which was worse: the crisply frigid winter over the Great Lakes, or the shelteringly humid summer climate of wherever they were currently at.

Anchored on the cliffside off the coast, he cautiously followed Theodore down a path leading to a hidden cave in the rock. The tunnel twisted deep, stuffy and airless, the blue glow of infused lanterns illuminating the passage every few feet.

The droning murmur of voices echoing off the walls slowly grew louder until the hubbub was more easily distinguished: talking, laughing, and even some strumming of instruments. The faint smell of cooked food wafted through another twist, and Benedict's stomach growled in response.

The tunnel finally opened to a wide area stacked with barrels and crates filled with various supplies. Tents were erected, scattered throughout, and a large campfire burned in the middle of everything, surrounded by revelers. Two men stood guard along the entrance, nodding their heads to acknowledge Theodore, who rubbed his hands together and eagerly rushed to grab some food, leaving Benedict behind.

Where was he? Who were these people?

"Welcome tuh di hideout, Captain," loudly rang an all-too-familiar voice.

The merriment turned to cheers, and Benedict's heart rate sped up a little with dread now that everyone's attention was on him. Ajani approached with an arm extended. Reluctantly, he clasped her hand and they shook, the brilliantly white grin on Ajani's lips something he'd never seen before while with Davies. In fact, none of this gaiety ever happened aboard the *Condor*.

"That was quite the clever plan you devised," he started, "reaching out to Madam Bonifrey."

"Jus' following orders," she admitted, leading him to the fire.

"Whose orders?" he asked, stopping in his tracks with a concerned frown. It couldn't be Davies—he was dead. Wasn't he?

"Mine," came a voice, and Benedict's heart skipped a beat at the sight of the almost-unrecognizable man before a grin found its way to his lips.

There before him, wiping his hands with a rag, was Mathias, clean-shaven, with his mop of black hair slicked back. Benedict stepped past

Ajani as the surgeon extended his hand, and he pulled him into a hug instead.

Relief washed over him to see Mathias alive and well. He hadn't realized just how much the surgeon *really* meant to him until that very moment. He wasn't alone in the world.

"Yours?" Benedict finally said, holding him by the shoulders at arm's length. "Who are *you* to be giving orders?" he jested.

"I'm the one with the money and the ability to either save your life or let you die," he quipped back with a chuckle. "I was against working with Madam Bonifrey since finding ourselves sold off . . ." he trailed off, clearing his throat near the end, "but your friend knew where Miss Ballou's family was, and with her gone, well . . ." Mathias lightly squeezed Benedict's forearms. "I'm terribly sorry for your loss, Ben."

He could only nod. His shattered heart hurt.

"Madam Bonifrey freely updated us on everything, including the fact that we're all wanted by the Crown," Mathias added dryly.

Benedict's brows pulled together, and his lips tightened in a thin line. He'd never wanted Mathias to be a wanted man; he had far too much going for him. His future was too bright. "I'm sorry," he said sadly, and Mathias only shrugged.

"I've made my choice," he replied. Then he said, "Come, let me show you around."

He followed Mathias past the delicious-smelling food toward a slope. "Are you really all right with this? You don't have to stay," he tried.

Mathias only looked at him for a few seconds before stepping onto the top few rungs of a wooden ladder peeking past the edge of the slope. Intrigued, Benedict followed him down past the thick stone, where it opened to an even larger room than above. At least a dozen airships of various sizes were anchored along a trickle of water from the sea.

"How?" was all he managed to say, to which Mathias's only reply was a grin.

Following him into a side area, he looked around the clean medical room—well supplied and well stocked, just as he would expect from the surgeon.

Mathias pulled a lever on a device along the wall, and a loud mechanism began grinding somewhere. He followed the sound out of the medical bay to the entire front wall chugging forward like an overhead factory door, pushing out and up to the water. They were hiding in plain sight, and the idea absolutely amazed him.

"Did you . . .?" He couldn't finish the rest of his thought as he stepped out onto the edge of the cliffside, his jaw still dropped.

"No, it was already like this when we came to claim it. Turns out Miss Ballou has an excellent photographic memory and could point us to all the hideouts."

His muscles tensed up at the thought. How many other pirates that were still loyal to Davies did the same? What if there were some mingling among the crew upstairs? Even Ajani could be a double agent.

"Where are we?" Benedict asked, recognizing the salty smell of the Atlantic Ocean.

"Somewhere off the shores of North Carolina," Mathias replied.

Benedict nodded in acknowledgment. "Frank was looking for you," he added, betting the lieutenant never thought about looking in North Carolina.

"And Lieutenant Darley can keep looking," Mathias replied, turning and heading back for the medical bay. "I'm wanted by the Crown, remember?" he called over his shoulder.

The lieutenant would never arrest his own brother, would he? Calamity sounded up above: boisterous laughter and cries of amusement bounced off the walls, distracting him from his thoughts.

"Come," Mathias said as the massive bay door chugged closed. "The chef's dinner is always delightful."

They made their way back to the main level, where pirates handed him platters of fragrantly spiced fish and various delectable vegetables.

It tasted far better than the food he'd eaten in prison—which, in turn, was infinitely better than anything he'd ever eaten as part of Davies's crew.

Ajani, sitting quietly on the other side of the fire, had turned out to be an asset in the end, helping him with Davies and keeping Mathias safe. But he needed to know more if he was to trust her.

"Ajani," he called out amid the festivities, loud enough to draw her attention. When she met his gaze from across the fire, Benedict motioned with his head for her to join him.

"Captain?" she said, standing straight.

"Have a seat," he offered, and she nodded, leaving the length of one person in between them as she sat on the log next to him. "What's your story?" he asked, his eyes dropping to his plate.

"Mi . . . story, Captain?" she asked, uncertainty in her voice.

"Kitch said Davies was holding your family hostage."

"Aye, he did. An he sen' dem away tuh keep mi on a tight leash. If mi cud nuh fine dem, den mi wud do his dirty work. Mi feel indebted tuh Madam Kitch fi finding dem, returning tuh mi fi mi freedom."

"Freedom to rule as captain?" he tried, looking back at her, testing her loyalties. "I mean, you've done a good job on your own with Davies dead."

A soft smile spread to her lips as she shook her head. "Only when yuh a nuh longer ah dis mortal earth," she said, slowly glancing at the pirates about the area before her eyes landed back on him. "Dees men waited on yuh, nuh mi."

"But they knew you better," he pointed out.

"Aye, but mi groomed dem fuh yuh." Benedict blinked in surprise. "Mi chat wid dem. Di ones dat hated him. Yuh did see mi. Mi did tell dem dat man dere . . . he will free us.'"

Benedict finally understood. All the times that he thought Ajani was monitoring him, she was actually getting the pirates on her side. It explained why the crew divided after Davies's death. She had played the double agent to keep her family safe—and she apparently had more trust and confidence in him than he had.

"I'll take your debt to Kitch if you'll allow it," he said.

"Mi will 'low ih." She grinned as they shook on it and finished their meals.

After dinner, Mathias and Benedict returned to the airship hangar, where Mathias walked him through everything: the locations of the hideouts around the world, the amount and type of ships they owned, the quantity of men and goods. Benedict flipped through the impeccable notes with a whistle. They were beyond well organized.

"Now that you're here, what we do will be whatever you need us to do," Mathias said. "So, what will you call your hearty crew?"

Benedict chuckled, thinking back to Mathias's great ruse upon the *Amaroq*. "The Doom Crusaders, of course," he said. "I thought you knew this."

Mathias smirked. "What are our first orders, sir?"

"Sir? Orders?" He jokingly eyed Mathias up and down. "Are you saying you've embraced this pirate life?"

"Hardly," he admitted. "But you tend to get shot and stabbed a lot, so you're going to need a surgeon to patch you up."

He grinned, clasping Mathias on the shoulder before heading toward the largest of the airships at the rear of the hangar: a carrack. "I'd like to explore the other hideouts. Make sure the crewmen still loyal to Davies aren't doing the same as us. Then go from there."

"Hmm," Mathias mused as he followed. "That sounds like work."

Chuckling, Benedict climbed the gangway and boarded the airship, following the rigging with his eyes. "It's only work for those who don't know how to make it up as they go," he teased, before his eyes fell back on Mathias. "Gather up a crew; we set sail at dawn!" Mathias saluted and began walking away when Benedict called out after him. "Matt!"

The surgeon turned back around, a brow raised in question. "Yes?"

He couldn't describe what the sensation was deep inside. It wasn't emptiness or loneliness, and it wasn't heavy. "I'm glad you're here."

The surgeon bowed his head before he continued to walk away. Benedict inhaled and exhaled deeply. He had gone through quite a bit since leaving London and grown plenty in experience and taste. He was looking forward to the freedom, to staying three steps ahead of the military for the sake of his crew, and doing what he wanted when he wanted. The pirate life wasn't so bad.

Disembarking the carrack, he paused in his steps. He had finally figured it out.

He was *happy*.

EPILOGUE

Have a good evening, Captain."

The steel point of Captain Fitzgerald's fountain pen scribbled audibly against the paper as he finished signing his name in the report, only offering the friendly soldier a wave as a reply.

He had one final meeting and wanted to be sure he could give all his attention. After all, it wasn't every day that one got to meet with a world-famous alchemist. He had met his fair share of famous people, but none as exciting as this one.

The slight static from the receiver on his desk spat out a few incomprehensible words. Setting the pen down, he picked up the device, fiddling with the antenna and adjusting the knob at the front to locate and hone in on the signal.

The voice traveling through the airwaves came in crystal clear for only a few seconds, and it was long enough for him to sigh at the news. Disappointed—even slightly irritated—he set the device back down and scooped up the report. A knock at the door interrupted him as the receiver continued to cut in and out about Benedict Keenan's escape from prison.

"Captain." A blond head peeked into the office. "Sir, there's someone here to see you."

"Let him in, Private," he replied, getting up from his chair and stepping to the shelving unit against the far wall.

Pulling out a box halfway, footsteps tapped nearby, pausing at his door as the captain placed the report inside, shoved the box back in place, and turned to his guest, extending his hand for the man to shake.

"Doctor Wilfred Beckford," he greeted enthusiastically as the alchemist clasped his hand. "It's an honor to finally meet you, and on such short notice before you return to Upper London," he added, sweeping his arm to the side. "Please, have a seat. How are your wife and children?"

"The family is well, thank you," Doctor Beckford replied, taking a seat across the desk from the captain. "Anna is well, Jacob has gone off to basic training, and Juliet is shaping out to be a wonderful young lady. She's developed an interest in alchemy, I'll have you know," he added, pulling the chair in.

"That's wonderful," Captain Fitzgerald replied with a grin. "I'm sure she'll make you proud with her discoveries."

"Speaking of discoveries," Beckford said, removing his wire-frame specs and cleaning them with a cloth hidden up his sleeve, "I hear that you have something for my own findings."

"Ah! Yes." Captain Fitzgerald peeled back the top layer of the square of folded fabric on his desk, revealing the two vials taken from Keenan upon his arrest. Handing them to Doctor Beckford, the alchemist inspected them closely after putting the glasses back on his face. "It's called Drapyltin."

"Where did you get this?" Beckford's brows knit together in deep concentration as he slowly twirled the vials toward the dying evening light from the window.

"There was an incident, and we were able to . . . *procure* some before they disposed of it," he half lied. "Doctor Garfield Marsden from London was the lead scientist in charge, but he sadly passed away."

The creases on Doctor Beckford's forehead smoothened out as he nodded sagely, his blue eyes still on the vials. "It's a shame. He was a brilliant young man," he mused halfheartedly. It was as if the contents hypnotized him. "I heard that the characteristics of the gas can change with alchemy."

Captain Fitzgerald quirked a brow. "Then I can think of no better man to test that theory than yourself."

"I'm flattered," the alchemist replied, still lost in thought.

The moment suddenly got awkward. Purposefully clearing his throat, Captain Fitzgerald added, "I wouldn't want to hold you back from your travels any longer, Doctor."

"Ah!" Snapping out of his trance, he reached for his pocket watch and did a double take before jumping to his feet and placing the two vials in his other pocket. "Yes, Anna would be worried sick if I missed the ship back home! I wouldn't want to be late."

Getting to his feet, Captain Fitzgerald walked the alchemist out, thanking him for his time as he climbed into the steam carriage, and waved before turning around to grab his things and go home.

THE END

THANK YOU FOR READING!

I hope you enjoyed reading *Rise of the Sky Pirate*, the first book in the Adventures of Captain Keenan series!

I love feedback! Tell me what you thought of Benedict Keenan and his adventures. I'd love to hear from you. You can write me at raine@swraine.com and visit me on the web at http://swraine.com.

And if you have a moment, I'd love if you left a review for *Rise of the Sky Pirate*. Reviews help build my credibility and integrity as an indie author, and they encourage new steampunk readers to try my books. They also make it easier for me to get my books into libraries and indie bookstores. Reviews don't have to be complicated! They can be as short and sweet as saying what you liked and didn't like about the book.

Thank you again, dear reader, for spending time in the world of *Rise of the Sky Pirate*! I am forever grateful.

OTHER BOOKS BY S. W. RAINE

The Techno Mage

ABOUT THE AUTHOR

Raine is Canadian, born and raised, and constantly moved in between Ontario and Quebec with her military family. She moved to Michigan, USA, in 2004, where she currently still resides with her husband and son.

She has always had a vivid imagination and loved reading and writing from a very young age. She took courses in Children's Literature through ICL in Illinois, and published her new adult steampunk debut in 2020. She has participated in NaNoWriMo for over a decade and is currently a Municipal Liaison for the Detroit region.

Made in the USA
Monee, IL
05 June 2024

58999477R20246